Moon Rises Harmony Falls

Moon Rises Harmony Falls

David Reuben

ISBN:	Softcover	978-1-4628-9260-0
	Ebook	978-1-4628-9261-7

This book was printed in the United States of America.

To order additional copies of this book, contact:
Xlibris Corporation
1-888-795-4274
www.Xlibris.com
Orders@Xlibris.com
98188

Dedicated to:

My beautiful wife Denise.

My five fabulous boys:

Dustin, Devan, Drew, Cody, Moe . . .

Without their loving support this work would not have been possible.

Additionally, special thanks to my son: Cody – for his creative input.

To Dad:

Love eternal . . .

ACKNOWLEDGEMENTS

Cover Design: Dakota Ryan

Interior Artwork: Dakota Ryan – *The Beast of Harmony Falls Page: 194*

My very special thanks to the following people:

Angie McCain

Nancy Crow

Susan Carter

Crystal Cooper

Tide Waters

Beloved ones presently past friendships
ceased all too fast
Tide waters rush in rush out
Loved ones whose tide waters
have rescinded
Pages torn chapters ended
Memorials to attend not to comprehend
Newborn children write new pages
born with eyes bearing more than traces
Tide waters rush out rush in.

David A. Reuben

ABOUT THE AUTHOR

David A. Reuben,

Is the author of ***Moon Rises Harmony Falls*** and the popular ***Blood of the Lamb*** series of novels. He is a poet, and inventor/ entrepreneur – David is married to his wife Denise, together they have five children, all boys.

David and his wife Denise reside in Southwest Washington State.

PROLOGUE

Fifteen Minutes

Madagascar – Spring 1991

TWO MEN STOOD shaking hands. One spoke in a very thick oriental accent. They both smiled while cameras flashed. This was it . . . The sort of thing that pastes your face across the covers of countless magazines. This was significant enough to land both of them guest spots on all the best talk shows. They might even soon find themselves waiting in the most famous green room of them all; watching a monitor. Listening for those immortal words – *here's Johnny!*

It was that big. But it wasn't as if it had come easy. Both men had suffered bouts of dysentery and malaria; relatively small expectable potential sacrifices they had both accepted during months of their communication's prior to the expedition. What they sought, if they could prove its existence they both agreed – would be worth nearly any sacrifice . . . Well worth it!

Both men had had their eyes on this particular ichthyoidal prize for years. One man to put an exclamation point to his long list of notoriety in his field. The other . . . This was his best chance to jump-start a severely stalled career. This was the chance of a lifetime he'd been looking for – praying for!

It wasn't that he was getting on in years. He was still a relatively young man. The problem was; the field of what some referred to as pseudo-science that he avidly pursued offered a very shallow window of time to prove yourself not to be a crank. To get stamped with that irrevocable label would be the proverbial *coup de grace* – the death blow; regarding any hopes of attaining additional grants to further his studies.

CHAPTER 1

Sic Semper Tyrannis

Present day

IT WAS LATE afternoon. The early autumn sky was dark and foreboding. It had been a fiercely windy day from the beginning. One of those days like so many others this time of year; where the torrents of sheeted rain seemed to further drown his existence. The stormy weather served as just one more excuse. It wasn't really what held him captured within the confines of his bleak existence. He'd become a prisoner of his own creation, the aftermath of a mental disposition of his own devise – one much more serious than mere seasonal unrest or cabin fever. He had fallen off the wagon or rather had leaped off months ago. He'd been sinking faster and further into the deep end of clinical depression until his brain was swimming in it. He was way beyond his depth with no shoreline in site. Desperately treading to remain a-float while grasping futilely at any would-be semblance of a life raft that always remained just out of reach. It had all been like a bad dream, a nightmare that he couldn't wake from. The loss of both his wife and teenage daughter two years ago at the hand of a drunk driver had in one ugly sweep of fate or cosmic karma or whatever, had seemed of late to be just another horrific allowance by God; if there even is a God he often wondered – that travesty, that sacrificial taking of the only two people he loved by the supreme seemingly absentee land lord had ruined his life . . . If God exists, he hated him!

He had been on the downward slope of a rollercoaster ride from hell like so many other deeply bereaved that he'd seen plenty of times over the years on talk shows. But now he knew with empirical certainty that unless a person has experienced something similar; all those sad stories heard almost daily leave us mostly unaffected. That is, unless a loved one or ones, should find themselves one day *zigging* when they should have *zagged*, either metaphorically or actually. Whereby random bad luck or perhaps even more cruel, some predestined cosmic fate should strike with a finality that up to that moment he never could have comprehended – that fateful day when the stars in his eyes, the hope in his heart was instantaneously extinguished leaving him feeling soulless or perhaps besides his bottomless remorse; it left him in many ways no longer feeling at all . . . He'd become a vacuum, void of all the light of the world. Nothing looked the same. His world had transformed from Technicolor to black and white. Nothing smelled fragrant or tasted sweet. He'd become – hollow. Everything around him seemed to be spinning out of control. His mind was caught in a continuous looped aging wearing-out video that played incessantly magic and tragic memories that lingered but were becoming out of focus like swirling smoky fading specters of what once was. He felt that nobody could ever comprehend the depth of his affliction . . . Which in common vernacular was a condition generally referred to as a *broken heart*. He hated people who used that phrase *broken heart* – like those two lady's from his wife's old church that came to visit him a few months after the accident . . . He made the mistake of inviting them to come into his house and to have a seat. After what seemed to him an eternity of them looking at him with their phony sympathetic eyes; as they thumped their thumbs upon their bibles that they held firmly upon their laps . . . *So that's where they got the phrase bible thumpers* he'd mused at the time . . . To him they were nothing more than cackling blue-haired old birds who liked to poke their beaks up other peoples business. The only thing they had to say that he could even remember was a lot of crap about faith and that old cliché – *time heals all wounds* . . . Who ever coined that phrase should have been shot on sight he often thought . . . His extreme mental pain and anguish which he'd been told by some Doctor was called *post traumatic stress and anxiety disorder* . . . He'd become convinced with certainty that to gain release there was but one cure, or rather, solution. The trouble was his method to date to achieve a solution was taking way too long. Suicide by drinking himself to oblivion as a means to achieve his own death, was depressingly slow and expensive. And he was rapidly running out of what little money he had left, and that too was terminally abysmal.

Today his depression was rapidly approaching crescendo as it held him tight within its vice-grip and was twisting and wrenching his gut. Tighter and tighter it squeezed and it wasn't going to let go. He was feeling lower than a snake's belly. And no amount of time, or church do-gooders with their kindly offerings of support and pep-talks, nor any amount of prescription anti-depressants, or even his medication of choice lots and lots of booze, had or would made one lick of difference.

He just set in his dilapidated twenty seven foot Airstream Argosy travel trailer circa 1986 presently situated in *The Dunes RV Park* – and stared blurry-eyed out at the torrential rain and gusting wind. The weather in Winchester Bay, Southern Oregon Coast had been much like a metaphor regarding how his life had been for the last two years . . . Dismally bleak and catatonically depressing!

Each long day brought the same result in his mind – just another useless waste of time. Which to him merely underscored the futility of any thoughts he might fleetingly consider – rare thoughts regarding any possibility of effecting positive change intended to gather momentum towards some semblance of beginning to live again.

He had moved out to the Pacific Northwest after the accident in a feeble attempt to dive back into his work. That too had been failing and he was nearly broke. Nearly as broke as his completely broken heart that by some cruel joke just keeps on beating.

It hadn't always been so. He'd once been for the most part a happy guy. Generally considered to be a respectable academician; though his shiny credentials often lost their luster among his peers – due to his notorious deviations from scientific pathways more commonly tread into the unhallowed halls of: Crypto-Zoology.

Shortly after the accident he'd sold their house in Sacramento and most of his and Janet his late wife's things. He moved away mostly as an attempt to leave the house and area that around every corner brought memories that tore at his soul until there wasn't anything left to tear at. He'd been living or rather surviving all around the forests of northern California and the Pacific Northwest for the last year . . . Semi-occupying some of his time by chasing any hint of a credible lead geared towards the ever elusive *Big Foot.*

Dr. Ian McDermott PhD seated in his very broken down swivel rocker-recliner sat slumped over in an alcohol induced haze reading the *help wanted* classified ads in the local newspaper. He had just turned *forty-two* not two weeks previous. He celebrated his birthday alone as usual. Alone, that is, unless you counted his house guests for the evening – Jack Daniels and a loaded thirty-two Beretta that he affectionately called *"Ole Caretaker."* He'd named his gun that name after one of his favorite characters from a movie he'd seen years ago – *the Longest Yard* . . . The original, not the remake . . . Generally speaking he hated remakes. *Some things are sacred cows and should be left alone,* he thought to himself.

The night of his birthday he'd become reacquainted with "Ole Caretaker." In the shank of that fateful evening amidst his rock bottom despair; his trusty Cyclops barrel-eyed thirty-two had stared him unsteadily between his eyes for one eternal minute.

To say in addition to his grieving, he was having a midlife crisis would be like saying, fish swim – over simplified but true.

Ian turned from the window and for the next several moments just sat staring at a framed picture of himself and the renowned oceanographic scientist Dr. Mitsuru Matsimoto, PhD from the University of Nagasaki. The two were posing for a photo. Shaking hands in celebration of their co-discovery of a previously thought to be extinct variety of prehistoric fish. The photo of them showed the fish lying on its side on the deck of the boat right at their feet. This particular variety of black finned blue Coelacanth showed signs of evolutionary traits that would later prove to pre-date on the evolutionary scale the previously discovered all blue Coelacanth found in Indonesian waters not six months earlier. Both varieties of Coelacanth had been thought to have been extinct for over eighty million years.

That photo had been taken just off the coast of Madagascar. Ian's participation in that scientifically significant discovery had served as what Andy Warhol had once in the sixties described as – a persons proverbial fifteen minutes of fame.

The rain had increased to nearly a thundering sound as it hammered relentlessly on the metal roof of the trailer. Ian, due to the noise, gave up on the idea of watching any television. He decided rather to just sit back in his recliner and let time tick away. He reached for what he'd been saving for this evening, but deciding it must be cocktail hour somewhere. He picked up the bottle still in its brown bag – his recently acquired reload of preferred spirits that he'd picked up yesterday from the local liquor store. With practiced precision without looking at what he held, he twisted the lid off and with a small flick of his wrist tossed it to the ground. Whereby allowing the escape of the sweet malted whiskey fragrance to perfume the air about him. Ian loved the smell of Jack Daniels in the morning, afternoon or evening . . . it smelled not like victory, more like *surrender* – he mused.

At the very moment he'd seized his chalice of choice. Inflated his lungs. Puckered his lips in preparation to blow any dust out that may have settled to the bottom of his ready positioned favorite whiskey glass. The glass which had set for hours neatly in place on the end table just within his reach – standing on the sideline faithfully waiting to be the media of libation delivery for this evenings non-celebratory drink-a-thon . . . It was just then that his cell phone began sounding off . . . Playing its too familiar irritating jingle which startled him to the point of nearly dropping his glass and bottle.

Ian cried out loudly in a silly voice that he'd do once in a while; never in the presence of anyone – an attempt at a surreal southern gentlemen's drawl. This time responding in a manner he figured Jack Daniel's himself would have; if faced with the same disturbance which nearly caused alcohol abuse in the form of spillage or heaven forbid, total breakage of *old number seven. "Why, disturbing a man from enjoying his libation – tyranny I say, bill collecting scoundrel no doubt. Why, who ever is behind this outrage should be summarily drawn and quartered . . .* ***Sic Semper Tyrannis!*** *– thus to Tyrants, I say . . ."* Ian was oblivious that his out cry, its vernacular, inflection and intonation – his funny voice intended only for purpose of self amusement. Was the recreation of a subconscious imprint left on him from his childhood. He without intention had just then and occasionally over the years had been doing a pretty decent vocal impersonation of the *Loony Tunes* cartoon character *Yosemite Sam* portrayed as a southern civil war officer.

After almost enjoying his proclamation of protest – Ian contrary to his better judgment decided to pick up his cell phone; the call said restricted. Whoever was calling disturbing his peace was anyone's guess – but for just a second he thought maybe, just maybe it might be that gal – *what was her name, Rosaline? That gal wore too much makeup in a poor attempt to hide her middle age. But she did have two redeeming qualities in the form of very large almost picturesque breasts.*

Ian had kidded himself into nearly believing that he'd been inadvertently flirting with her yesterday up at the counter at the liquor store. With half hearted belief that it would ever amount to anything. He'd gone as far as to tell her where he was staying. And when she had turned her head away from him he stealthfully placed his business card on the counter, then slipped out the door not looking back. He thought she did look to be worth spending at least twenty minutes with.

"Hello . . . Yeah, this is Doctor Ian McDermott, who wants to know . . . ? Okay Sheriff Bud O'Brien . . . What does the Sheriff of Harmony County Washington want with me? Yeah, that's what I study. Yes, I have been chasing, doing this sort of thing for a long time – my field, it's called Crypto . . . I'm a Zoologist – yes . . . Untypical species or sometimes thought to be extinct . . . Yes, that is what I specialize in . . . Yes, that was me in those old articles. Yes, I was . . . I am known to be an expert in my field . . . You still haven't said what this is all about?"

On the other end of the phone Sheriff Bud O'Brien sat in his office with one foot atop his desk. He held the phone to his ear with one hand and in the other he held an old copy of the magazine, ***Explorer.*** As he talked and listened, he gazed at the second magazine that sat on top of his desk (the ***National Geographic***). Both magazines had Ian's face splashed across the covers. Bud had asked an old friend of his, Molly Keener, who worked part time at the Vancouver, Washington, public Library – to dig up and send him any article's she might be able to find featuring someone whose credentials might pass as a credible professional investigator of non-typical possible predator animals. He had promised the town council; especially the more superstitious members, that he would leave no stone un-turned no matter how improbable it might be. Especially in the wake of the recent heightened surge of wild stories abounding of *Big Foot* sightings and the alleged Sasquatch attack of a local logger.

Even though Bud had grown up in the Northwest and had lived his entire life in quote *Big Foot* country – Sasquatch was a subject that Bud could barely give any serious thought to. But pressure had been mounting on him regarding a couple of tourist hikers that had gone missing for a couple of weeks now. And no amount of conventional wisdom regarding his coordinated efforts with other county's Sheriffs departments, Police departments and Search and Rescue professionals had offered any answers. So due to the incessant coaxing from the town council; and sheer numbers of the bizarre reports. Bud reluctantly decided that there was little harm to his reputation to consider remote possibilities (conventional or otherwise) since all inside the box investigative procedures had so far failed to turn up any answers to the fate of the hikers or explain what animal was responsible for the very real viscous attack on Rob Richards a local independent logger.

Bud was further encouraged down the path of extreme possibility by his deputy Charlie Redtail. Bud figured he would humor Charlie; primarily because he knew the local Indian legends of Sasquatch held sway many of the locals. So he decided to at least pretend to consider the possibility that they could be dealing with some rare thought to be extinct at least to the region, predator such as a wolf, or more likely a cougar . . . or more fitting to the description of his only eye witness to the attack, the victim – a large bear . . . But even Bud who was largely a skeptic, even he wasn't willing at this point to totally rule out the tiny possibility that he might be dealing with something else entirely.

One thing seemed too apparent though – there is or at least was something out there in the woods. And it could mean more trouble than he already had to deal with now down the road.

Rob Richards' story had to be taken serious; excluding any exaggerations or hallucinations that could have stemmed from sheer terror and trauma to his testimony. He had in fact been savagely attacked by something that was certain. He'd said he was attacked at a job site just above mile marker thirty eight. An area well known by Bud, he'd hunted that area many times – it was very near the south base of Mt. St. Helens. Rob had said the attack happened shortly after dark as he was stowing some chain saws and other rigging into the back of his truck.

Bud thought to himself for a moment – *the attack happened at night, but there was a lot of moonlight that night . . . these things happen so fast! You know how reliable eye witnesses can be, especially ones under fierce attack by a wild animal, or . . .*

Rob Richards had shown up last Thursday night just before midnight pounding on the front door of the very small ***Harmony Falls Medical Clinic*** – Rob was desperately attempting to wake Doc Matthews who lives in an apartment upstairs; before he lost consciousness from blood loss and trauma. When Doc came downstairs and opened his clinics front door and found Rob; he immediately noted that Rob was all tore up, but his primary wounds were to his chest and right arm. Doc was able to stabilize Rob whereby saving his life. Later Friday morning after getting Rob transported by helicopter to Portland, Oregon, Saint Vincent Hospital, Doc Matthews told Sheriff Bud O'Brien that Rob's wounds mostly resembled canine bites and tears; though he couldn't rule out bear or cougar. Regardless, the bite radius of the wounds was so large they could have only been inflicted by a very large animal, larger than any known around these parts. Most probably something like a hybrid wolf-dog let loose into the wild. Or some extremely large feral dog – perhaps a Husky or German Shepherd or some like breed. Whatever it was: Dog, bear, or cougar . . . Whatever had attacked Rob, it was a very large, very dangerous force to be reckoned with. It had laid Rob out with ease. And Rob was a large, strong, rough and tumble logger and skilled backwoodsman. A man who had a deserved reputation for knowing how to take care of himself in the wilderness or in a bar fight. Doc said the last thing Rob Richards said to him before he lost consciousness on his bed in the clinic was . . .

"Doc, I swear what got me, it weren't no regular animal. But it weren't no man neither . . . I mean it stood like a man, but it was big, Doc, it was huge! I mean Doc, it looked like some kind of monster . . . ! Doc, you got to believe me, I know this is gonna sound crazy, but I think it was *Big Foot!*"

What had happened to Rob Richards was the proverbial straw that had broke the camels back, or at least the voice of reason – which had led him to this point, to make this phone call with Dr. Ian McDermott.

"All right, Sheriff, understand that I get two-hundred fifty a day plus expenses to investigate; with no guarantees – I mean no refunds if I can't help turn anything up . . . That is agreeable? Okay then – I'll come on out to your neck of the woods and poke around a bit . . . Just as long as you understand that regardless of what I turn up or whatever, well, usually these things have perfectly logical explanations. Okay, okay, I'll see ya tomorrow. Yeah, that's right, I'm currently residing on the Oregon coast so I'm just a few hours from you . . . Right, right I look forward to meeting with you . . . Thanks for contacting me, right . . . Bye!"

Ian hung up the phone, reached down and picked up the screw cap that he'd tossed earlier and re-screwed it back onto his bottle. He then took a deep breath, slapped his knees with both palms and suddenly found himself momentarily smiling a genuine smile.

CHAPTER 2

Big Foot Country

TRAVELING EAST ON Lewis and Clark State Highway 503 – Ian had been driving for the last fifteen minutes along the shoreline of beautiful Lake Merwin, a twenty-six mile long damned reservoir of the Meriwether Lewis river; a tributary of the mighty Columbia river. He stopped to rest at the Speelyai bay recreational day-use park to stretch his legs and use the restroom. Checking his Tom-Tom global positioning system, Ian was pleasantly relieved to see that he was less than a mile from the town of Harmony Falls. He'd phoned ahead last night and made reservations to stay at the only RV park within miles of the little town. After viewing the properties website www.firlaneresort.com from his laptop. He'd discovered the modestly quaint resort offered a cluster of six rental cabins, a dozen tent camping sites as well as eighteen full hook-up RV pull through sites; all nestled under a blanket of tall fir trees. The little resort had all the amenities that he would require for a stay that he doubted would be more than just a few days. Amenities which included a shower-house with clothes washers and dryers; there was even a little restaurant right next door; which pleased him since he rarely cooked for himself. That particular eatery sounded especially pleasing to him because mentioned on the resorts website, that restaurant boasted homemade northwest berry pies; specialty of the house Marionberry – which happened to be his favorite.

After the short break at the day use park Ian got back on the road and had only been driving his 1993 Jeep Grand Wagoneer heading further east for just a few minutes; when he spotted the sign he'd been on the lookout for. He slowed his vehicle way down and turned his Jeep and trailer left off of the highway and up the private road entrance to the ***Fir Lane Resort and RV Park***. His Jeeps odometer which had maxed out, returning once again to its starting point of zero's more than three years ago; that now reflected just a little more than eighty thousand miles wouldn't fool anyone as to its obvious care-worn condition. But to Ian his Jeeps engine still sounded strong with plenty of compression. He thought his engine sounded tough, regardless of its age and mileage. Especially strong since its catalytic converter and most of its tail pipe had gone missing in action while crossing over the Siskiyou mountain range near Mt. Shasta a few months back.

Faithfully in tow was his equally tired Airstream trailer. Both Jeep and trailer clanked and squelched loudly. Ian was mostly oblivious to the noise. Unabashed by the spectacle he and his worldly possessions had created while pulling into the resort. Very apparent to all other on-lookers was the fact that both his Jeep and its tow were suffering acutely from metallic rust-tinoma cancer – which obviously even to the laymen's eye, had systemically metastasized throughout their wheel-wells and undercarriages. Additionally, adding to the Jeeps long list of ailments was its chronic vehicular fatigue syndrome in the form of worn out shocks, struts, u-joints and soon to no longer be legal, balding tires.

Shortly after registering with the park's office, Ian parked his trailer in site number eight. A beautiful spot located near a large creek that ran not thirty feet behind his camp-site. After unhooking his

Jeep from his trailer, Ian opened the driver's door of his Jeep and retrieved his cell phone from its resting place; a cup-holder on the consul between the two front seats. Ian had been moving pretty fast readying his camp and had subsequently become momentarily out of breath. He stopped, bent over and with hands on his knees took a deep breath – a gasping re-fill of high-oxygen enriched fresh mountain air. Ian straightened up and stretched his back . . . He then proceeded to call Sheriff Bud O'Brien.

Ian dialed Bud's number . . . the phone began to ring through, once, twice, three times . . .

"Harmony County Sheriff's Department – Sheriff Bud O'Brien speaking, how can I assist . . . ?"

Ian chuckled to himself . . . for some reason the professional tone of the Sheriff of this tiny burg surprised him. Ian had in his mind that he'd be speaking with some *good-ole-boy* sounding yokel who probably would speak similar to the sixties television character from the Andy Griffith show – Sheriff Andy Taylor of Mayberry . . . by starting the conversation with a hearty home-town *"howdy!"* But he quickly decided that after such a formal answering of the phone that he'd start the conversation with a title of his own.

"Hello Sheriff O'Brien this is Doctor Ian McDermott . . ."

Upon hearing his voice Bud began rapidly swallowing his prune-Danish and replied, "Oh yeah, McDermott, good to hear from ya . . . When you going to be arriving to our fair community . . . ?"

"Well Sheriff, I have arrived . . . I'm staying at your local five-star resort, the *Lone Fir,* or *Fir place* . . . uh, Fir, something?"

"Oh yeah, you're at Molly's place, *Fir Lane Resort* – nice place, though we both know it ain't no five-star resort . . ."

They both laughed simultaneously as tensions eased considerably.

"Say McDermott, why don't you come join me? – I'm grabbing a bite of lunch . . . I'm just up the road from ya, bout a couple minutes from where you're staying . . . I'm at the *Lakeview Bar and Grill.* It's in plain site on the right side of the road bout a half mile from where you're at. Like the name suggests, it's got a nice view of the lake and good grub. Anyway, you can't miss it . . . We'll get further acquainted and I'll get ya up to speed with what's been going on.

"Yeah, sure Sheriff that'll be fine – I'll meet up with you in a few minutes . . ."

CHAPTER 3

First Impressions

IAN HAD ONLY been driving for a couple of minutes when he saw up ahead the sign he'd been looking for. The restaurant-bar was just as easy to spot as Sheriff Bud had assured him it would be. Ian switched on his right turn blinker and proceeded ahead until he reached the gravel driveway that led to the restaurant parking lot. Upon pulling into the parking lot he immediately noticed another thing that Sheriff Bud had told him just minutes ago – the place did indeed have a beautiful view of Lake Merwin.

After parking, Ian slowly climbed out of his Jeep and just stood looking for one long moment out at the lake. It was a mostly cloudy and briskly windy day. The wind had the lakes surface pretty kicked up. But for the moment the sun was shinning brightly through a cloud break – creating what to Ian looked like millions of brilliant shimmering shards of golden light that gently kissed the slightly white capped surface as they danced across the glacier melt blue-green water. Everywhere he looked, Southwest Washington sub-alpine flora in all indigenous varieties comprised every color and texture imaginable.

Ian stared up at the trees and was mesmerized by the abundance of heavy moisture laden leaves on branches that swayed back and forth in the breeze. Ian marveled at the shades of fiery yellows and burnt oranges that though typical of the fall season was none-the-less to him, beautiful to behold. Ian couldn't help but smile just a little as he took notice of the thousands of leaves that had lost their battle to hang-on and had joined their comrades in helping to form the ever-growing blanket that partially covered the ground at his feet; creating to him what resembled a colorful expanding organic tapestry all about the parking lot and beyond. The brilliant natural pallet of colors that surrounded him in every direction reminded Ian of a time years ago when he'd visited Vermont in the autumn. Somehow, what surrounded him now was even more beautiful than that and it brought a momentary smile to his face. But it was short lived. Ian's customary facial expression which generally reflected a dismal demeanor began once again to take hold. He began intellectualizing all of his surroundings as picturesque as it is; as just the mere changing of the seasons that in short order would all just rot and wither away. After a protracted discontented moment of reflection Ian did finally concede to himself that all of the beauty wasn't doomed to merely rot-away; as he gazed across the lake to the other side at the nearly timeless existence of the massive stand of ancient evergreen forest . . . *At least the sections that hadn't yet been clear-cut,* he mused – which to Ian appeared as a dense dark green monolithic foreboding presence; alive and watching his every move. The gentle swaying treetops gave him the eerie impression of the trees breathing, somehow taking in, devouring or at least hiding all life. Suddenly, Ian felt a slight chill up the back side of his neck – he quickly turned away from gazing at the forest beyond the lake. Ian spotted the entrance to the bar which was located in the backside of the restaurant and began walking towards the entrance. Just as he reached the door, Ian turned to gaze once again out upon the lake and the mountainous hillsides beyond. From his present vantage point the densely forested hillsides across the lake looked to go on forever. Ian suddenly realized with clarity how isolated and primal this area was . . . and how small one man could feel.

Ian thought to himself – *if ever there was a playground for Big Foot. Or, some type of predator that could exist largely undetected. Undetected by virtue of existing in an area that offers hundreds of miles of vast expanses of ancient forest for habitat, this is it!*

He entered through the bar-entrance to the restaurant. It took a couple of seconds for his transitions adjustable lenses in his glasses to lighten up enough to see around the bar-lit room. After a long uncomfortable couple of seconds of standing in the open doorway had passed, just as he could see well enough to proceed on in he heard a familiar voice bounding from across the room . . . The voice was calling his name . . .

"Hey, that you McDermott . . . ?" Ian shook his head yes and gave a reluctant smile. "Well, come on over and cop a squat, with a cop . . . ha!" Bud O'Brien just thought that one up at the moment of its delivery.

Ian walked over to Sheriff Bud's table, smiled and shook the Sheriffs hand. He then pulled out a chair and took a seat across from the Sheriff. Then without hesitation Sheriff Bud O'Brien jumped into the conversation.

"Hey, McDermott . . . your first name's Ian, right . . . ?"

"That's right Sheriff."

Sheriff Bud then smiled a very large warm smile.

"Well now, how bout we forgo any further formalities and you call me Bud and I'll call you Ian, no more to do with titles and such – that sound okay by you?"

Ian replied with a smile and sigh of relief, "That sounds good by me!"

Right out of the gate Ian liked Sheriff Bud's laid back style. Ian hated people that were full of themselves, people with over inflated ego's.

"Well sir . . . Ian . . . The food here's good. But say, if you like meatloaf sandwiches, well ole Gracie, she owns the place, and does most of the cooking . . . anyway – she makes the best god-damn meatloaf sandwich I ever tasted, comes with mashed taters and beef gravy . . ."

Without even looking at a menu Ian smiled at Bud . . .

"By God Bud, now you're talking – that sounds better than great! Say how's their pie . . . I read online that the little eatery next to where I'm camped has good homemade pies."

Bud slid back slightly from the table relaxing his abundant stature into a more comfortable posture.

"Yes sir, they do got pretty good pies – but tell ya the truth, Gracie here's got em beat. Got em beat hands down – especially if you like homemade berry pie."

Ian spoke up eagerly, "You mean local berry pie like . . . Marionberry . . . ?"

"Why hell yes, Ian . . . You like Marionberry?"

Ian with wide eyes shook his head yes and replied, "That's my favorite!"

"Ya don't say – hell Ian, that's my favorite too. And just so happens to be a specialty of this here place . . . Well sir, we'll just have to get us a slice or two, to go with our eats."

Both men smiled brimming smiles at each other . . .

Bud turned his head towards the young gal that was tending bar.

"Say Sally – go an tell your mom that me and my guest here will have us a couple meatloaf sandwiches and a couple slices of Marionberry pie Ã la Mode."

Bud looked over at Ian and immediately saw by Ian's smile, that his Ã la Mode idea met with resounding approval.

As Ian sat there directly across from Sheriff Bud O'Brien; he had to fight back a grin in response to Bud looking just exactly as he had imagined him from their first phone call yesterday. Ian surmised, as he mentally took inventory of the man who sat before him, that Sheriff Bud years ago, was probably quite the high school athlete. He still looked tough and he definitely had that ex-jock look of confidence about him even though he now sported somewhat of a rotund midsection. But definitely tough as the pig-skin leather he probably used to pass around and carry for touch-downs; big Bud, the Football star, would be a sure bet. *Probably de-flowered the Prom Queen after the big homecoming game* . . . Ian mused. Ian went so far as to surmise, by the very aged wedding band worn on Bud's left hand, that Bud probably married his high school sweetheart. He probably nailed down the Prom Queen right after graduation, Ian figured. Ian had always prided himself of his ability to size people up. Good powers of deductive reasoning had over the years served him pretty well. In the field of Crypto-Zoology, you had to be a good observer as well as clever investigator. He further deduced that despite Sheriff Bud's abundant belly, that his shirt had a hard time keeping covered as it was tucked in above his flab folded over belt-line; that by the size of Bud's arms he could no-doubt handle himself very handily in a physical scuffle against pretty much any of the local logger rough-necks. There was just something behind the *good-ole-boy* exterior that led Ian to understand almost from the first moment he'd met Bud; that this small town Sheriff was no run of the mill hick. Ian figured Bud could probably shoot the wings off a fly on the wall from thirty paces with the Smith and Wesson .357 magnum that he sported in plain view holstered to his utility belt. Additionally, his utility belt housed plenty of ammo, a set of cuffs, as well as a telescopic night stick and the customary can of *mace* brand pepper spray.

Bud looked Ian up and down while sporting a sly but convincing smile.

"So tell me Ian . . . exactly what is your educational background? I mean what's it take to be a hunter of the, well let's say, the unusual animal variety . . . ?"

Ian not being the sort that likes uncomfortable silences was actually glad that Sheriff Bud was a direct to the point kind of guy. He was ready for this line of questioning, the kind which comes up time and again when discussing his somewhat unorthodox profession.

"Bud, I have a doctorate in Zoology and a minor in Biology – I've also studied Primatology, extensively specializing in forensic

Anthropology and Paleontology. Additionally, I had begun studies a few years back – in Psychology and Parapsychology. You already have my phone number, but here's my card for your file or records, or whatever . . ."

Bud reached halfway across the table and accepted the business card from Ian. As he looked intently at the card for a long moment he developed a perplexed questioning look on his face that Ian tried hard to read . . . Bud then spoke once again straight from the hip . . .

"Say there, not wanting to sound too ignorant . . . If I understand ya . . . and no disrespect intended. You're sort-a like that Indiana Jones character from those movies . . . cept you look for the Lock Ness Monster, Big Foot or the boogie-man . . . instead of buried treasure or bones like most characters with your credentials, PhD and all – But what in hell's creation is Parapsychology? Isn't that something like them ghost hunter fellows I seen on late night T.V . . . ?"

Ian smiled a genuine smile; not offended in the least by either the expression on Bud's face nor by his question.

"Well, yes in a way I suppose – but actually it can mean many things . . . I mean many different disciplines of research; like say, the study of psychic abilities. Or, well anything along the lines of people, places or things that don't exactly fit into what most people consider conventional wisdom I suppose. But understand that really isn't what I do. Like it says on my card . . . my business is Crypto-Zoological investigations. In other words, I look to verify or debunk reports of animals thought to be extinct – or I search for hard evidence of the existence of creatures, for lack of a better word, that are generally considered to be myth but in fact just might be very real . . . I keep an open mind and let the facts speak for themselves. In my investigations I do a lot of out in the field work, collect evidence, interview people. I do, I assume, much the same as what you no doubt do in your field of law enforcement when you're investigating a crime. Hence, the name of my business – **McDermott Cryptid Zoological Investigations**."

Bud looked up from Ian's business card and stared directly into Ian's eyes, then replied, *"Cryptid Zoological Investigations* . . . the search for strange or yet to be proven animals so to speak."

Ian interjected, "Yeah, that about sums it up."

"Hmm – well, sir, Ian, I'm glad you pointed that out. What with all the liberal wacko jobs out there. Hell, I might have figured you to be some sort of animal Coroner who investigates the cause of death of critters who die in the Zoo or some such."

They both laughed at that notion.

"Tell ya the truth Ian – I pretty much knew what ya do for a living before I called ya in the first place . . ."

Ian looked intensely back at Sheriff Bud and fired a question that had been burning his mind since their first telephone conversation . . .

"Tell me Bud – how'd you come to be calling me in on whatever you're hunting, or investigating, anyway?"

Bud sat back in his chair and grinned at the question that he'd been anticipating would inevitably come up.

"Well now, that is a fine question there Ian . . . Ya see, I don't readily buy into all the local talk of Big Foot or monsters and such . . . I figure what we got here is a case of mistaken identity, ya know of a bear or wild dogs or such . . . It's no doubt blown way out of proportion due to frightened people with overactive imaginations. Imaginations fueled by a host of local Indian superstitions and such . . . But here are the facts . . . I've got some tourists gone missing without a trace . . . I got a local man all torn up lying in a bed in the hospital in Portland; who by the way ain't no greenhorn when it comes to the back country, spouting tales of his attack by Sasquatch . . . I got wild tales buzzing all round-town . . . crazy talk. And I'll admit up till now my investigations regarding those missing tourists and my banged-up local yokel, ain't turned up squat . . . Anyway, to answer your question; I've a friend who helps me time to time check into things . . . She works at a library in Vancouver . . . You know the one here in Washington next to Portland, not Canada . . . . Anyway, I asked her to check through her library's archives and see if she could come up with a reputable name of someone that investigates – well, investigates strange phenomena regarding animal attacks, or . . . such like that. Meanwhile I did some checking around on the subject of fellows like yourself who investigate strange creatures and such. Your name was right at the top of the list. You're considered by the scientific community to be slightly less crazy than most in your field. You actually proved that one fish still is around; you know that one that scientists said was extinct."

Bud laughed a small laugh. He didn't mean to offend Ian – he didn't.

"Anyhow, some days go by . . . My librarian friend she calls me, tells me she's sending me a couple of prestigious magazines that I needed to check out that had you plastered all over them. Magazines telling of you being an expert in your somewhat dubious if I may, field. Well-sir, I figured it might be in the best interest of the fine people of my little town here that all channels be considered. A feller like yourself just might add a different perspective – you know maybe offer some insight on the very outside chance that we might be dealing with something, well, lets just say out of the ordinary. Ian, I don't mind telling ya this is becoming a very high-profile situation . . . I'm getting lots of unwanted questions and pressure from the media. Ya see – the tourists gone missing just happen to be the daughter and son-in-law of a prominent Seattle attorney, Mr. Walter P. Shultz. And if that ain't bad enough, Mr. Walter P. Shultz, he just happens to be the son of Washington State Senator Hamilton Shultz. Needless to say, I got news vans with their reporters microphones in hand crawling all over – one in particular, a Ms. Marsha Steward, KATW channel thirteen news. She just yesterday, crawled so far up my ass that if I was to fart it would no doubt be quoted on the six o'clock news . . . and out of context far as that goes; anyhow, back to the subject of you. After I did a little light reading of them magazines regarding your escapades capturing that prehistoric fish, I figured if I was gonna even consider extreme possibilities you were my guy. So I got on my computer, *Googled* for your last known locale and contact digits; found ya, called ya up . . . here we are . . . Say, you're famous bout what you do, or at least once were . . . right?"

Ian grinned sheepishly, then with a slight sigh replied . . .

"Yeah, well I had my time in the spotlight I suppose – But Bud, that was a long time ago . . . I mean, make no mistake I'm not saying that I don't stay busy . . ."

Ian was now smiling, attempting to display sublime confidence regarding his past reputation and present aptitude to aide Sheriff Bud with his investigations. Whereby warranting his not yet paid salary for services not yet rendered. All the while Ian knew he was about to cross the line from embellishments to lies . . .

"Well, yes it's true that I have attained a certain level of notoriety as an expert in my field. Which, is a field that covers many aspects; and it's a big world with lots of unexplainable reports of strange or thought to be extinct animal sightings around the globe . . . keeps me very busy. I'm continuously on the move, traveling place to place. Fact is the only reason that I accepted your invitation to check into things here for you; is that it just so happens that I've been actively researching the Big Foot phenomena throughout the Pacific Northwest and Northern California for the last several months. This seemed to fit with my ongoing investigations; and well, here I am at your service. For the fee we discussed previously, of course."

Bud looked Ian over then winked a sly wink back at him.

"Of course, don't expect a man of your prestige and notoriety to work pro-bono!"

They both laughed – they jointly were becoming more relaxed with one-another. It would have been clear to any third party that right from the start somehow they shared a respect of one another.

Just then during a fractional moment of silence their mutual admiration was interrupted by a heavily gray bearded elderly gentlemen dressed in street vagabond attire; including the customary Vietnam vintage soldiers jacket. The man was seated against the wall, slouched over an empty glass – poised as if he were a fixture of the place; over the years that was nearly what he'd become. But this fixture could speak, though he did so rarely – mainly merely to beg for liquid scraps from the occasional tourist or more commonly from local patrons of the establishment.

"You that Big Foot hunter feller people be talking bout . . . ?"

The tattered, silver bearded man – who had once years ago served his country with honor; and in doing so lost most of the mobility of his left leg due to shrapnel received from a North Vietnamese antipersonnel mine; glared with care-worn, liver-spotted face – first at Ian, then the Sheriff, then back at Ian . . .

"I seen him . . . I seen the Big Foot . . . Cept he ain't no ape-man like what people say . . . People say he be more scared of them then they be of him – Bullshit! The Big Foot ain't scared of nothing!"

The old vagabond was talking in spurts. Often too loud or too soft to readily understand. To make matters of understanding him worse he was moderately intoxicated and slightly slurring his already heavily accented words . . .

"It ain't like they say, no mistaken reared-up bear or such, the Big Foot be Loupe-Garou . . . Say, that's all ya get from me fer free, hey city feller . . . Mister big time Scientist – you a monster hunter? You come prepared to battle the monster . . . ? Cause if ya ain't, you best high tell it back to where ya came . . . The names Fournier, Tom Fournier. I seen that monster what folks call the Big Foot – and lived to tell about it. Tell ya all about it if'n ya buy me a *wild turkey* straight-up!"

Ian looked over at Bud and spoke just above a whisper for Bud's ears only. "I could be mistaken, but doesn't that old timer have an Acadian accent, Fournier he's French . . . Cajun?"

Bud grinned and replied, "Very perceptive of you Ian – I can see you're a man who takes note . . . Yep, we got a lot of descendants of the French settled in these parts. Most come down here by way of the fur trade from Canada. Some come up from Louisiana when logging and saw-mill jobs were plentiful . . . Ancestors originated from Quebec – France before that. This area like so many places have our little immigrant concentrations . . . Why take across the Columbia over in Clatskanie Oregon – mostly Fins over there . . . and we got areas with German towns and such . . . Fact is we got."

At that instant the side door of the bar burst open interrupting Bud mid sentence – there in the doorway stood a man in uniform. The same uniform that Sheriff Bud sported; but this man was obviously a Native American. He stood there tall with long ebony hair that was salted with just a smattering of gray; an abundant mane that was pulled back into a pony-tail. Ian immediately made the man in uniform to be around six foot one or two in his late thirties or early forties . . . The uniformed figure stood in the doorway proudly with shoulders back obviously of fine vigor. Equally obvious to Ian, and to all present for that matter, was the uniformed mans extremely excited urgent demeanor.

In a deep husky voice the uniformed officer called out for the Sheriff as he removed his very dark wire rimmed sunglasses. It had taken Ian a few seconds for his eyes to adjust from coming in from the bright outdoors to the dim bar-light – but the officer obviously knew exactly which table the Sheriff would be seated at, his usual . . .

"Bud, you need to finish up what you got or take'ur with ya – we got to role . . . We got an anonymous call telling us . . . Well, I'll tell ya about it outside."

Bud had worked with his depute for over four years and knew when to take him serious – Bud knew this was serious!

"Sally, tell your mom to wrap them sandwiches to go and please be quick about it; we gotta get going straight away, duty calls!"

Sally could tell by the tone in the Sheriff Deputies voice as well as by the deputies apparent excited state that she needed to move fast – and move fast she did. She headed back to the kitchen and helped her mom get the Sheriff's order ready to go . . . She then came nearly running out from the kitchen brown bag in hand.

"Here Bud, mom's put you and your friend here's lunch on your tab . . . Oh no, I forgot your pie . . ."

Bud looked kindly at Sally. "Now gal don't you fret about that – me and Ian here, we'll be back soon enough to enjoy some of your mom's pie."

Bud reached out and took the lunch bag from Sally. He then turned to Ian. "Come on Ian, lets get out of here and hear what's got my depute all fired-up!"

The three stood next to one another for a moment at the doorway to the side parking lot.

Sheriff Bud, seldom one to concern himself with political correctness or mincing words for that matter continued . . .

"Ian let me introduce you to my Deputy Charlie Redtail – he's my Tonto so to speak."

All three men grinned slightly at Bud's attempted levity.

Ian held out his hand to the Deputy.

"Ian McDermott . . ."

The Deputy, with guarded smile, shook Ian's hand and replied.

"Charlie Redtail – hmm . . . Ian McDermott, I've heard about you. You were famous once, right . . . ?"

Ian didn't answer he just gave Charlie a small reluctant grin. He wasn't sure if he'd just been praised or insulted. By the tone of the Deputies voice the latter was probably the case – Ian mused.

The three men then quickly exited the bar. Charlie Redtail still in a very excited state stared suspiciously up and down at Ian as he spoke.

"Bud, can we talk shop in front of this man?"

Bud smiled and nodded yes to his Deputy. "Yes-sir Charlie... we got us a real bona-fide expert here. As I explained to you yesterday – Ian, by my invitation, is here to observe; and no doubt do a little snooping around on his own as well I suspect. Anyhow, he's here to give us his take on things. We're gonna share any pertinent information with him that we got relating to what's been going on. Now that said – what in hell's going on?"

With assurance from Bud, Charlie told both men what was burning his tongue to tell.

"Bud, back at the office – Jenny took a call about ten minutes ago from an anonymous male caller. The caller told her there are bodies of a man and women at the north end of the lava tubes. That's all he told her before hanging up."

Bud looked at Charlie and without saying a word began marching to his car.

"Come-on Ian you ride with me. I'll drop ya by here later to get your vehicle which I'm guessing is that Jeep sitting over there by its lonesome . . ."

Bud nodded towards the Jeep; Ian smiled and nodded back to Bud that he was correct, it was his.

"Charlie, we'll meet ya up at the tubes – mind ya . . . flash them lights and blast yer siren, lets get there double-quick."

Ian climbed into the passenger seat of Bud's late model Chevy Blazer – Charlie Redtail got in his well worn Chevy Malibu; in an instant the tires of both automobiles were tearing up the gravel as they sped out of the parking lot.

CHAPTER 4

Lava Tubes

RACING UP THE roadway, at near ninety miles an hour, the two Sheriff Department vehicles sped with their cop-lights flashing and sirens blaring.

"Say Ian, I see a ring on yer wedding finger. You got a little women tucked away somewhere? Any kids . . . ?"

Ian replied in a soft monotone voice with a blank expression on his face.

"Once . . . she died. They're both dead. My wife Janet and my daughter Sue Ann. They died in a car accident a couple years back. Just can't get out of the habit of wearing this old wedding band. The ole finger feels naked without it . . . How bout you Bud, you married? – happens I noticed a ring on your finger as well."

"Ian you'd make a fine detective . . . Seems we're both widowers – lost my lovely wife, God rest her soul, three years ago to cancer of the female parts. It ate her up bit by bit. In the end there wasn't much of her body or mind left to eat – then, when she finally went, well, she was gone and I was alone . . . We never had kids . . . My wife . . . May, was her name. She didn't have a fertile womb. Something bout an incompetent cervix or some such thing . . . Anyways, there ain't a day goes by I don't miss her something terrible . . . I can't bring myself to take the damn ring off neither. It's my memory of the good times I suppose – ain't we a pair . . . ?"

Ian glanced over at Bud just for a second then replied . . .

"Yeah, ain't we a pair . . ." As they sped up the road under Bud's very expert handling of his car – they both sighed and shared a moment of reverent silence. Silence honoring their individual attempts at repressing memories they both knew were too painful to dwell on.

Bud cleared this throat, then proceeded to change the subject.

"Say Ian, back at Gracie's the old timer that was talking. He's a regular, you know, every place has its town drunk. Anyway, he said something – something like Big Foot ain't no bear . . . it's a Guru, or some such . . . ?"

Ian smiled and chuckled just a bit as he shook his head no.

"No – Bud, he didn't say Guru – that's like a Yoga instructor, or . . . No what he said was Garou . . ."

Bud replied the second Ian had finished saying the word . . .

"Guru, Garou . . . sounds pretty much the same to me – okay, what in hell's a Garou?"

Being a crypto Zoologist Ian knew the answer to Bud's question; even though the answer even to Ian was . . . crazy! But Ian decided crazy or not he'd answer as best he could.

"Bud what the old-timer said back at the bar I believe was Garou . . . as in Loupe-Garou the French word for a mythological anthropomorphic wolf-like creature."

Bud interrupted, "Anthropomorphic, hmm big word . . . Man, just spit it out – yer talking bout a monster, a werewolf . . . The Indian folk round here they call that sort of superstitious nonsense – shape-shifting, or some such shit."

Then followed a drawn-out uncomfortable pause of silence between the two men. A silence that was finally broken when Ian replied with a sly grin. "Yeah, that's right Bud – werewolf!" Both men laughed . . .

Then Bud changed the subject back to what was at hand.

"Ian, when we get up to the tubes – supposing this weren't a crank call. You can identify skeletal remains or such if need be? I mean if the bodies are say without clothes and are heavy chewed on by some of our local wild life.

Ian smiled a shallow smile, "Yeah Bud, I'm trained to do that, should it be necessary."

Bud cleared his throat then suddenly sounded very serious.

"On the outside chance there are bodies up there – Ian can you tell me if they are victims of natural deaths or, well foul play or such . . . ?"

Ian replied quickly and honestly to that question. "Maybe Bud . . ."

Bud glanced over at Ian to better read Ian's body language regarding his last question and Ian's reply to it.

"Yeah, well – if foul play would turn out to be the case – I'd be notifying crime scene investigations out of Vancouver anyhow . . . Along with dozens of calls and mountains of paperwork regardless of type of death – could mean a massive man-hunt though . . . Well, it's all speculation until we get there. Like my Daddy used to tell me – don't get the cart before the horse . . . If there are bodies up there – poor folks probably got lost and exposure got em, or injuries or such . . ."

Ian took a deep breath, and shook his head in agreement.

CHAPTER 5

Ape Caves

"WELL LOOK WHAT we have here . . ." Bud said to Ian as he glanced into his rearview mirror.

Ian turned his upper body, neck and head to the left as far as his seat belt would allow – enabling him to have a look back at whatever had caught Bud's attention.

Neither Bud nor Ian spoke another word for one extended moment. Then Ian spoke, "Channel thirteen news van – hmm . . . Bud, it looks like we've got company."

Bud took a deep breath then let out an equally large irritated sigh. "Yeah, that's that news lady whose been a big pain in my ass . . . She's persistent I give her that. The woman's been crawling up my backside further then under-shorts with worn-out elastic."

Charlie Redtail, first to arrive, rapidly exited his car – unlocked and pulled back the gate which had boldly posted on it . . .

Warning:

This Area Closed Until Further Notice

Unsafe/Unstable Conditions

Harmony Falls Sheriffs Department

Charlie got back into his car. Now right behind him were two other vehicles driven by: Bud O'Brien and Tom Iverson mobile cameraman for investigative reporter, Miss Marsha Steward – all three vehicles in parade-like succession pulled into the parking lot of the Mount Saint Helen's lava tubes; better known to the locals as the "Ape Caves."

Bud took another deep breath as he pulled into a parking spot alongside his deputy. He then got a very serious look on his face as he exhaled and stared straight into Ian's eyes.

"We had to shut this area down, the tubes I mean; a few days before them hikers went missing round these parts . . . due to Miss St. Helens having a bad case of indigestion. Caused some of the cave siding to give away; still a bit unstable down in there the geologists tell me."

Ian looked at Bud, smiled then replied, "By indigestion I take it there was a significant seismic event, right?"

Bud looked at Ian with just a little surprise in his eyes, that of, what else . . . ? "Yeah Ian, that's right – a significant seismic event; as in a pretty good shake-in-bake earthquake . . . But not really much more than what normally happens around these parts now and again . . . Far as this place and it being shut down, well, sometimes you get lucky . . . This area being shut down made it a whole lot easier to keep the lookers-on away during our initial sweeps of the area looking for that missing young couple. But maybe, they like others managed to pack on in regardless of posting's or roadblock's . . . I really don't think we're gonna find anything here – it's been searched and searched good. Even had dogs up here sniffing about. All sorts of law enforcement involved – yours truly included . . . rescue teams and the like. We concentrated our efforts about four miles from here as the crow flies.

Up at Little Merwin and the falls . . . Seen evidence of someone setting up camp there, but could have been anybody. Well, guess it won't hurt us none to have another look-see around again I suppose – since that anonymous caller, who knows? Mind you now Ian, you're here by my invitation, so I trust you'll stay as far from that television lady or any media folks as you can. If, or when they do get you cornered; you say *no comment* to their questions and keep marching as far from them as your feet will take ya . . . We clear on that?"

"Yeah Bud, we're crystal on that – I've had plenty of unpleasant experiences with the media . . ."

Bud smiled hearing that response from Ian – the two then exited Bud's Blazer and joined Charlie who was standing at the rear of their vehicle. Charlie was growing anxious to discuss with Bud where they should look first for bodies. And he too was stressing a bit regarding the sudden presence and potential scrutiny of the media. Charlie spoke first with an affected smart-alecky tone to his voice . . .

"Bud, I see you've invited your girlfriend . . ."

Bud took his Sheriff's cap off his head and wiped the sweat from his forehead. He replied with a not subtle irritation reflected in his voice.

"Okay, chief talks-a-lot, here's what we're gonna do."

Bud paused with his talking long enough to open the rear hatchback of his Blazer. He reached in and brought out two, two-way radios. Bud handed one to Charlie and began to explain his plan to both Charlie and Ian.

"We're gonna have to keep in touch via walky-squawky. Cell phones are no good up here, no reception."

Bud then took on an entirely new expression and posture – a look that Ian had never before seen in him, but one that came as no surprise. Ian had known somehow from the beginning that beneath the good-ole-boy exterior that was Bud O'Brien, beat the heart of a true law enforcement professional – Bud had his game face on.

"All right, gents, this is how we're gonna play it. Charlie you and Ian are gonna fan out in different directions . . ."

Bud took care to point in every direction except that of the entrance to the lava-tube caves.

"Now, once you're out of sight from here, you're gonna double back and rendezvous with each other down yonder at the cave entrance – go on in and have a look- see."

Bud was waving his arms all around as he spoke. Mainly intent on creating a little theatre – perhaps create some misdirection to the peering eyes of his media nemesis Marsha Steward. Marsha had already bounded out of her news van motioning instructions to her cameraman Tom Iverson to zoom in on Bud, Charlie and Ian – to hopefully catch wind of what they were up to.

Bud motioned with his eyes to a pair of flashlights that were laying in the back-end of his Blazer. Charlie and Ian stealth-fully retrieved and stuffed them into their pockets carefully keeping their actions out of the line-of-sight of the media. Flashlights would have made a statement loud and clear that they were going into the caverns. Charlie closed the Blazers hatchback, took a deep breath, and nodded to the Sheriff that he knew exactly what to do.

Bud smiled at them for taking his cues . . . He then continued explaining his plan.

"All right then gents . . . We're gonna play a little Three-card Monte with our little media gal and her camera-jockey. I'll run interference . . . I'm gonna walk right up to em and start chirping like a little bird about this and about that . . . Giving you time to give the main cave a start at a good once-over . . . Now Ian, that there lava-tube cave over yonder it's the big one, the granddaddy size-wise of the tubes. That's as good a start as any . . . The other couple of caves are tiny by comparison . . . The big one it's around three miles long, so be prepared for a little hike. We don't call em the *Ape Caves* for nothing – you need to be some kind of monkey to climb around in some of em . . . Now mind you both – since that earthquake, there's a lot of fallen rock and some of the otherwise easy going, well, now, it might not be so easy. You may have to climb up and down hill and dell inside there. Be damn careful. But I want every square inch looked over best ya can. We'll worry about the smaller caverns later on – am I understood . . . ?"

Charlie and Ian both shook their heads yes . . . Bud continued . . .

"After I'm done jawing with that news lady – I'll do some looking around here topside all about . . . Once you're both a ways down inside the tube give me a holler over the radio – the code to tell me you're okay is – Ah hell, just tell me you're okay . . . By that time I don't give a good god-damn if that news lady hears us or not . . ."

Charlie almost laughed at Bud; he knew every inch of the cave system. He'd been all through them countless times as a boy and young man – and he was still nimble as a mountain goat.

Charlie looked straight into Ian's eyes, then spoke . . .

"Sure Bud, whatever you say – long as this white-boy can keep up, no problem!"

Ian, who had done plenty of cave spelunking in Mexico and South America though years ago, remarked with a confident voice . . .

"Don't worry about me – I'll keep up!"

CHAPTER 6

Darkest before Dawn

After nearly an hour had passed, Charlie and Ian were deep within the cavern and Ian was beginning to rapidly fatigue. He stopped for a moment and propped himself up against the cavern wall to rest. Ian noticed and began studying various abundant cave drawings that were prevalent all around where he stood. One large grouping of rock art was located high above him near the cave's roof.

"Wow, look at all these magnificent drawings – my God, there's both Pictographs as well as Petroglyphs all around this section . . . By looking at the difference in the art styles; and I mean the difference in the clay and charcoal drawings versus the engravings in the stone . . . Well, taking into account the greatly varied symbols one from the other – I'd guess these somewhat cuneiform-like drawings and etchings are from more than one culture. Cultures probably separated by hundreds perhaps thousands of years . . . One group of art . . ."

Ian pointed with his flash light up at the symbols located directly above his head. Hoping to perhaps make points with his Indian companion by demonstrating his expertise, he began to elaborate more fully. "One group is definitely Native American, maybe ancestors of yours. By the looks of the pictures depicting hunting and fishing, they were no doubt Kawlic peoples of the Cowlitz tribes . . . But some of these Petroglyphs would suggest . . ."

Charlie interrupted Ian mid sentence, "Look professor white eyes . . . We're not here to look at the pretty pictures drawn by my ancestors . . . Let's stay focused. The cave goes on for a ways yet."

He motioned with his flashlight for them to get moving onward. Then after taking a few steps forward; Charlie stopped mid-stride. Staring, straining his eyes as hard as he could. Trying desperately to focus ahead on what had suddenly caught him by absolute surprise.

There was light – light where there should be none! Around a hundred yards up ahead was light – the type of light that, even at that distance, the eagle eyes of Charlie knew, with reasonable certainty, wasn't from any flashlight or lantern.

Charlie looked back at Ian who was about ten feet behind him. He motioned, waving his flashlight, signaling Ian to catch-up . . .

"Mister Scientist man – you might have some usefulness yet . . . Cause something's going on up ahead that's more than peculiar."

"What . . . ?" Ian replied, sounding slightly short of breath.

Ian ended his rest and quickened his pace; in seconds he was caught up to Charlie.

"Charlie, what . . . what do you mean . . . peculiar . . . ?"

Charlie never glanced away from what he was focused on.

"Up ahead there . . . You see that light with those expert eyes of yours?"

Ian was beginning to get fed up with the way Charlie had been talking to him. Fed up regarding the condescending, even racist references thrown his way. But for the time being he chose to keep his temper in check.

"Yeah, what about it . . . ?" Ian replied, with little concern.

Charlie glanced just for a moment at Ian . . . With a disgusted look on his face, he fired back – "What about it? What about it? I thought you were an educated Scientist or some such shit . . . That light, up there, it . . . It can't be – that's all."

Ian knew from what he'd already been told about the lava-tubes – that they were dead-end caverns . . . He also had seen the faint light a moment earlier. But it hadn't registered with him.

Charlie didn't let on to Ian how surprised he actually was. "Something wrong with your white-eyes . . . ? That don't look like no light from a flashlight or lantern – that's the proverbial light at the end of the tunnel, so to speak . . . Problem is, the cave comes to a narrow end just up ahead. No opening to the outside."

The two quickened their pace as they moved forward heading towards the ever increasing light.

The cave was progressively narrowing as they moved ahead another seventy feet or so. There was loose rock and upturned sizable stones and churned earth all about them. So much disturbed cave wall and ground that you wouldn't need to be a Geologist to understand that it reflected a recent occurrence.

"This is . . . was the end of the line. Must have caved away – must have opened from that earthquake – this right here's been the end of the line for hundreds or maybe thousands of years."

Ian began looking around and shook his head in agreement. "This is all newly disturbed granite and soil – other than dynamite, no other explanation beyond a significant seismic event could have caused such collapsing of the thick rock wall."

Charlie and Ian began to make their way up and over the large stones and churned earth; into what was now an entire other chamber. A never before known part of the lava tube cave system – they glanced at each other as they both supposed that they might very well be the first human eyes ever to view what they were seeing.

CHAPTER 7

Tomb

CHARLIE AND IAN kept moving forward into the no longer narrowing, now large open cavern. The light grew brighter as they moved forward. They switched off their battery powered torches and began looking all around the large chamber. Charlie and Ian marveled at the abundance of ancient rock art and Indian artifacts that lay strewn all about. They both realized without exchanging words, that they were standing on a site of enormous, perhaps monumental, Archeological significance. The abundance of never before discovered or tomb-raided hand crafted antiquities was beyond either's comprehension.

All around them were spears, arrowheads, and woven baskets. Artifacts that though partially covered in dust and debris – otherwise looked nearly like new. Silver and turquoise jewelry sparkled in the dim light. The entire chamber was filled with ancient lower Columbian Indian wares. A people who had once flourished since time immemorial in the area, but now had few surviving descendants – Charlie being one of them. Ian, a little short of breath, began to speak.

"My God . . . this is . . . all of this is just . . . . unbelievable!"

For the first time since they'd met, Charlie didn't have a sarcastic or condescending reply – Charlie shook his head in agreement as he spoke.

"You got that right! – man, this part of the cavern hasn't been accessible or even known about . . . for . . . I don't know, pretty much forever! I heard stories when I was just a kid told to me by my Grandfather – of a secret ancient burial place for what he called the "old ones." A burial place that was rumored to be somewhere around this area. But understand when in comes to legends of my people; more often than not they're nothing more than stories. And as far as my Grandfather or any of our tribal elders talking about whether it even really existed and thought to be located somewhere around this area. Well, that could mean practically anything! The concept of distance in terms of miles was a vague concept. Distance was measured more like . . . It's a one or two day walk in this or that direction, if you get my drift. There's all that, and I learned at a very early age that you have to take certain things my Grandfather has to say with a grain of salt; especially when it comes to his often exaggerated stories about our ancestral people . . . Anyway . . . Where I was going with all this, is . . . in one of his many stories he told me of a burial ground of the "old ones" – a place that holds the graves and treasures of Chiefs from the beginning of my people up to when the white European fur traders, explorers and settlers first began their invasion into our land. A burial chamber whose secret location was never to be spoke of to the white man or ever written down – so it would never be discovered and desecrated. We'll, I guess the jigs up now . . . All we can do is try and keep this quiet and close off this cavern to the public, until the right authorities determine what to make of it all – and keeping anything . . . especially something as big as this on the down-low, well, in these parts, that ain't gonna be easy!"

Charlie and Ian were becoming nearly giddy by all that surrounded them . . . Both were excited as little boys in a candy store. Charlie took a deep breath then continued.

"Bud or I will have to notify the local tribal council and all the proper authorities. Then, with any luck, before all the arrow-head collecting vultures catch wind and rob this site blind – Archeologists and museum people can find a proper place for it all . . . I'll tell you this . . . From now on – I'm gonna start giving more credence to my Grandfather's stories!"

Blank-faced, Charlie took another deep breath as he looked direct into Ian's eyes. But within seconds his upper lip began to quiver until he could maintain his poker-face no longer . . . Charlie began grinning. His smile began small, but it soon overtook him as he began exhaling his deep breath. Charlie began beaming a huge smile as he slowly shook his head side to side . . . Ian couldn't help himself. He smiled big in return while nodding his head yes; indicating Charlie's Grandfather may well be a wealth of previously untapped or at least underestimated wisdom. Wisdom at least pertaining to what they had just discovered.

After a few seconds of mutually exited light-heartedness . . . Charlie suddenly stopped shaking his head and became still as a statue.

"Wait, you hear that? That faint sound, it sounds like . . . rushing water! We're approaching or are at least near, well, Harmony Falls would be my guess – if I'm right that would put us back on reservation land which borders the falls and little Merwin . . . Anyway, again if I'm right, and we are near the falls . . . That would explain why this all has gone undiscovered . . . Well, that, and the fact that the cave never had that opening we came through before the earthquake . . . Anyhow, nobody . . . no Archeologists or such has ever been granted permission to dig anywhere around here. Little Merwin and Harmony Falls is sacred land to my people – and now I'm beginning to understand why this is sacred land – sacred burial grounds that is! Ian listen, we take nothing, we disturb nothing, we tell nobody but Bud about this . . . are you clear on that?"

Ian was point of fact a little perturbed at even the suggestion that he would disturb such a site of historical significance; tribal land or otherwise – he took a shallow breath, became wide-eyed, then stared straight into Charlie's eyes before answering.

"Crystal clear! . . . Charlie, you don't have to worry about me . . . I wouldn't dare touch a thing – this is of course too important to history as well as to your tribal elders and people . . . This is the stuff for professional Archeologists to excavate, catalog and put into some museum. But know this . . . Once the news of this site leaks out – and believe me somehow it will, and sooner than you think – not by me, mind you . . . But it's not if . . . it's when, it does . . . You and Bud are gonna have your hands full just trying to keep tomb raiders and hosts of weekend warrior cave spelunking ravagers and arrowhead collectors out."

Charlie was finding it increasingly difficult to maintain his initial instinctual dislike for Ian. Charlie believed Ian was sincere when he assured him that he would not take anything from this site – nor discuss what they had found with, anyone.

"Well white boy – at the very least when we do lift the gag on this. You'll once again get to see your name in the papers as co-discoverer . . . And I guess for a guy in your line of work that kind of publicity might just end up payment enough, right . . . ?"

They both laughed . . . Then Ian replied, "Yeah, a little positive press never hurts business . . . And hey thanks . . . I mean you will include me as co-discoverer, right . . . ?"

"That's right white boy – hell, maybe I'll stay out of the lime-light altogether . . . Give you full credit . . . Ah, who am I kidding – screw that, of course I'll take the credit!"

Again they both laughed.

Charlie looked over eye to eye at Ian. He then motioned for them to continue forward in the direction of the light and the increasing sound of distant rushing water. As they progressed forward the cave floor now had ever increasing in quantity and size, puddles of stagnant water. The cave walls steadily bled moister – the caverns ceiling dripped droplets of water that splattered ever increasingly in their intensity down upon their neck and head. And there was a rapidly growing stench; almost indescribable and growing stronger each step they took.

After walking ahead for what seemed to Ian to have been maybe another seventy-five yards; a hike that was now heading steadily up hill at what he estimated to be about a four percent grade. They came upon another even larger open area of the cave – beyond that not thirty more feet ahead from where they stood was the source of the light and sound they had been heading to . . . It was there at the threshold of the source of illumination; stood an enormous boulder. One that at first glance seemed to be rolled aside exposing a crescent moon shaped doorway to the outside world. From their present vantage point Charlie immediately estimated the opening to be around eight feet high and maybe four feet wide. As they approached the massive stone – it became evident that the opening led to the back side of a considerable water fall . . . There simply was no other waterfall of its size anywhere around the area other than Harmony Falls . . . They stood at the threshold of a subterranean back entrance to Harmony Falls. Charlie and Ian looked at each other knowing that this also was another first. Charlie knew of the giant solid granite boulder that was behind the falls; but to his knowledge nobody had ever dreamed that there was a cavern behind the massive rock – the great boulder behind the falls had never suggested that there may have been any kind of entrance to a cavern behind it. At no time of the year was there even room to stand behind the cascading water and get a good look at the giant stone – an apparent natural formation that seemed to fit precisely into the backdrop of the falls.

The water from the falls pounded with fury just beyond where they stood. Thunderous noise echoed all around them. Even when shouting, the intense noise made it very difficult to hear each other speak.

Harmony Falls boasted approximately a seventy-five foot vertical drop of cascading extremely frigid glacier melt-off. In no way was it the largest falls in Washington State, but it did present itself as a beautiful display of falling pristine water in all its power and visual glory.

Charlie just stood there at the threshold behind the falls, totally astonished. Before the revelations of the day, he'd always prided himself in otherwise knowing the area like the back of his hand – but regardless as impossible as everything had been that they had seen this day and now saw before them . . . He felt justified about being right about one thing . . . His earlier guess of where they might have been heading – they were in fact now standing on reservation land, never before discovered subterranean land, but reservation land none the less.

The lava tubes, the caves, they now went all the way from the Ape Caves parking lot which was miles west from where they now stood; all the way to reservation land . . . Ian came over to Charlie and both stood there captivated, so mesmerized by the moment that they hardly noticed that the falls heavy mist had nearly instantly soaked them both – they slowly nearly unconsciously began to shiver. They stood drenching wet as they looked back from the falls all about this part of the caves walls and floor. Which was dankly covered with moisture saturated vines, cave moss, and small varieties of ferns and ivy that abounded everywhere; seemingly clinging parasitically to suckle from the caverns life force. All of the plant-life amidst the damp dankness created a humid steamy mist that hovered about six inches above the ground all around. The mist nearly covered their feet and swirled all about as they walked.

Charlie and Ian each ran their hands through their soaked hair and wiped the accumulating mist from their eyes. They began focusing on the massive slab of granite which had served as blockage to their newly discovered cavernous world. They both surmised without uttering a word regarding; that such a mammoth stone must weight several tons. But the ground at the near wheel shaped monoliths base appeared disturbed. It revealed tracks in the mud and sandy ground. Tracks which would have indicated to anyone expert or lay-person; that the mighty stone had either rolled probably due to the recent earthquake – or, as far fetched as it would sound; had been forcedly rolled over at least a quarter to have created the doorway passage now open to or from the falls . . . Both Charlie and Ian were totally intrigued as well as confused by the sight and thought of it.

"God Charlie the smell, I don't know how much more I can take of it – starting to make me feel sick!'

"'Yeah Ian, I hear that . . . Smells, I don't know like concentrated road kill."

They both laughed a small nervous laugh regarding Charlie's remark. It was then, at the height of their confusion – Ian began stepping backward to gain better perspective of what they were viewing. After a couple moments of staring at the great rock, Ian stepped even further back out of the well lit open area, backwards and to the side of the massive boulder – into the darkness Ian backpedaled seeking to prop himself up against the cave wall. As he approached in the reverse the caverns side; the stench became nearly more than he could bare. Ian desperately needed to balance himself against something to enable him to lean over and stretch his back. His lower back had begun to spasm from all of the unrehearsed exercise. Just as he'd back-stepped his way nearly to the side of the cave he stepped toe to heal onto something that nearly rolled his ankle over. And as it did made a crunching sound as it squished into the soft sandy dirt beneath his foot – Ian looked down . . . What he saw at that instance caused him to grow two shades whiter than the white-boy Charlie teased him of being. He then uncharacteristically let out an uncontrollable, unimaginably terrified – scream!

"SHIT . . . !OH . . . MY . . . GOD!"

There laying at Ian's feet – were the partially intact blood soaked nearly fleshless skeletal remains of what had once not long ago been a man and a women. There was enough male and female identifiable shredded tattered clothing still clinging to the bodies to make that much instant identification. A small portion of the perhaps blonde women's hair – though it was impossible to be certain of the hair color in the darkness . . . with all of the gooey rancid blood and mud that nearly covered both bodies. Regardless of her hair color; Ian could not take his eyes off of the spectacle of how it somehow managed to remain clinging to the back of her partial remaining skull. The hair had been pulled into a semi-pony tail through the back side of her chewed and much bloodied but still recognizable, Seattle Mariners baseball cap. Charlie now standing next to Ian also stared slack-jawed at the aftermath of what had probably been beyond anyone's worst nightmare. A ravenous carnivorous assault that one could only pray brought swift death to them both. All of their major organs had been removed, presumably eaten by some kind of large predator at the time of the assault – or, perhaps what lay before them now represented not just the initial kill, but further later feasting could have taken place by the initial predator or other lesser carnivore as well – neither Ian nor Charlie even suffering from the instantaneous horror of what they witnessed needed any forensic pathologist to tell them whatever had attacked these two poor people was much more than they could have stood a chance against. Their guts were probably the first things eaten. Then their skulls finally succumbed to massive crushing from the jaws of what at first glance could have been imagined to have been from a bear or cougar; perhaps though rare even a pack of wolves or wild dogs.

Charlie began panning his flashlight all around Ian and the bodies. Within moments of searching the parameter with his electric torch he motioned to Ian to look just a few feet beyond where they stood corpses at their feet. To both of their horror driven minds just a few feet away from where they stood was a mound of older much cleaner picked human as well as animal skeletal remains. Ian and Charlie beyond shock-struck! Neither for one very uncomfortably long moment could muster even a single syllable as convulsive quivers undulated up and down their spines. It was only then that the horrid stench from the rotting cadavers even took issue with their sensibilities.

Charlie cleared his throat and managed to speak.

"Ian . . . There's something not right here – I mean besides the obvious . . . Look, no drag marks on the ground. It's a cinch they didn't buy it here . . . I mean I'm pretty sure this is that couple of hiker-campers that we've been searching for . . . But no gear – where's all their hiking gear and tent and all that? Ya see they were brought back here to this animals den – but any animal that I know of would have dragged em in here. Ian, there ain't no drag marks on the ground!"

Ian looked at the ground all around then stared straight into Charlie's eyes. "Yeah – you're absolutely right . . . Shit, whatever tore these poor folks apart carried their bodies into here from somewhere out there . . ." Ian pointed towards the massive boulder and the light of the outside world beyond the cave.

Charlie stood up straight and gathered his composure . . .

"All right, Ian . . . We're gonna get the hell out of here – don't touch a thing. Soon as we get out of this cave and can reach Bud by our radios; we'll get him up here to see this all for himself. Then we're gonna lock this son-of-a-bitch down tight and try and find whatever has done this . . ."

Ian replied with a mildly surprised look on his face . . .

"Okay – but as soon as possible; I want to take some bite radius measurements and maybe even try and collect some saliva residue, hair, or any viable tissue for its DNA that may link us to the animal – before the Feds or other so called experts take over, and whisk all the physical evidence away . . . I know a guy, Matt Larsen up in Vancouver B.C., who has a lab. He and his partner can help us with identifying what animal, or animals that did this – unless maybe it was done by some kind of homicidal maniac . . . No . . . It looks pretty self-evident that these are canine type bites."

Ian was now down on his knees looking at the bodies very closely – he nearly gagged when he saw all the flies, maggots and worms that were crawling over, feasting on what little flesh and fat cell remains that was left of the dried blood and mud soaked young couple. With his flash light held firm in his right hand he panned the white LED light up and down the victims as he rubbed his chin with his left hand deep in thought . . . Ian spoke again, this time expressing his evident confusion.

"Hey, I thought you guys already had this place closed-off due to the Earthquake and the man-hunt . . . ?"

Charlie with a notably disgusted intonation to his voice fired back.

"Yeah, well obviously it hasn't been shut down tight enough – else we wouldn't have got that anonymous tip to come up here about this unfortunate couple. Someone's been here before us . . . Don't know who, but I'm sure as shit gonna find out! Anyway, no doubt in my mind the same animal that attacked Rob Richards, one of our town folk, killed this here couple as well . . . Rob's up in the hospital in Portland all tore-up from what he described as . . . Well, hell, he said it was Big Foot that got him!"

Ian looked blank faced at Charlie, "Big Foot . . . ! No shit . . . ?"

Charlie shook his head slowly side to side, "No shit . . . !"

"Wait just a minute look; over there . . . Ian waved his flashlight towards the pile of bones; my God, there . . . we have it . . . tracks! Prints from the beast – in this soft ground there had to be tracks right . . . ? But my God, look at the size of them . . ." Ian and Charlie walked over to the bone pile to have a closer look at the impressions in the sandy dirt.

Ian bent down onto one knee to better study the tracks.

"Charlie look, look at the size of these . . . Big Foot indeed and no pun intended . . . But take a look here. The impressions look like some form of canis lupus track but much too large; I mean these are enormous. An animal would have to be beyond freakishly large to make these tracks. And by the depth of the prints this animal would have to weigh – my God, hundreds of pounds. Maybe close to four or five hundred or better. And check this out, there is also some kind of – well heel type impression it looks like. By the look of the tracks impression it seems to be . . . Christ, it seems to indicate a gate of heel to toe . . . And apparently bipedal as well . . . Jesus . . . Here take a look for yourself!"

Charlie shook his head in agreement to all Ian had said . . . Without further discussion he grabbed Ian's shoulder and motioned for them to get moving. Ian stood up and both without speaking another word began to make their egress from the darkness into the light.

Charlie and Ian made there way out of the cave, through the waterfall and around the west bank of Little Merwin Lake. They were both still shocked by what they'd seen and were dripping wet and shivering cold. Charlie reached for his walky talky radio . . .

"This is Charlie for Bud, come back . . . This is Charlie for Bud do you read . . . ?"

"Yeah, you got Bud, what the hell have you two been up to all this time – why's it taken so long for you to contact me – come back . . ."

Ian looked on while Charlie continued talking to Sheriff Bud.

"Bud, we need you to drive to Little Merwin and pick us up – we got us a real situation up here . . . I'm not gonna discuss it on the radio – might not be secure. So don't ask me any questions; just come and get us right away . . . Understand – you copy?"

Bud scratched his head as he stood alongside his Blazers open driver side door. Left foot propped up on the door jamb of his rig, right foot on the ground – he'd been stretching out his arthritic left hip when the call came over his radio.

"Little Merwin – how the hell did you two get all the way up there? Never mind, don't answer . . . I read ya, could be other ears listening . . . Stay put – I'm on the way . . ."

CHAPTER 8

Discovery

BUD COULDN'T FOR the life of him figure how Charlie and Ian managed to get up to Little Merwin Lake. He'd seen them both enter the caverns himself. Regardless, it would take hours and hours to hike to Little Merwin from the Ape Caves parking lot area. Bud pondered the question over and over in his mind of how the hell they got up there – as he drove nearly sixty miles per hour up the gravel road; rocks, dirt and dust flying behind him. He lit out like a house a fire to avoid any chance of being followed by the press, namely Marsha Steward. Bud had sped out of the Lava tubes parking lot so fast Marsha and her sidekick had no chance to get their equipment loaded back into their van. Bud knew he had them dead-bang by surprise. He knew the odds were hundreds to one that they would ever catch up with him or have even a clue which road he'd soon be taking to head up to Little Merwin . . . The roads around these parts riddled the hills like a spider-web maze; a myriad of gravel roads that for the most part all looked about the same. Mostly they were Weyerhaeuser Company logging roads that led here and there all the way to Mt. Saint Helens and beyond. One wrong turn and they could be traveling for miles and miles; heading to God knows where . . . For a moment Bud almost felt bad about that – but he soon got over it.

In less then ten minutes after leaving the Ape Caves parking lot. Bud came bounding in his rig into the very small dirt parking lot located at the west end of Little Merwin Lake. He immediately spotted Charlie and Ian, and at first glance could see they were definitely worse for wear . . . Bud laid on his horn as he sped towards them; coming to a stop along side them both – without hesitation a very confused Sheriff Bud parked his Blazer and climbed out.

"Well aren't you two a couple of sorry looking sites – Jesus in a Cracker Jack box what in tar-nation happened to you fellows? – far as that goes, how in hell's bells did you manage to get all the way up here . . . ? Normally a hike from the caves up to here would take nearly a full day . . . Not that you ain't been gone half of that . . . But I never seen either of ya come out of the cave."

Neither Charlie nor Ian was quick to respond – they both had somewhat far away eyes with blank expressions on their faces as they both stood not ten feet from Bud.

"Are one of you two sub-geniuses gonna tell me what in the hell is going on?"

Charlie took one step closer to Bud putting himself between Bud and Ian.

"Bud, you are not going to believe what we've seen – first off, we found bodies. Most likely the bodies of the two missing hikers."

Bud shook his head reflecting his legitimate sorrow in hearing that . . . Charlie took a big gulp of air, gathered his composure best that he could and began.

"But Jesus Bud – that ain't even the half of it . . . So listen up and listen good . . . Cause I ain't in the mood to be repeating myself; not just yet anyway. I mean the amount of paperwork I'm gonna have to fill out. And the number of questions I'm gonna be answering over and over to you and maybe the Feds; and God knows who else, is gonna be enough to fill two books."

Bud interrupted, "Okay, all right, Charlie let's just stick to the facts of what you've got to tell me right here, right now – let's hear it plain, slow and simple!"

Bud then looked away for an instance from Charlie over directly into Ian's still shock glazed eyes. "And Ian, don't you be shy about laying it out straight for me neither."

Charlie took a deep breath and cleared his throat. He didn't know if he was going to be able to sum up all that he and Ian had seen. But he was going to try his best.

"All right . . . Bud, me and Ian we did like you told us. We entered the lava tubes from the parking lot and proceeded to check out the big cave beginning to end. All was normal until we got near the end and well, now there ain't no end! It's been opened up probably due to that earthquake – opened up to an all new chamber where we found lots of artifacts and such . . . and . . . now there's an opening from the outside into the cave from behind the falls . . . next to where that giant boulder's always been."

Bud scratched his head as he looked over at Ian . . . Ian shook his head in agreement with all that Charlie was saying . . . Charlie continued, "Bud, in the new part of the cave we found bodies. A young man and woman most likely the hiker couple we've been searching for. They fit the general description – well, what's left of them fit's the description that is."

Charlie paused to catch his breath and maintain his composure. Ian seized the opportunity that afforded and spoke up . . .

"Bud, of course it all was as Charlie says – but I got to tell ya . . . Something attacked that poor couple and whatever it was. It was big, powerful, and now has a taste of human flesh. I need to get back in there as soon as possible and look further around for other evidence of prints, claw marks, saliva . . . bite radius . . . And whatever else might be useful in determining what animal or animals did the initial kill. I say initial kill . . . Because by now there probably have been other lesser carnivorous scavengers that may have joined in on consuming the bodies after the fact."

Bud, now with sweat beads forming across his forehead took his Sheriff's hat off and wiped the sweat away with his right hand shirt sleeve before replying. "Okay, okay . . . Charlie you stay here and call dispatch to get the County Coroners up here. Use my cell phone it gets some signal from right here where we stand. I checked a few minutes ago. Not a strong signal, but it should be enough. No way it will hold signal up at the falls."

Bud handed Charlie his phone. "Better notify the state cops too! Meanwhile . . . Ian, you're gonna take me to where ya'll say that entrance behind the falls to the cave is. I'll have a look around myself while you do what it is that you need to do – just mind ya, we need to leave the scene as non contaminated by our presence as possible under the circumstances . . . That will be about impossible I know. And we'll no doubt take shit from someone regarding. Anyhow, let's get going. By the looks of you two, I'm about to take a shower in the falls, am I right?"

Charlie had already gotten on Bud's cell phone and was making the necessary calls . . . Ian responded while shaking his head and mustering a very small non-sincere smile.

"Yeah Bud, you're gonna get wet – you don't happen to have a couple respirators or gas masks in that rig of yours do you . . . ?"

Bud looked confusingly back at Ian.

"Gas masks . . . Oh right, the bodies are starting to get pretty ripe no doubt!"

CHAPTER 9

Confirmation

BUD JUST STOOD looking at the bodies and all around for tracks. He held a handkerchief over his mouth and nose. The stench from the rapidly decomposing corpses was almost more than he could take. As far as tracks – there was plenty of what he sought. Large prints of what looked like canine type tracks but they were different. Too large and very unusual.

"Okay Ian, now you're the expert here . . . I've seen plenty of all kinds of animal tracks in my day . . . I used to do a lot of hunting around these parts . . . But hell, I ain't never seen no tracks that look like these here. Except maybe some plaster casts of phony foot prints taken by hoaxers and crackpots over the years; you know, the typical Big Foot crap that's been turned into my office time to time."

Ian smiled at that thought. He'd seen lots of that junk himself in his line of work. Every single one tavern logger town throughout Washington, Oregon, Idaho and Northern California that he'd ever visited regarding Big Foot investigations had plenty of the typical plaster cast foot prints to ponder. Usually brought out from behind the bar as tongue and cheek conversation pieces much the same as the equally typical Jackalope that stands stuffed and mounted on the wall. The castings for the most part were generally really bad fakes; but occasionally he'd be shown one that was at least intriguing, manufactured by probably a taxidermist with at least some basic knowledge regarding primate skeletal anatomy.

"Bud, these prints, these tracks are amazing! Nothing about them looks to be fake . . . I guess we should take some plaster castings of them . . . Unfortunately wait and see; now like me, you're gonna know what it feels like to have people thinking you're a nut case or perpetrator of a hoax or both . . . You'll see it in their eyes regardless of what they say."

Bud was already one step ahead of what Ian had just said. He knew that stories whether fact based or otherwise around these parts tended to grow larger down the line.

The last thing that he wanted was to get any reputation as a "crack-pot." That could devastate his career. Or, at least severally damage his much deserved reputation as a level headed law enforcement professional – as well as jeopardize his status as being a highly respected member of his tiny community; and that meant everything to Bud.

"Yeah Ian, we'll get some casts made of these prints . . . But say let's keep this tuned to the down-low if you get my drift. Stay away from saying anything to the media about any of this, we clear on that . . . ?"

"You bet Bud, no problem – I know why I'm here and who's paying the bills . . . Besides there is the bigger picture here. The total mutilation of that young couple over there."

Ian pointed back a few feet over at the decaying corpses of the hiker couple.

Bud then suddenly felt bad about not sounding more concerned regarding the case of the deceased; rather than worrying if reporting weird tracks could potentially damage his reputation or not.

"Yeah Ian, of course you're right . . . Much bigger picture! That must of sounded pretty cold on my part . . . Hey, anyhow, I trust you to do the right thing regarding a gag-order bout all of this."

Ian smiled a small smile and shook his head in agreement to help ease Bud's concern. He knew this was a lot of pressure for the small town Sheriff to shoulder.

Ian continued to look all around the cavern walls and proceeded back over to the large boulder that appeared to serve as a would-be doorway. One that leads to the outside world through the waterfall into the light.

"Jesus Christ! Bud get over here and take a look at this!"

Bud got up from his kneeling position. He'd postured himself stooped over the couples bodies to get a closer look at their remains. In response to Ian's plea Bud quickly stood and nearly ran over to where Ian stood staring slightly upwards.

Ian had his flash light focused on the left side edge of the large boulder about seven feet above the ground.

"Bud would you take a look at these massive what appears to be scrape-marks in the stone – and mind you this is solid granite! You see that, you see the blood, a bit of what looks like dark gray animal fur, and . . . Holy shit look up there, just a little higher up; that looks to be maybe . . . like a broken claw-nail, buried in the stone?"

"Good God oh-mighty Ian, I believe it is . . . Can your reach it?"

"Yeah, Bud I think I can . . . Here hold my flashlight I'm gonna try and get to it – I've got a knife-kit with multi-tool on me . . . The small pliers should do the trick."

Ian retrieved his handy multi-tool from its sheath that was fixed to his belt and began to stretch as high as he could to reach whatever it was that was lodged into the boulder. Ian had already before calling Bud over to have a look, stealth-fully collected some blood and hair samples from the boulder. He had tucked the samples into a small glass vial that he habitually kept on him in his field vest for just this sort of thing.

"There . . . Bud, I got it! Good God . . . you got to look at the size of this thing, and it appears to be just a broken-off piece of nail!" Ian thought to himself – *nice! We've got plenty of DNA to use to identify this thing . . .*

Bud smiled with relief that Ian was able to get the sample without hurting himself. Ian had had to climb up the rock a number of feet to be able to pull and pry the object from the boulder with sufficient force to remove it.

"All right Ian, good job . . . Get it down here so I can have a look-see!"

At that very moment Bud and Ian heard faint voices from just the other side of the falls. The voices echoed and reverberated from the intense sound of the cascading falls . . .

"Bud, Ian . . . It's Charlie, I got the Coroner, Dan Sparling with me . . . We're coming in!"

Bud looking surprised by how fast Charlie and the Coroner had arrived. Quickly glared emphatically direct into Ian's eyes. "Ian, quick . . . stow that claw, or whatever the hell it is, in your pocket."

CHAPTER 10

The wait

IN THE BACK parking lot of *Harmony Falls High School* stands a teenage boy nervously pacing back and forth. The boy glances at his watch, it is 7:37 pm – he thinks to himself that she is now more than a half hour late. He suspects due probably to her father, he's been stood up. But just as he climbed back onto his nearly vintage partially restored Kawasaki dirt bike; there she came rolling into the parking lot in her shiny like new Honda two-door civic; a birthday gift from her well-healed, over protective, prejudice to the extreme father. Her father hated him. Hated him for who and what he is.

"Shit Katie, I've been freezing my ass off waiting for over a half hour! What kept you? As if I don't already know!"

"God Jeremy, you know how he gets . . . Fuck, he drilled me with a thousand questions about where I was going. But it's cool . . . I told him I was going over to Becky's to help her with homework . . . He can't stand Becky's parents so no-way he'll call them. If he calls at all it will be my cell and I just won't answer. I'll tell him I left it in the car."

Jeremy laughed and shook his head while he flicked what was left of his two-thirds smoked cigarette down onto the pavement.

"Yeah, right. Like he's gonna buy you not having your cell in hand at all times . . . Christ Katie he knows you'd like go into some kind of spazz attack if you couldn't text your friends every few minutes."

Katie flashed Jeremy a flirtatious smile as she cocked her head to the side. She ran the fingers of her left hand through her long blonde hair, twisting it around and around . . .

"So what was so important that you couldn't text or call me about – what's with all the secrecy? You know if you just wanted to get me alone you didn't have to sound so mysterious or desperate even. I don't hold out on you; well not for long anyway . . ."

Katie was nearly shocked that her attempt at signaling her present mood for overt promiscuity didn't have the effect she'd hoped for.

"God, you are in a mood aren't you? Anyways, what's so important that it couldn't wait to tell me at school tomorrow . . . ?"

Katie was ready and willing to take matters into her own hands – she rushed up to Jeremy and wrapped her arms and right leg around him as she kissed him passionately.

Jeremy responded with equal enthusiasm – after several long seconds he gently backed her from him a half arms length and sighed. "Listen to me . . . I may be in trouble! – I don't know for sure."

Katie could tell by the very serious expression on Jeremy's face that play time was over; at least for the moment.

"Trouble, what do you mean trouble? What have you gotten yourself into now? You haven't like fucking stole something have you?"

"No . . . Give me a break! – if you can shut up long enough I'll tell you why I need to talk, needed to see you . . ."

Katie stepped back and put her hands on her hips. Her typical *all right lets hear it* pose.

"Okay, tell me what's got you so weird-ed out?"

Jeremy cleared his throat and took a deep breath . . .

"Right, uh, where do I start . . . Just a couple days ago I was up at the falls. I got this big idea to carve our names into that giant boulder just behind them. This is the only time of year that you can get to it. The water flow over the falls is at its lowest cause all the melt off is pretty much over – well, shit you know . . . Anyway . . ."

Katie interrupted with a playful laugh while batting her eyelids in a semi-mocking fashion at Jeremy's expense.

"Oh, how romantic! You know you're awful cute when you're like this."

"Like what?" Jeremy replied, beginning to get irritated.

"You know kind of scared and I don't know, vulnerable I guess."

"Yeah right, whatever – Katie listen to me this is important . . ."

Katie stopped with the kidding and nodded her head gesturing that she'd behave and listen to whatever he was about to tell her. Jeremy could see that she was now serious about listening.

"Okay, where was I – oh yeah, anyway, I made my way around the lake bank to the back side of the falls, then over behind the falls to the huge rock. I got out my knife and began to scratch our names . . . But then I saw what I couldn't believe. I saw the giant rock was not where it's normally. I've been up there a million times and right away I could tell the fucker had moved . . . Moved just enough to allow me to enter a cave that I guess has always been there hid behind it."

Katie couldn't help herself, "What do you mean entrance to a cave? There's no cave . . . I've been there before too you know . . . Or, did you forget skinny dipping last July . . . ?"

Jeremy held up his right hand gesturing Katie to once again stop talking.

"Look you're not listening . . . I tell you there is a cave entrance . . . But that's not even the point – I mean that's not what I need to tell you."

Katie took a deep breath and again rolled her eyes, she was growing more impatient by the moment. "So what about this cave . . . It sounds sick – you want to show me, right? That's what this is all about? – I'm in."

"No Katie, I mean not now anyway . . . Look, inside the cave I found two dead bodies – the bodies of a man and a women . . . Probably the missing hikers – you know the ones that all the hypes been about."

"Jeremy you're fucking kidding me, right?"

Jeremy looked her dead in the eyes and with a serious as a heart attack expression on his face shook his head, no.

"God Jeremy did you tell your Dad and Sheriff Bud?"

"Sort of... Well, what I did was... I called Dads work and left an anonymous tip about them, the bodies."

Katie looked at Jeremy and shook her head as if to say – not a good idea!

"Don't worry, I was smart about it . . . I covered the phone with a towel and talked in a deep voice. Dad can't ever know I was up there. With all the warning signs and road blocks that say stay out cause of all the investigation and that earthquake thing. Well, I sort of promised my Dad I wouldn't go anywhere near there... But holy shit Katie you would not have believed all the blood – I mean those, those hikers were totally fubar. Man they were torn to fucking shreds!"

The moment he'd uttered those words Jeremy was instantly seized by a shudder that ran from the middle of his back up his neck . . . For an instance before he regained his composure Jeremy began to tremble. This was the first time Katie had ever seen Jeremy scared of, anything!

"Oh my God Jeremy – you're telling me the truth, aren't you . . . ?"

Jeremy mustered a small smile as he raised his right hand. "Yeah, nothing but the truth."

"Jeremy take me up there – we can get through all the barricades or roadblocks with your bike – just like you did . . ."

"Oh man, Katie, I don't know . . . There's something up there in the woods and it's killing people . . . If something happened to you . . ."

Katie interrupted with one of her typical smart remarks.

"If something happened to me my Dad would kill you, ha!... Say, you got a smoke?"

"That was my last cigarette; I'm quitting . . . Got to get in shape for track – I never was much of a dedicated smoker like you, anyway . . ."

They both laughed – Katie shook her head in agreement.

"Yeah, I should have never got you started . . . cigarettes, that is – but that's not the only thing I've corrupted you with or introduced you to, now is it?"

Katie, playfully ran her hands across her breasts . . .

They both laughed once again as they climbed onto Jeremy's bike – Jeremy handed Katie his spare helmet. One that bore her name in small letters written across the back. She strapped it on . . . they were off . . .

CHAPTER 11

Delilah – Part I

IAN WITH TIRES squelching bounded into the *Lakeview Bar and Grill* parking lot. He wanted or rather needed a drink – after the day he'd just had not many would have blamed him.

Ian had seen enough today to give a stronger man the willies. As he sat in the parking lot in his parked Jeep. He decided to check his wallet to see if his concealed weapons permit was still legal-tender, not expired. Upon checking the date Ian noted that it was still good for another month; he sighed a grateful sigh of relief. Ian then felt around under his seat for *"Ole Caretaker"* his trusty thirty-two caliber Italian companion. Truth be told over the years; his little friend had helped get him out of more than a couple dicey touch-n-go situations with indigenous wild life, both foreign and domestic. But from what he saw today he figured he'd need a hell of a lot more stopping power than afforded by his small pistol – *but something was better than nothing* he figured, if the shit was ever to hit the proverbial fan.

Ian strapped his pistol and its ankle holster up under the inside of his right leg jeans trouser. It was well concealed. From this point on he had no ambitions to go anywhere around these parts not packing heat.

Ian than climbed out of his Jeep to go inside intent on getting a bite to eat and a whole lot to drink.

He entered the restaurant bar through the side parking lot entrance – the one that lead straight to the bar. He immediately sat down at the first empty table. Not thirty seconds passed before Ian was greeted.

"You look like a man who could use a drink . . . What can I get you?"

Ian looked up at the bartender-waitress – who was wearing a screen-printed t-shirt that had the name of the establishment *Lakeview Bar and Grill* artfully done up with a nice picture of Lake Merwin nestled among fir trees in the background – her name was printed just below the logo.

"Good evening Sally – you got that right; I could definitely use a drink!"

They smiled respectfully at each other.

"Give me a Jack-n-Coke . . . Light on the Coke and heavy on the Jack . . . and I'd love a menu, I'm as hungry as I'm thirsty . . . well, nearly anyway . . ."

Sally once again smiled at Ian. "How about I bring you a couple shots of Jack, a Coke, and a third separate glass – one you can use to mix to taste . . . and I'll get you a menu – but if you like prime rib it's on special for the evening . . . Just fourteen-ninety-nine for a twelve ounce, mashed potatoes and veggies."

"My God Sally, perfect! You're an angel, no need for that menu, you had me at prime rib!" Ian thought a moment about the wisdom of his choice to eat red meat . . . But his hunger outweighed the slight residual stomach squeamishness he was still experiencing regarding the gore that he'd seen earlier in the day.

Sally left to get Ian his drinks. Just then the side bar door opened and in came the one person Ian was hoping not to run into . . .

She walked into the room like a model on a cat-walk. All eyes in the room fixed on her every move – it wasn't every day that anyone of any amount of celebrity visited their small burg.

She walked straight up to Ian's table almost as if it had been scripted.

"Have you room for company . . . ?" She asked Ian with a sly confident voice; like something he would have expected to hear watching an old black-n-white Bogart movie – Ian mused.

Ian was caught completely off guard. People were watching. Despite all of Sheriff Bud's warnings he couldn't be overtly rude . . .

"Uh, sure . . . Please . . . uh, have a seat . . ."

Ian stood up and stepped a couple steps over to the opposite side of his table; pulled her chair back and seated her like a gentlemen.

Without hesitation Ian returned to his seat and spoke.

"You're that television reporter aren't you?" Ian already knew the answer; he just wanted her to say it.

"Yes, that's right . . ." She extended her right arm across the table to shake hands. Ian responded accordingly.

"Marsha Steward . . . And you are . . . ?"

Ian smiled, she had a charm about her.

"Ian McDermott, pleasure to meet you . . ."

Marsha smiled, "Well, it's nice to meet you . . . Ian."

Without as much as ten seconds delay – Marsha began going straight down the path that Ian feared most to travel.

"Say, I could beat around the bush, but I'm a direct person . . . Tell me Ian, what's your connection with the local Sheriff's department? That was you I saw with Harmony Falls finest this afternoon wasn't it?"

Ian knew lying, at least at this point would be pointless.

"Yeah, I was with the local Sheriff today – I'm an independent investigator brought in to lend a hand. Though quite honestly my services are probably not necessary. The local Sheriff and his deputy have matters well at hand . . ."

Marsha looked suspiciously, directly into Ian's eyes.

"Do they now? I wonder . . . Say, that was pretty cute how you all played me and my cameraman today."

Ian tried to muster a genuine look of confusion. Though he knew exactly where she was heading with that statement.

"Played . . . ? I don't understand?"

Marsha smiled a cunning smile, "Oh Ian, I think you do . . . I mean the misdirection. That was played very well. My cameraman-driver he is very good at what he does. You all lost us with apparent ease. Granted the locals know these hills no doubt like the backs of their hands . . . I was not offended mind you. I realize the press isn't always popular among law enforcement. But understand the people have the right to know that the investigation of those missing tourists is being conducted in the best possible fashion. And it's my job to report the news. Given the profile of the family of the missing persons, this story is very important to my . . . It's important!"

Ian mixed his Jack Daniels and Coke . . . Looked into Marsha's eyes . . .

"Uh, say, can I buy you a drink or something to eat? I've ordered my dinner it should be coming up in minutes – you hungry? I'll get Sally over here to take your order."

Marsha replied with a chuckle in her voice while reflecting a semi-flirtatious grin.

"My . . . already on a first name basis with the local gals . . . I'm impressed!"

Ian continued, attempting to reflect little emotion or expression of any particular interest one way or the other in his voice.

"Yeah, well, anyway you hungry?"

"Yes, yes I am – thank you . . . And I'd love a glass of chardonnay . . . What did you order?"

"I ordered their house special – prime rib . . ."

Marsha smiled a genuine smile, "That sounds lovely . . . I'll have the same!"

CHAPTER 12

The Rock

JEREMY AND KATIE finally made it to the small dirt parking area at Little Merwin. A small mountain lake not much more than a very large pond; that was known as a scenic picturesque favorite day use area that boasted the beautiful Harmony Falls; which served as a favored swimming hole for both locals and tourists during hot Summer days. Jeremy's motor-bike's headlight had been dancing around wildly from the rough heavily tracked, pocked and pitted dirt and gravel road which led to the small lake tributary. Little Merwin from this point flowed down the mountain to the valley as a creek; eventually emptying into Lake Merwin less then ten miles below.

"God, let me off this thing my ass is killing me . . ." Katie exclaimed as she nearly sprang off the back end of the motorcycle.

Jeremy laughed at her as she rubbed her backside.

"Yeah, sorry bout all the bumps – but hey if you need me to rub the kinks out of your ass, no problem!"

"Yeah, you wish! Say that's not a bad idea!" Katie exclaimed, as she began unbuttoning her blouse while walking slowly towards Jeremy.

She sashayed her hips to and fro in an exaggerated cat-in-heat like fashion intended to generate maximum effect; and it worked!

Jeremy after several minutes of intense petting and making out managed to skew-up enough self control to at least temporarily over-ride his glandular charged passion. He slipped just out of her grasp, took a very deep breath of brisk mountain night air . . .

"Oh my God, Katie, holy shit slow down! This is not why we're here – I mean this is great, but . . ."

"What's wrong Jeremy, don't I do it for ya?"

"Fuck, you kidding? It's just, it's just I don't want us to be up here any longer than necessary. Come on . . . lets go check out the cave."

Suddenly that was enough to get Katie to slow-down with her immediate agenda. She began buttoning her blouse . . .

"Fine . . . your loss! All right . . . lets go see your stupid imaginary cave . . . You better have not got me all the way up here just to see our initials you carved in some fucking rock!"

Jeremy took the lead with Katie just a close one step behind him as they made their way around the small lake bank over to the falls . . . Jeremy pointed ahead . . .

"See Katie, look . . . Now tell me there's no cave!"

"Oh my God Jeremy, you weren't making this all up – let's go inside . . ."

"Fuck . . . you're kidding right? Shit there could be a bear or cougar in there! Not a good idea!"

Jeremy saw the begging look in Katie's eyes . . . He hated it when she gave that look. The look he could never say no to.

"All right, all right . . . But stay close and go slow! It's gonna be pitch dark in there . . . All we got is this one stupid small LED flashlight. We're lucky there's nearly a full moon tonight – or, we'd of had trouble just getting up here . . ."

"Okay Jeremy, what ever you say . . . But let's go in!"

CHAPTER 13

Delilah - Part II

"IAN WOULD YOU excuse me I need to visit the little girls room."

"Uh yeah, of course," Ian considered for a nano-instance standing up as she backed herself from the table. But he decided otherwise – there were limits to his practice of table manners. Especially formalities geared towards impressing his initially unwanted female companion. Companionship that had he been completely honest with himself at that moment was becoming increasingly easy to endure; as the booze began kicking-in.

Ian maintained at least for the moment enough presence of mind to remind himself of what Marsha no doubt really wanted from him – the exclusive inside story of the now publicly acknowledged recovery of the missing back-packing couple. Ian knew this all too well . . . What he didn't know is that she didn't need to use the restroom or powder her nose at all. What she did need to do was use her cell-phone away from his ears.

"Hi, hi Tom . . . Say, I might have the break we've been looking for! Let's just say I'm working on it as we speak . . . Where am I? I'm at that little dump of a restaurant-bar down the road from our motel."

"You're where . . . ?" Tom had been napping – he was trying desperately to clear his head.

"That's not important – just have all the equipment loaded in the van and be available for anything! We're on stand-by alert . . . You understand?"

"Yeah, yeah . . . Stand-by, ready for anything . . . got it!"

Marsha continued, "That's right . . . You want me to bring you back something to eat later?"

Tom replied, "No, no I grabbed a couple of hot-dogs from the little gas-n-go up the street bout an hour ago."

Marsha smiled to herself. She was relieved to hear that she didn't have to pick any food up for Tom. "Okay then – bye!"

Marsha checked herself in the bathroom mirror. She applied a little lip gloss and then proceeded to return down the hall to the bar . . . Once back in the bar Marsha smiled a flirtatious smile directed across the room at Ian. She exuded a nearly palatal aura of sexuality; one that held the attention of every male present as she crossed the room. Marsha a tall slender stunningly attractive thirty something woman – stood around five foot ten in heels. She had thick, apparently natural red hair and jade green eyes. Eyes that to Ian could penetrate hardened steel.

Ian knew being here with her, talking to her could potentially be real trouble. He actually considered leaving while she was in the bathroom . . . But he just couldn't bring himself to it. Their prime ribs and drinks had just been delivered – and he couldn't escape the fact that she was . . . *Beautiful!*

Marsha re-united herself with Ian and sat down at the table, smiling a seemingly genuine smile as she spoke. "Now that does look yummy! Who would have thought this place would serve such a beautiful prime rib dinner. Ian, I am impressed!"

Ian seriously doubted that anything shy of a five-star restaurant could possibly impress his guest. Regardless he couldn't help but smile back at her. The dinners did look very good and she looked . . . gorgeous!

The next couple of hours passed by like minutes to Ian. Lots of small talk . . . more drinks. Ian had been shocked that Marsha hadn't asked another question about the investigation. She had kept conversation light and . . . fun! That was until the clock reported it to be eleven forty-five bar time. Then like a batter expecting a fast ball but is thrown a curve instead, all was about to change.

"Ian . . . Would you like to follow me back to my motel? Well, it's more like a cabin really . . . I could make us some drinks and we could listen to some music or watch some T.V., whatever you . . . desire!"

Ian without hesitation or any consideration of what Sheriff Bud or anyone for that matter might think, smiled a huge Cheshire cat-like smile and replied, "Uh . . . sure!"

Ian paid the tab and left a reasonable tip. They collected their things and left for the side bar door which led to the parking lot.

He walked Marsha to her car. They both were staggering just a bit. The moon was bright nearly full. It was there leaning against her Mercedes that they dove into each others arms and shared a lengthy very passionate kiss . . . both out of breath they laughed . . . Marsha spoke up.

"Okay now, don't you get lost – be right behind me . . . We're going to the ***Firlane Resort*** just up the road a bit . . ."

Ian laughed as he thought to himself – *wait . . . that's where I'm staying – just in the crappy RV part; in my even crappier trailer, ha! . . . Small world, well, small town anyway!*

CHAPTER 14

Monster

THEY MADE THEIR way through all of the heavy falls spray and over to the cave entrance.

Jeremy grabbed Katie's hand with his left then with his right hand he gently pressed his index finger to her lips gesturing for her to be quiet as they entered – he then whispered . . .

"Katie, no doubt they've moved the bodies out of here by now – least I sure as shit hope so . . . But I'm warning you it stinks in there something terrible!"

As they began to enter the cave, there was an ever increasing smell. A horrific stench that to Katie smelled like that of rancid rotting meat.

"Katie began to gag from the smell, "Oh God Jeremy, forget this – I'm not going in there, it smells worse than shit!"

A very relieved Jeremy shook his head in agreement with her. They both turned around and began their egress from the cavern as fast as they'd moments earlier had begun their ingress . . . It was then they heard the first of a series of bellowing howls. Howls that had begun sounding as though they were coming from far away; but were rapidly becoming louder and louder . . . Instantly Katie and Jeremy became terror stricken. They stood momentarily frozen from fear as they looked with terrified eyes at each other. Katie was first to break their silence as she let out a scream that Jeremy immediately tried to muffle with his right hand. One instant later they began to run as fast as they dared in the moonlight. Jeremy's flash light's light bounced wildly as they ran towards the dirt parking lot – towards Jeremy's bike . . . The howling was getting louder and louder as it seemed to be rapidly closing in on them.

They both now sensed with clarity that they were running for their very lives!

Katie was crying almost hysterically as she ran. Charged with adrenaline she ran faster than she'd ever ran before in her life. Jeremy too was scared beyond rational thought . . . But he still managed to yell up at her as they ran along the lake bank.

"Run Katie . . . keep running as fast as . . . we're almost to the bike . . . keep going fast as you can!"

They continued running as fast as Katie could all the while tree branches slapped at them stinging sharply as they struck their faces. Huckleberry bushes and tall lion-grass seemed to grab at their ankles and knees like hands raising up from below intent on tripping and dragging them down; to hold them captive for the beast or whatever it was that was rapidly closing on them. They now could hear branches snapping and the panting, snarling and growling of whatever beast or beasts was running them down.

In their desperate fright and flight . . . thoughts, panic stricken thoughts of the hikers that had come to this area before them swirled in both their minds. Terror driven thoughts that this could be it for them flashed in Jeremy's burning head. Desperation was rapidly setting in on both of them equal to their fatigue – but just as it began seeming all may be lost; they both spotted the clearing and just ahead of that the bike; their only hope for salvation.

At that sight Jeremy kicked into some other gear that he didn't even know he possessed. He passed up Katie like she was almost going backward. Jeremy knew their only chance was for him to get to his bike, get it started, grab his girl and get the hell out of there as fast as possible – hopefully out running whatever it was that nearly had them.

Jeremy, after crossing the parking lot with Katie maybe now thirty feet behind him; leapt onto the bike and started it up. He revved the motor, dropped the clutch and spun his wheels throwing dirt and gravel as he sped ahead towards Katie and the beast or beasts beyond; as he raced towards her he saw clearly for the first time what was chasing them – but his eyes could not believe what he saw. Chasing after Katie only around sixty feet behind her was . . . a monster! – and it was closing on her fast!

Jeremy ran through his gears with the skill of a professional dirt-bike racer as he sped towards Katie. He screeched to an abrupt side-drift stop as he grabbed her and whisked her onto his bike. Their helmets had fallen onto the ground when Jeremy had abruptly taken off. There was no time to retrieve them. Jeremy power slid a fast one-eighty degree spin tossing dirt and gravel; two-cycle engine exhaust bellowed from his tailpipe as he revved his loud high pitched rapping motor. Jeremy popped his clutch grabbed second gear, and they began their speeding dash . . .

They were doing around thirty by the time they hit the main road. Jeremy could see faint head lights coming towards them a ways up the road. The sight of headlights was somehow comforting to him – a little taste of civilization. Just then Jeremy started jittering almost uncontrollably regarding what he'd seen or thought he'd seen back at the lake. He drew in a deep breath as they began to pick up speed. They both began to somewhat catch their breath; Katie's loud crying had turned to mainly shivers and shakes as she clung onto Jeremy with all her might. They both began to realize they'd made it . . . at the very moment they realized they'd out ran the thing that had almost got them, it sprang out onto the road just in front of them from the deep wooded roadside – Jeremy swerved his bike as hard and fast as he could to avoid running straight into the beast . . . but he swerved too hard and too fast. The riders toppled end-over-end into the tall grass and mud-bog shallow creek which ran alongside the road; the bike flipped and skidded down the road rapidly transitioning into a mass of twisted metal.

CHAPTER 15

Delilah - Part III

IAN LAID ON his back looking up at the ceiling. He began counting tiles . . . Ian began to realize that unfortunately with his ever increasing sobriety came the ever increasing realization of where he was and what he'd done. He was in bed with the enemy in the truest sense of the phrase. Ian began planning his egress from the situation – just as he had skewed enough courage to begin his stealthiest moves to exit the bed without waking her.

"Ian, you're not sleeping?"

"No, I . . . I'm kind of antsy – I probably should leave so you can get some sleep."

Marsha seized the opportunity, like the seasoned under covers investigator she was.

"Well, since neither of us are in the mood for sleep, I have just a couple questions that I want to ask – you don't mind do you? I mean now that we've so little to hide from one-another . . ." Marsha giggled more for effect than levity. She had opened with a strong hand . . . one that deliberately was intent to make it very difficult for Ian to pass, fold, or otherwise avoid.

"Uh . . . Sure, I mean I guess – Marsha, what's on your mind?"

"Well, Ian, I've already been informed that you were there when the Sherriff and his deputy discovered the bodies up near little Merwin. And I know that the bodies were severely mangled, perhaps victims of some large predator animal . . . What I don't know is were they actually killed by some animal or pack of animals, or did they die of something like exposure and later were . . . Well, scavenged on by animals, or whatever . . . ?"

Ian abruptly raised up from bed and set on its edge. He reached down towards his feet and grabbed his underwear and pants that were laying piled on top of one another where he'd tugged them off and carelessly flung them; before the two of them subsequently piled themselves on top of one another. Ian quickly put his shorts and pants on while shaking his head in slight disgust indicating that he wasn't pleased with Marsha's suddenly cutting directly from the chaff to the wheat.

"Well, Marsha, now those are good questions . . . Ones that I'm really in no position to comment on – and even if I was able to comment on them; I really wouldn't have any definitive information for you . . . now I trust that anything that has transpired between us . . . is going to be held completely confidential – off the record, right?"

"Of course Ian – we are consenting adults!" Marsha giggled and rolled her eyes.

Ian figured the only way anything would be held in confidence with this beautiful yet potentially very dangerous women, would be for him to give her just a little information – not much, just enough to keep her at bay wanting for more; but under his terms. Rather than allow her to blackmail him with threats of exposing their rendezvous to the Sheriff. Bud would probably believe that he'd told her whatever she would say he did true or otherwise. Which would undoubtedly exclude him from any further collaborative efforts regarding the investigation – and get him ran out of town nearly by way of the proverbial rail, whereby crushing any hopes of revitalizing his dismal livelihood such as it is.

"Marsha, really I don't know much . . . I was up at the caves with the local law as you know . . . and I was there with Sheriff Deputy Charlie Redtail when the bodies of those two unfortunate hikers were found. But neither myself or Deputy Redtail performed any investigation of the bodies other than casual observation. It did look like the bodies had been mauled, but when and how – I have no idea!"

"Okay, Ian I buy that. But how in the heck did you get from the caves up to little Merwin Lake without going past me . . . Did you guy's somehow double back to another vehicle that you called for; and were picked up down at the main road or something?"

Ian thought about what Marsha had just said. He figured that he'd better be very careful not to begin a lie that would only serve to open the window for many more questions that would have no possible answers that wouldn't eventually blow-up in his face. Ian decided to tell the truth, but to be very to the point – and offer no more than the basics.

"The Sheriff, Deputy Redtail and I responding to an anonymous tip; one that got us up there in the first place . . . Deputy Redtail and I headed into the main cavern to investigate while the Sheriff searched above ground all around the parking lot. Hey, you sure this is completely off the record, right?"

Marsha shook her head yes and crossed her heart as she smiled an innocent smile.

It was her uncharacteristic innocent smile that made Ian even more nervous to speak than he'd been previously; but all the booze he'd drank earlier that evening made his lips a bit loose non-the-less.

"All right, anyway, the Deputy and I we headed into the larger of the two caves; the ones the locals call the Ape Caves, to search around. The cave we entered was suppose to go for a couple miles or so and then come to a dead end . . . But, do to that earthquake that happened some days ago the cave wall gave way at its end. It now opens up . . . The once cave is now a tunnel – it has a second opening to the outside world up at Little Merwin straight behind Harmony Falls. So that's how we ended up there . . . at the falls. That's why you never saw us come back to the parking lot from the cave . . . It was inside the cave near the new opening that we discovered the bodies . . . After finding the bodies, we called the Sheriff and that's about it!"

Suddenly Ian, even in his present alcohol hazed and heavily fatigued condition, realized he'd said too much – way too much! *Ah Christ! If she goes up there poking around; I just gave her the exact location of the Indian artifacts . . .*

Marsha just set there propped up in bed contemplating all that Ian had said. Ian put the rest of his clothes on, leaned over and kissed Marsha more out of expectation than for any other reason . . .

"Well, I've got to get going . . . I've got to meet up with the local law again first thing in the morning . . . Uh, hey I had a great time . . . Uh, well I'm gonna get going . . ."

Marsha didn't say another word – she just smiled a shallow smile as she stared blankly past him.

Ian could nearly feel the wheels turning within her head; it made the hair on the back of his neck stand on end. He was suddenly filled with dread.

CHAPTER 16

Semi-Savior

HE'D BEGAN APPLYING his air-brakes to slow down after spotting what looked like twisted metal strewn across the road. Now captured in his headlights shimmering in the twilight moon-glow was the clear and apparent fragmental remains of what once represented itself as a motor cycle.

Not a split second later, "What the Sam-hell . . . ?"

Something very large and very hairy had sprung from the forest right in front of his truck.

WHAM-BAM . . . !

"Jesus holy jumped-up palomino! – what the hell did I hit! Christ on a crutch must have been a bear!" He said out loud to himself . . . He then smirked as he further thought to himself . . . *less it was one of them Big Foots! Man alive wouldn't that be something!*

He continued bearing-down on his brakes while down-shifting as fast as he could. Finally with one last big blast of air he managed to stop his big rig without jackknifing it which probably would have meant loosing his load, or perhaps worse.

He then reached behind his head and grabbed his rifle from its rack. He climbed down from his rig and looked all around for what he assumed must have been a trophy-sized road kill.

He checked the front of his rig. Sure enough there was blood and some fur lodged into the grill from the hit. But no beast in sight. Just then he heard moans from the side of the road . . . Moans that sounded not like that of a beast but rather from . . . someone!

"Hey, help . . . We need some help over hear!"

The trucker ran over towards the cry for help . . . It was then the trucker could see partially illuminated by his rigs headlights – two teenagers. They were laying about ten feet apart from one another on their backs in the shallows of a mud enriched boggy creek bed.

Immediately he put two and two together . . . That was their bike that lay in ruins on the road. He called out as he raced as fast as he could towards them.

"Hey, you two okay? – should I fetch my first aide kit?"

The truck driver was now close enough to them to tell that one was a boy the other a girl . . . The girl was now screaming loudly. The boy held onto his knee with both hands and was rocking side to side obviously from pain.

"Mister . . . Oh man, thank God – check on my girlfriend and hurry she might be really hurt!"

The young man sounded almost hysterical to the trucker.

"Mister hurry! – we got to get the hell out of here! There's some kind of monster that jumped us . . . Mister, if we don't get out of here and quick, it's gonna kill us all!"

The truck driver knew there was some kind of big animal about, he'd just hit it. He began considering that an injured animal like a bear might be even more dangerous now that it was hurt. So he began panning his eyes around while closely holding his rifle. He made his way over to the girl. She seemed to be relatively in good shape. He helped her to her feet and together they went over to get the boy.

"Mister, thank God you came along! – I think I sort of twisted my knee or something. But I think I can get up, with some help . . . I'm pretty sure I can walk."

The trucker helped the boy to his feet. The boy was limping badly as the three made their way back to the truck as fast as they could.

It was just as they were climbing into the truck that the three heard the loudest most horrifying sound they'd ever heard in their lives. A series of blood curdling howls that sounded close, very close! Again the girl began to scream crying hysterically. The trucker managed though with some difficulty; to get his capacity loaded double trailer logging truck turned around in the road. After turning around, without further delay he began rapidly accelerating, up-shifting through the gears as the three sped away in the opposite direction that the trucker had initially been traveling in. Away from the blood curdling howls . . . The trucker knew the only medical facility in the area was back in Harmony Falls. He then shook his head as he once again spotted the bike laying in pieces strewn across the road. He was totally amazed the kids hadn't been more seriously injured than they appeared from their accident. But he'd been around long enough to know appearances could be deceiving.

"You two are god-damn lucky you were slung from the road into that shallow creek . . . Not much for rocks down there just mostly soft mud . . . your bike, wasn't so lucky . . . god-damn lucky is all I can say bout that! My names Mike Rousseau, my friends call me *Big Mike*. I'm the best damn log trucker on the road, if I do say so myself."

Big Mike began to laugh in hopes his levity would help calm the girl . . . she was beginning to calm slightly. She had begun calming due to their getting away from the source of the howling; and to the truckers kind face. A face that was somehow appropriately fitting for him; as it was substantially hidden behind a more than full salt and pepper colored beard. Which gave him one of those somehow trust-worthy Santa like looks. Big Mike had what appeared to be a balding head; though it was difficult to be certain due to his head being partially covered by a red and black checkered wool hat. One that perfectly matched his suspenders.

"Say, what's you two kids names and where'd you say you were from . . . ?"

"Uh, I'm Jeremy, sir . . . and this is my girlfriend Katie. We live up the road a bit, in Harmony Falls."

Jeremy looked over at his girlfriend and took her hand in his – "Katie, you okay?"

Katie tried desperately hard to suppress her sobbing. "Yeah, yeah I'll be fine . . . How bout you, Jeremy did you hurt your knee bad? It looks to be bleeding pretty bad through them torn-up jeans . . . ?"

"Nah, I'll be fine . . . It's actually starting to not hurt so much, no problem!"

The trucker interrupted Jeremy, "Well, you two try and relax. I'll have you back in Harmony Falls in just minutes. I think maybe we should get you to that medical clinic ran by ole Doc Matthews – have you both checked out to be safe."

Jeremy gasping just a little from pain spoke-up. "Mister, I mean . . . Big Mike – you don't look familiar to me; you're not from Harmony Falls are you?"

"Once upon a time I was . . . Grew up there . . . moved to Woodland bout twenty years ago – but I'm still up and down this here road least a couple times a week. Still lots of logging up this way. Hell, ole Doc Matthews, he fixed me up more than once when I was bout your age – used to raise a bit of hell back in the day."

Big Mike laughed at what he'd just said. Jeremy managed a half laugh, mostly out of manners. With the pain he was in and his state of mind from having the hell scared right out of him not a half hour before – he really was in no laughing mood. Katie, was no longer crying. She just sat there staring blankly straight ahead, until she too finally spoke.

"I don't care if it sounds crazy! It was a . . . Monster! It jumped us . . . made Jeremy crash the bike – it almost got us! I tell ya . . . it's a . . . Monster!"

Big Mike tried to keep his voice very calm. “Well, look here little missy, I believe ya! Mind you, I didn’t get much of a look at it – but I know ya saw something . . . I know, cause I’m pretty sure I hit it with my truck, and hit it good! Anyhow, that monster – well, it is, or more likely it was, a bear . . . Too big to have been anything else I can figure . . . It was a trophy size animal, a real monster just like you say! Cept, I’ll admit, I never seen or heard of any bear that size round these parts, I give ya that . . . anyhow . . . after I smacked it and good – I’m guessing it crawled off and died. Those loud sounds were from it bellowing in pain, a-for it keeled over.”

Jeremy spoke up, “No disrespect Big Mike . . . But that was no bear. Katie’s right . . . it’s some kind of, well . . . monster I guess is as good a thing to call it as any . . . I seen it plain and clear. Kind of looked like a bear and wolf mixed together, I know that sounds crazy! Man it had these yellow blood shot eyes and fangs and, well . . . God, Big Mike, you must of heard the howls too – when we headed to your truck!”

Big Mike didn’t answer just then, but he did shake his head in agreement to the howls.

“Hmm . . . monster you say. Well, hell, I don’t know exactly what to say bout that . . . But the facts are something must of jumped you and what I hit was awful big! Maybe it was one of them Sasquatch’s – friend of mine says he seen one once . . .”

Jeremy interrupts, “Big Mike it wasn’t no Sasquatch, Big Foot or whatever! – I’m telling you if I had to give a name to what I saw, I’d say it would be . . . I guess I’d say uh, werewolf!”

“Werewolf, Loupe-Garou, hmm . . . ?” Big Mike ran his right hand through his beard . . .

Jeremy now very confused spoke up, “What did you say, Loupe-what? What the hell, that French or something?”

“Loupe-Garou’s what I said . . . it’s been a very long time since I even thought bout them words . . . when I was a kid my Granddaddy told me of Indians around these parts that were said could shape shift into wolves, or wolf-men . . . he called them “Loupe-Garou,” means basically – werewolf. But say, you're obviously Indian or at least partial – you must of heard them shape shifting stories from your Granddaddy or old man too right?"

Jeremy shook his head in agreement. "Yeah, I've been told all kinds of stories about in the old days some of my people had such powers, but I always figured that stuff to be sort of like fairy tales . . ."

Big Mike spoke up attempting to divert the conversation which was not helping Katie to calm down.

"Ah, let's not go carrying on no more just now about monsters . . . You two just sit tight I'll get you back to Harmony Falls lick-it-tee split . . . Gonna take yah to Doc's clinic, get you all bandaged up and such!"

Both Jeremy and Katie offered up some protest to that idea. But they could tell straight away that any further argument about it would be futile. Big Mike was going to take them to Doc Matthews' clinic to get checked-out regardless of whatever they would have to say to the contrary – he was a good man.

CHAPTER 17

Town Hall

BUD WAS HEADING to his Blazer . . . It had been one hell of an emergency town meeting at the local grange hall regarding the discovery of the bodies and reports regarding follow up investigations pertaining to any possible predatory threat that may exist in or near their beloved township. Bud was last to leave – he'd stayed a while after everyone had gone home or elsewhere to shut the place down and lock it up. For three hours straight he'd been in the hot seat having to field many more questions from the town council than he'd answers for. It was now just past eleven o'clock, and he was beat! The ***Grange Hall*** shares a common parking lot with the ***Harmony Falls Medical Clinic*** – just as Bud climbed into his rig, drivers door still open. He looked up in response to the roar of a big diesel that was coming through town fast on the main road, too fast. He couldn't help lifting his eyebrows and jumping back out of his Blazer in reaction to the fully loaded logging truck which came bounding into the parking lot downshifting hard as air-brakes squelched and hissed. Finally with one extended blast which expressed itself as the disconcerting load noise created by the sudden release of compressed air – the truck came to a sudden stop. Bud was thankfully relieved at the sight. Not more than a split second earlier the truck looked to him to be heading to completely remodel Doc Matthews' recently partially renovated clinic.

A short moment later the drivers door of the logging truck opened. Out came a man that could not have looked more stereotypically the part of trucker. Bud began walking towards the log truck at a pace that was only slightly less than a bum-hip limping jog.

"Hey there, what's got you in such a toot?" Bud called out to the trucker.

The trucker was glad to see that Bud was a Sheriff. He yelled back to the Sheriff, "Got me a couple of kids here in my rig – one looks like he could use some mending from Doc Matthews."

"Don't say . . ." Sheriff Bud called back to the trucker now just around forty feet away and closing fast.

The trucker walked around the front of his rig and opened the passenger door – he helped Katie out . . . And then with a little more effort helped Jeremy to climb down out as well."

Bud joined the three at the side of the truckers rig.

"Why Jeremy, Katie . . . What the hell happened to you-all!" Bud could see the tear and dirt smeared face of Katie . . . He then spotted the blood dripping from around the knee area of Jeremy's jeans.

Bud immediately assumed the lead of the situation.

"Come on you all follow me . . . Jeremy can you walk on your own?" Jeremy shook his head yes.

"Okay then, let's go wake Doc . . ."

The four of them made their way over to the front-end of the medical clinic . . . Bud pressed the buzzer-button once that was located just below its associated intercom. He then pushed the buzzer a number of times in rapid secession. A moment went by with no answer – Bud repeated . . . he knew the buzzer was wired to buzz in the apartment that Doc had upstairs as well as inside the clinic. Bud had already took note that Doc's Cadillac was parked in its marked parking spot – Doc was there all right . . . hopefully not passed out from too much medicinal tonic typically labeled Canadian Mist.

"Who is it – what do yah need?" A very groggy sounding Doc Matthews spoke over the tiny sounding intercom.

Bud pressed the button and informed Doc of the situation . . . In less than a minute Doc came downstairs, turned the lights on to the clinic. He then opened the door.

"Come on in and let's have a look at you two. Jeremy you climb best you can up on that exam table over yonder . . . Katie how bout you, anything hurt?"

Jeremy crossed the room and with little difficulty made his way up onto the exam table.

Katie shook her head no to Doc's question. She once again began to sob. "Go Doctor, go help Jeremy!" She spoke to Doc Matthews as she headed to her boyfriends side.

"Okay, all right, so you took a tumble on your motorcycle did you . . . ?" Doc spoke as he proceeded to cut-away Jeremy's jean leg to be able to have a look.

"Now then, that's not so bad . . . could use a couple-few stitches. You just lay back I'm gonna stick you with a needle that'll take most of the pain away for a couple few hours anyway – gonna numb it up good after I clean it up a bit first that is. So how'd your little spill happen anyway?"

Big Mike spoke up first, "Well, I found these kids pretty close to the turn-off up to Little Merwin and the falls . . . not too far from Harmony Falls-Ape Caves junction. Any-ways, I hit some animal with my rig . . . Big son-of-a-bitch bear I think. I spotted these two over on the side of the road laying in a muddy creek. I also saw what was left of Jeremy there's motor-bike. It didn't fare as well as these two . . . it was in pieces all over the road. I'm telling you Doc, Sheriff . . . these kids were plenty lucky!"

Katie spoke up just as soon as Big Mike had finished . . .

"What Big Mike here doesn't realize is, it wasn't no bear he hit . . . what he hit was after us . . . it made us crash! – it's a monster plain and simple! I mean I didn't see it, I only heard it up at the lake . . . but I saw it when it jumped out at us on the road – a monster I tell you!" Katie began crying hysterically . . .

Jeremy spoke up immediately to support what his girlfriend had just said.

"What she said is the truth I swear it! It was no bear or cougar, or whatever you may say or think – I'm telling you it was . . . it is a monster! From what I saw of it . . . I don't think Big Mike hitting it with his truck did much more than just piss it off!"

Big Mike spoke up once again. "Say, I think whatever it was, or still is, I mean whatever's left of it – it left some of itself on the grill of my truck . . . come see Sheriff, I'll show you."

CHAPTER 18

Grilling

BUD FOLLOWED BIG Mike outside to his rig to have a look at the remnant DNA evidence.

"Just a second I'm gonna go get me a flashlight out of my Blazer." Bud said to Big Mike. Less than a minute later the two men stood looking at the front grill of the logging truck.

"I don't know about you Sheriff, but to me that don't look like no fur of no bear or big cat neither . . . it's kind of tough to be certain but the hair, well fir, it looks mostly dark gray in color."

"Yep, I'd say that's bout right – mister, what did you say your name was? You look mighty familiar to me. You pass this way hauling logs often, stop and have some chow now and again?"

"My names Mike Rousseau. And yep, I've been hauling logs from operations on the east ridge for the last couple weeks straight. But that's probably not why I look familiar to you . . ."

The Sheriff took a long look at Big Mike. "Say there's a number of folks round these parts with your last name – you got family around these parts?"

"That's right Sheriff, grew up here... my folks moved to Woodland when I was still a kid."

Bud smiled then replied, "That a fact!"

"Sheriff I remember you . . . you're Bud O'Brien right?"

Bud looked at Big Mike a little surprised, "That's right!"

Big Mike smiled a big smile, "Bud you was just a couple years older than me when me and my folks lived just out of town; down the road a ways – hell Bud, we went to school together back in those days."

Bud smiled a big ear to ear smile, "By God I knew there was something bout you looked familiar . . . How bout that . . . Say Mike would you do me a favor and stick around just a little longer – I'm gonna make a couple of calls and get my Deputy and another feller out here to have a look at this hair and blood on your grill. And by the way, I can't thank you enough bout what you did for those two kids. Fact is the boy's my Deputy's son . . . yeah, the shit's gonna hit the fan when my Deputy finds out where those two had been before they took that spill . . . Jeremy's dark butt's gonna get a bit more of a tanning from his Dad, unless I miss my guess."

Big Mike replied "Suppose they be in double deep cause of all them posted **do not enter** warning signs I been seeing all round those parts. Still, hope his old man, nor the young gals folks for that matter, they don't be too hard on them two. Those two seem like real nice kids. And well, kids will be kids. Anyhow, we done worse-n-that back in the day . . . right, Bud?"

Both Sheriff Bud and Big Mike laughed in mutual agreement to that one!

Bud called up both Charlie and Ian. The two met up with him and Big Mike nearly at the same time; arriving at Doc Matthews clinic in just minutes after receiving their calls.

Once Charlie and Ian stood alongside the logging truck with Bud and Big Mike – Charlie and Ian both began more intensely wondering what was so important that they all gather here of all places, this late at night. Bud hadn't said anything to them on the phone other than it was very important for them to get to Doc Matthews clinic as fast as they could. Bud didn't want Charlie to worry un-necessary about Jeremy. And Ian, well Bud figured it was more important to get him here to the truck for a look-see than jabber about it on the phone.

Before any questions from either Charlie or Ian could be asked or answered – Bud orchestrated all of the polite introductions . . . he then told Charlie a bit of what had taken place. Charlie raced inside to check on Jeremy and Katie . . . Bud called Katie's parents, her Dad was on his way to pick her up.

After watching Doc thread the last of fourteen stitches into Jeremy's knee . . . Charlie re-joined Bud, Big Mike and Ian outside at the front of the truck.

The four of them now stood in front of the logging truck pondering and discussing just what type of big animal would have dark gray fur.

Bud looked at Ian, "Looks an awful lot like that fur we seen back at the cave don't it?"

Ian shook his head in agreement, "It sure does! I'll get a sample of this here blood and fur."

Ian slumped over and bowed his head slightly . . .

"Oh, by the way I must confess, I collected some samples back at the cave . . . I mean extra ones that neither you or Charlie knew I did."

Both Bud and Charlie frowned a bit about Ian taking anything from the cave without their knowledge.

Ian continued, "Sorry about that . . . but believe me I collected the samples for all the right reasons. Now looking at what we got here, I'm damn glad I did. The sample fur taken up at the cave and looking at this fur here – just at cursory glance look to be the same in both color and general texture. But we'll get my other samples of blood and fur along with what we got here and get it all to an expert I know . . . The guy, Matt Larsen, is a PhD in genetics. He and his partner specialize in this sort of thing; tops in their field of DNA research and all that – and believe me, he knows how to keep things discreet. His lab ***Helix-Tech***

I believe it's called; is not far . . . it's up in Vancouver, B.C. We can send the samples tomorrow via overnight express. Should get the results in just a few days! They'll do all the necessary tests and sample comparisons – of course its gonna cost . . ."

Bud spoke up, "Cost, yeah right . . . Of course it will cost. Don't worry Ian we'll get the costs covered. I was told in no uncertain terms at the town council meeting a few hours ago, that I better do whatever it takes to get this all sorted out and fast. Or, I'll be out on the bricks if you get my meaning . . . I may even have to go up north to Seattle tomorrow. I was asked to be prepared for that . . . might just take the train, then taxi it from there. Don't know my way around up there. So far they haven't demanded it, just strongly recommended it. Maybe I'll go, maybe I'll wait and see if I got to. Might have to answer some questions rapid fired at me by some fancy lawyers about the deaths of them hikers. Don't know why exactly, they've got my reports, they know bout as much as I do!"

Ian changed the subject back to the DNA evidence he wanted to send off to have examined. He assured Bud, Charlie and Big Mike too; that the scientist he spoke of would get them the answers they needed.

Ian skillfully collected some samples from Big Mike's grill; soon after Big Mike said his good-byes and was off on his way. Bud, Charlie and Ian went back into Doc Matthews clinic to find: Doc, Jeremy, Katie and now an extremely irate Katie's father.

CHAPTER 19

The Parting

STILL STANDING IN Doc Matthews portion of the parking lot – Bud, Charlie and Ian finally said their good-night's . . .

"Okay you two – we'll get back on this first thing tomorrow morning at the office."

Ian then spoke in reply to Bud's declaration of continuance in the morning – it was in fact technically already morning as they spoke . . . it was now 1:45 am.

"Sounds good Bud – I'll have the samples properly labeled and ready to send up to my guy up north."

Charlie who hadn't spoke since finding out about his sons escapades and subsequent injury finally spoke.

"Yeah, that sounds good . . . Ian don't you ever hold out anything on us again. But me and Bud we'll let you slide on this one. Specially since it looks like you're gonna make it worth while. We got to know what the hell we're gonna be dealing with. Or, maybe better said – what we're gonna be hunting before someone else gets hurt . . . oh, and Bud – when I left you guy's to check on the boy . . . he told me it was him that called in the anonymous tip about the bodies. Seems he's been sneaking off up near the outskirts of the reservation near the falls more than once! Don't worry he ain't gonna be doing nothing like that again. Me and the boy aren't finished about this . . . not by a long shot! And as far as him continuing to see his gal-friend Katie; well, her old-man he chewed the boy and me out and good. Said in no uncertain terms that my boy wasn't good enough for his daughter. He then threatened my boy; told him to never see his daughter again, or else! Whatever that was suppose to mean . . . went so far as to threaten suing me bout the accident. Know what I told him about that? I told him he could kiss my ass. As far as them two kids – nobody gonna keep them apart. They got love in their hearts . . . harder you try and keep two with love in their hearts apart . . . more they gonna sneak around to be with each other. Me I likes Katie, and I love my son . . . like I said . . . her old man can kiss my ass! And that's all I have to say about that!"

Both Bud and Ian smiled at Charlie's words and the obviousness of his love for his son.

Bud was compelled to add his two cents, "Charlie, Jeremy's a good kid, hell, I don't have to tell you how I feel about him and you and your wife. Why up till a couple years ago Jeremy used to call me Uncle Bud, and tell you the truth I kind a liked it. And Katie, well now, she's a good kid too! I'm behind you and those two young kids one hundred and fifty percent!"

Those words touched Charlie – he immediately smiled and shook Bud's hand.

Ian could see the bond between those two men was indivisible, and he too was touched by it. They were much more than just co-workers; they were best friends! Charlie's family was probably the closest thing that Bud had to family of his own. Suddenly Ian felt a rock hard pit form in his stomach – at that instance he felt more alone than he could handle. Thankfully to Ian, the two men before him couldn't see in the darkness the tears that had instantly welled up in his eyes.

Bud looked at both Charlie and Ian and smiled, "Well we best stop a jawing out here in the cold night air. Let's call it a night and put our heads together on this thing first thing in the morning."

Charlie and Ian shook their heads in agreement. What they didn't know was that Bud had one more task on his nights agenda yet to be executed before he was to go home.

The three men said their goodnights and began walking to their vehicles . . . but, then Bud turned around towards both Charlie and Ian.

"Say you two go on now. I'm just going back inside for a moment and jaw with Doc, I won't be but a moment. We'll all meet up at the office around eight . . . Charlie stop off at your store first thing before you come in – grab us some of them famous doughnuts of Elaine's." Bud turned to Ian, "Ian – you ain't lived till you've tasted Elaine's fresh baked doughnuts."

Charlie smiled in agreement to pick up some doughnuts; he and Ian waved good night to Bud, climbed into their rides and left to their awaiting beds.

Bud walked around towards the front of the medical clinic until both Charlie and Ian were long gone. He then walked briskly back to his Blazer, climbed in and fired it up, then headed out of town towards the mountain. *Can't leave motor-bike parts laying all over the road – could get someone killed.* Bud thought to himself; as he attempted to rationalize why he was about to do what he had his mind set on. One thing Bud had never had, was a lack of curiosity – a trait that had proven to serve him well as a law-man many times over the years.

The truth was Bud wanted to look around the area while it was fresh for any additional animal tracks. He just had to know if they would resemble the very strange tracks that he and Ian had seen up at the falls cave.

CHAPTER 20

Alone In The Dark

BUD SPOTTED BIKE wreckage here and there strewn all around on the roadway just ahead of him as it shimmered from his headlights. The remains were just exactly where Big Mike had said they'd be. Bud even spotted big-rig skid marks no doubt created by Mike slamming on his rigs brakes when he'd hit, whatever he hit.

Bud pulled his Blazer over to the side of the road – turned his vehicles four way's and law-lights on. They spun round and round flashing red, amber, and blue. The last thing he wanted was to get ran over as he pulled the bikes remains well off the roadway; over into the side ditch.

Bud returned to his Blazer and went around to its rear. He opened the hatchback and unlocked a gun case that was bolted to the floor of his rig. Inside the case he grabbed a beautiful assault style, carbon-fiber stock, twelve gauge pump shotgun that he and Charlie had only ever fired a couple of times on the gun range. It was fully loaded with magnum double-ought buck-n-slugs for maximum stopping power.

Bud always figured if a situation ever arose that would necessitate him to bring out the big gun – then big gun it would be!

Shotgun in arm, Bud proceeded off of the road over to the general area he figured the kids had taken their spill. He knew the area like the back of his hand and their description of the creek and boggy mud meant only one place. Bud walked stealth-fully though the tall grass listening to every abundant sound the forest had to offer. Frogs were crocking, crickets chirped, birds and squirrels made quite a racket until his presence became known to all the forest creatures – which then created a very eerie deep silence. He saw the expected occasional fruit bat swooping around. He even saw a good size buck freeze from his flashlight for a couple seconds before it bounded off into the forest. But then he saw what he came to see. There were more of the un-typically huge paw prints of some animal he couldn't readily identify. Bud couldn't help thinking that the huge prints could easily be thought of as being made from a *Big Foot*... and what Big Mike apparently ran into by his description was large and hairy – again ... *Big Foot?*

Upon Bud's closer observation, the prints appeared to be just like the ones Ian and he had seen up at the cave – they were just as Ian had aptly described; they looked like tracks of a dog or wolf; but they were different in certain ways. These tracks were fresh – and like the ones at the cave, these too had the additional indentation of what resembled sort of a heal-like imprint. But the prints were just too large. The size and formation made no sense. The most unnerving part to Bud was prints of this size so deeply imbedded into the soil would mean that proportionately the animal would have to be incredibly heavy and enormous beyond belief! Bud suddenly felt a chill come over him; he shuddered at the sudden realization of where he was and what might still be lurking near by. It was a brightly lit moonlight night; very nearly a full moon with little clouds. But even still, with only the visibility that the flashlight he clip-mounted on his shotgun afforded. His attempts at looking deep into the dense evergreen forest was nearly futile – Bud strained his eyes staring with all his might as he looked all around off into the abyss. He couldn't help feeling unnerved at the knowledge that no-doubt there were a thousand tiny eyes staring back at him with much greater success. And Bud also knew too well that animals of the predator persuasion were blessed with near perfect night vision. He was becoming increasingly convinced after speaking with Jeremy and Big Mike; and after seeing the prints all around him – that there may be at least one predator around that even packing his small cannon he'd rather not meet, not alone, not at night . . .

All at once Bud saw the impossible – small to medium size trees started snapping and breaking all around not thirty feet in front of him. The trees and foliage suddenly parted like Moses had parted the Red Sea. Bud prayed it was a herd of Elk creating a new would-be animal trail. But his prayers fell to deaf ears, or ears that could have given a shit; as he heard the deep low growling of something beyond fierce. Bud's legs became like lead-weights, he'd heard stories of people who claimed to have been frozen from fear; but he'd never before personally known it to be possible. He then felt the ground shake from impact tremors. Tremors that shook the ground in perfect synchronization like that of a massive marching army.

"Oh my God! . . ." Bud screamed loud and shrill at the sudden emergence of a massive dark silhouette that supported unholy mirror-like reflective retinas. It was reared up and moving on two legs as it leapt out of the black darkness directly upon him. Bud managed to pump-off three rounds of heavy load directly into the chest of the beast. The shotgun blasts impacted the creature hard, knocking it back a couple of feet. The beast bent over, bellowing and gasping for air – as its blood spew . . . but ultimately the direct hits effected nothing more than slowing the beast, only momentarily.

Now tackled and utterly shock-seized. The last thing Bud felt and saw was the panting of thick hot breath and saliva that dripped from the monsters jaws into his face. Unable to move, Bud was completely pinned. Staring down at him were two insidiously yellow and red-veined eyes – growling and snarling ferociously, the monstrous aberration posed with intensely drawn back heavily flexed facial muscles. The beast's gums now fully retracted revealing massive ivory colored canine swords and shark-like incisors which tore into Bud's throat; ripping and devouring it with thrusts of supernatural force and ferocity – until there was no throat left to sever. Momentarily satisfied, the beast backed off from him and just stood examining its kill – then it looked up at the Moon and let out an un-Earthly series of howls. Bud's head rolled from his body down the sloped embankment, coming to rest in the shallow muddy creek below . . . The beast then bit down onto the trunk of Bud's heavy bleeding decapitated body; picked it up and held it firm in its jaws. Then dropped from moving on two legs to quadruped as it crossed the road.

CHAPTER 21

What If . . . ?

HIS ALARM-CLOCK BLARED its incessant buzz, buzz, buzzing . . . the morning came too early – way too early for Ian.

Ian had fallen into shallow sleep while semi-watching an old black and white horror movie on his television. He had sprung for the works, full hookups at his RV campsite which included cable; since the good people of Harmony Falls would be footing the bill.

The movie he'd been semi-watching was the second of a creature double feature. Aired as a salute to Universal Studios classic horror films of the 1940's – both films starred Lon Chaney Jr. portraying the deeply troubled Lawrence Talbot. A man eternally cursed by the mark of the beast.

Ian figured he must have finally dozed off around three-thirty It was now seven-fifteen.

The last thing he could remember of the movie was an old Gypsy reciting a poem . . . *something, about how even a good man when the moon was bright could turn into . . .*

Still very blurry-eyed and fuzzy headed; Ian grabbed a shoe that was laying next to him on the floor of his trailer's semblance of a double wide bed. Which was made-down, transformed from its alternate self as it existed before, as the dinning table.

Somehow the thought of this, his bed, and how it can be transformed from one thing to another and the old movie started Ian's mind racing . . .

What if Big Foot was actually a . . . Loupe-Garou, like the old drunk at the bar had said – a werewolf . . . Nah, that's ridiculous! Ian's mind was swimming with all sorts of fleeting wild thoughts. Desperately attempting to form some rhyme or reason that might aide in the investigation. *Maybe that would account for why no body of a Sasquatch has ever been recovered?*

Ian couldn't help himself, his imagination had totally gotten the best of him . . . *Every culture around the globe has its stories of some type of shape-shifting phenomena – the American Indians have, or at least had very strong beliefs regarding such things . . . God what am I even thinking here . . . I must be loosing it! There's a logical explanation, just got to be the first to find it! I wonder if I even suggested such a possibility to Charlie, if he would think I was crazy and have me run out of town on a rail . . . ? One things for certain, I sure as shit wouldn't suggest it to Bud!*

Ian managed with some difficulty to drag himself out of bed . . . He splashed a little water on his face and headed out of his trailer and climbed into his Jeep. Ian figured he'd catch a shower in the park's men's bathroom and shower house later in the day. Right now he had to get a move on to not be late . . . Ian had his problems, but being late to the dance had never been one of them.

He first glanced up at the sky as he pulled out of the park onto the main road. Ian frowned when he saw though it was dry at the moment, the light gray cloudy sky was getting darker not lighter as the morning progressed. The clouds moving in were dark and thick. Major weather was heading this way; that meant heavy rain was a certainty and it was coming fast. Ian then glanced at his gas-gauge and noticed that his gas situation was starting to get serious. Ian began thinking of what his best morning strategy would be . . .

I better get some gas and pronto. We'll no-doubt be heading back up to the falls to do some more poking around . . . Charlie's wife's store is the only place I've seen in town to get gas. Probably outrageously high prices. But since their picking up my expenses who the hell cares . . . Maybe I'll meet up with Charlie – he was suppose to stop and pick-up some doughnuts; I guess I could spring for the coffee's since I'm gonna save my receipts and bill-em for whatever, anyway!

Moments later Ian pulled into the ***Merwin Mercantile*** . . . He immediately noted the price of regular gas was a good ten cents a gallon more than he'd paid just a couple days ago in Lincoln City on the Oregon Coast – and he thought those prices were ridiculously high even for a tourist town!

Ian began thinking to himself . . . *Boy what a racket Charlie and his wife have going. If you need gas while you're hell in gone up here – you've got no choice but to pay whatever price for gas they ask . . .*

Ian drove to the gas pump islands located just left of the store; he then proceeded forward up to pump number two . . .

He then spotted Charlie's car parked towards the back of the store. Ian smiled now knowing he wasn't going to be much if any later rendezvousing with Bud than Charlie would.

Ian hoped out of his Jeep and walked briskly up to the stores ingress – he spotted Charlie picking out doughnuts as he opened the heavy glass door and crossed the threshold into the store. Right away he took note of all the usual grocery items; beer, pop and lots of snacks . . . Ian was moderately impressed as he noticed they carried a pretty respectable selection of fishing poles, rods, lure's and related gear . . . but he couldn't help but smile and shake his head when he spotted the assortment of tourist-trap ***Mt. St. Helens*** and ***Lake Merwin*** screen-printed caps, tees and sweatshirts . . . Ian actually chuckled out load when he read the ***I survived the Ape Caves*** t-shirts. That was until the idea of the two unfortunate hikers crossed his mind, then the shirts suddenly lost their humor to him.

"Hey Ian . . . there anything we can do you for?" Charlie called out from the other side of the store upon spotting Ian looking around.

"Oh, hey Charlie . . . I mainly came by to get some gas . . . I see you're grabbing some of those world famous doughnuts Bud talked up."

"Ian come over here I want to introduce you to my wife."

Ian walked across the store over to the check-out counter . . .

Charlie took the lead with the introductions, "Ian, I'd like you to meet my gal here . . . Elaine, this is Ian McDermott, he's an out-of-town expert that we've brought in to help in the investigation . . . he's been a lot of help – hey, I'll be back in just a few . . ."

Charlie then headed off to the back room of the store.

Ian smiled and shook Elaine's hand, "Very nice to meet you Elaine." He was stunned at the nice words from Charlie to his wife regarding him . . . but it made him feel good. Charlie's attitude towards him had taken a three-hundred-and-sixty degree turnaround since those first very uncomfortable hours he'd spent with him in the caves.

Ian once again began gazing around the store; that somehow now seemed much larger to him then it had initially looked from the outside.

He spotted a glass case over in the corner that held what even at first glance was readily recognizable by him as Indian artistry. Ian walked over to the case; he began staring at the jewelry held within. He was genuinely amazed at the intricate artwork represented in each and every piece.

Elaine came over and stood behind the case, "Ian, can I bring anything out for you to have a closer look at?"

He couldn't help himself noticing what a beautiful Native American women Elaine was . . . she was slender and tiny, maybe five foot four. She had a near flawless completion, jet black eyes and long silky ebony hair that she wore tied in a pony tail that draped over her shoulder across her left breast . . . Ian had to momentarily look away from Elaine to not be caught gawking. The last thing he wanted was to offend her or Charlie for that matter, who would be returning any time now.

Ian regained his composure, "Uh, the jewelry here, it's very nice! It looks like sterling silver and the stones those are turquoise aren't they?"

"Why that's right Ian . . . you familiar with Native American jewelry?"

Ian smiled at Elaine, "Well, I know a little. I did some related research regarding Native American art, and such, but that was a long time ago. Don't bother bringing anything out right now, but maybe I'll pick something up later."

Elaine returned Ian's smile, "Okay, great, give it some thought."

Ian changed the subject, "Say Elaine, what I really need right now is some gas . . . I'd like to fill-er-up! – you take Master Card, right?"

"Yeah, master card is fine! Just go on out when your ready and fill up. Then come back and I'll run your card."

Ian replied, "Great, perfect . . . oh, and hey can you set me up with three large coffee's and some cream and sugars to go?"

Elaine once again smiled, "You got it!"

Charlie who had been in the restroom for the last couple minutes re-joined Elaine at the counter. He then called across the room at Ian who was beginning to open the door to head out to his Jeep.

"Okay, Ian, I'll see you in a few minutes at the office!"

Ian glanced back over his shoulder towards Charlie, smiled and nodded yes.

He then pushed opened the glass door and headed straight to pump two located adjacent to his Jeep.

CHAPTER 22

M.I.A.

IAN PUSHED THE heavy glass two-way door open with his elbow, trying desperately not to spill hot coffee on himself. He held three filled to the brim cups of fresh brewed in a small to go cardboard carrier, along with several small packets of sugar, cream and three small red straws.

The secretary and receptionist Jenny Hovermire sat at her desk just inside the small Sheriff 's office. To Ian's surprise, somehow Charlie had arrived a few minutes earlier and had informed her to be expecting him.

"You must be Ian . . ." Jenny said with a slightly forced smile the moment he'd managed to navigate the doorway into the office.

Ian looked at the middle aged heavy-set women with some surprise, he thought she was looking at him just a little, oddly.

"Yeah, that I am . . . Uh, is the Sheriff or Deputy Redtail here? . . . and, oh by the way – I have this little pouch, potential evidence that we collected needs to go to a lab . . . it needs to be sent up to Vancouver, Canada. It's addressed and ready to go, uh, it's sort of a rush – can you arrange to have UPS or FedEx, some overnight service pick it up?"

Jenny instantly replied with little enthusiasm, she had never been much of a morning person, "Yeah sure, I'll take care of it . . . Ian go ahead on back . . . Charlie's here, first door to your left."

Ian headed on back. He chuckled to himself when he noted there were only two doors that he could have chosen, one on the right, one on the left . . . each had name-plates on their doors.

Ian tapped lightly on the door on the left which bore the title and name *Deputy Charlie Redtail* . . .

"Come in . . ."

Ian opened the door and gave Charlie a big smile – he was feeling good about himself that he came bearing coffee.

Upon seeing Ian with the coffee which Charlie recognized as coming from his wife's store he returned the smile with equal enthusiasm.

"All right Ian, nice, you brought coffee . . . Jenny put a pot on in the little kitchenette in the back; but tell ya the truth it don't hold a candle to my wife's java. But keep that to yourself . . . believe me Bud will thank you!"

Both men laughed small laughs . . . Ian was really starting to like Charlie, which a day ago he would have thought would have been out of the question.

Ian then reflected to himself maybe that was it – *hmm, she saw the coffee, that was the reason she looked at me funny when I came in, must of pissed her off a tad . . .*

"Ian take a seat, Bud usually gets here around seven-thirty he beats me in bout everyday . . . huh, It's nearly eight . . . I tell you, the man's dedicated. He's never been late without calling, or missed a day of work in his life that I know of anyway . . ."

Ian sat down and handed Charlie a coffee, "I didn't know how ya take your Joe, there's cream and sugar in the box here." Ian sat the small box on the edge of Charlie's desk.

Charlie took the coffee from Ian and replied with a straight poker face, "I take it as is . . . I like my coffee like I like my women – dark and hot!"

Charlie then broke his poker face and began to chuckle.

Ian laughed, paused as he thought of a snappy comeback . . .

"Yeah, well, I take mine with cream and sugar – cause I like my coffee and women light colored and sweet to taste!"

Charlie almost choked on the sip of coffee he'd taken at the very moment Ian had retorted with levity of his own . . . Charlie laughed loud and hard. "Ian, you've got a sick sense of humor just like me, I like that!" Ian shook his head in agreement, both men laughed regarding their alike wit.

Both men sat sipping on coffee and eating doughnuts. Occasionally they would enter into some light conversation, it was now eight-twenty.

"Okay that's it – I'm calling Bud to see what's up!" Charlie exclaimed as he took the phone on his desk from its re-charge pedestal. "Bud don't have a land-line at his house . . . all he uses is his cell . . . so we'll catch him where-ever he be."

Charlie dialed Bud's phone number, a recorded message came on proclaiming that the phone was not currently in service . . . Charlie was stunned.

"Three things Bud don't never do . . . One, he never lets his phone's battery go dead; he's fanatical about keeping it charged. He even keeps a spare battery in his rig if that ever became an issue. Two, he don't ever go nowhere without his phone cause he's always on call. And the third thing is . . . he don't never, never turn his phone off for the same reason. And like I said before, he's never late . . . hmm, something's up and I don't much like it! Ian let's go for a drive, see if we can find him, hopefully just shacked up with some ten dollar hooker and too embarrassed to get up out of bed."

Ian scratched his head. Regardless of Charlie's small attempt to make light the situation he could tell by the look on Charlie's face that he was more than just a trifle concerned.

"Where you planning to look first?" Ian exclaimed stretching his arms and back just a bit as he stood up from the front side of Charlie's desk.

"Well, now that's a good question . . . Knowing Bud well as I do . . . I can't help but entertain the notion that he might have . . . Tell you what. First we'll swing by his place and pray he didn't up and have a heart attack or something. If he ain't there. We're gonna head back up towards the falls, maybe the caves too. The hair on the back of my neck is telling me he just might of got a wild hair up his ass. He may of gone to check out where my boy trashed his bike. You know, to have a look around for any physical evidence of whatever jumped the kids and that trucker says he hit . . . you know, while any signs are still fresh. The radio weather-man, he did say last night that it's suppose to rain today . . . I even thought about heading up there last night myself but then came to my senses. Bud's got the nose of a bloodhound and the curiosity of a cat. What's got me worked up is we both know how that worked out for the cat!"

CHAPTER 23

Fallen Comrade

AFTER CRUISING BY Bud's place Charlie didn't even bother going up to the front door and knocking. He new that Bud habitually kept his porch light switched on whenever he was gone day or night, and the light was on – furthermore no Blazer was parked in its typical location in Bud's driveway.

"All right, that's it . . . now I am worried! We're going to the falls, the caves, to hell and back if necessary!"

Ian shook his head in total agreement – he too was getting very nervous about the whole thing.

Charlie turned his cop-lights on. He even turned his siren on. He let out of town like he was in hot pursuit. They were making lickety-split time until . . . there it came just as forecasted. The dark sky flashed lightning off in the distance, thunder rumbled and then the heavens opened up. The rain started slow, but the further up in the hills they got the harder the rain began pounding down in huge drops. Charlie was forced to slow down a bit once the rain began challenging his wind-shield wipers to keep up. Visibility was made worse by heavy morning fog they began encountering just a few miles from the turn-off that headed up mountain towards Harmony Falls. All four eyes strained as hard as they could to see up the road as far as possible. Though it was difficult to see any great distance due to the water-blurred windshield that was further obstructed by the high-speed flipping wipers that sloshed rain-water to and fro – further complicating their vision was the fog that hung thick like a light gray cotton blanket across the road.

Finally they both spotted at the same time what they were looking for, but still dreaded to find. There, less than a quarter mile from the falls turn-off was motorcycle debris that had obviously been neatly dragged off the road into a ditch. As they slowed down and continued up the road; just beyond the bike wreckage around another forty yards ahead was Bud's Blazer pulled over on the right side of the road. His tail lights still vaguely were on, and even his cop-lights were still spinning and flashing, but they were noticeably growing very dim.

Charlie instantly knew that Bud's rig had been there for hours. Bud's Blazer was equipped with an extra heavy duty deep cycle battery that would way out-last the normal car battery and it had just about given up.

Charlie slowed way down and pulled his car over and parked it directly behind Bud's Blazer.

"Ian, this ain't no good . . . this ain't no good at all!" Charlie exclaimed with a noticeable heightened tone in his voice; his elevated anxiety also reflected heavily on his face.

It was then that Charlie said something to Ian that caught him completely off guard, "Up here in the sticks, it isn't like the city, there ain't no calling for no back-up . . . Ian you're my back-up. Raise your right hand." Without thinking Ian did just that, "Consider yourself temporarily deputized! Now grab that little pop-gun you got strapped to your leg and follow me. Mind now, you don't do nothing stupid like shoot me in the back!"

How the hell did he know I'm strapped with heat? . . . Ian couldn't believe the powers of observation that Charlie had . . . he knew his ankle-strapped weapon was nearly unnoticeable . . . *Nearly!*

"Okay, I got your back. I want you to know I've got a license to carry my gun."

Ian replied now getting very nervous about the whole thing . . .

"Yeah, well we'll discuss that later. Now come on follow me . . ." Charlie started to open his door, "Say, I've got a rain parka in the trunk if you like, otherwise you're gonna get soaked!" Ian shook his head no, "No thanks, I'M okay."

"All right then . . . Ian you hang about six feet back, behind me, you keep your eyes peeled and stay alert! Like Bud always says . . . expect the unexpected. Be ready for the worst . . . and pray it's nothing!"

Both men exited the vehicle and immediately drew their weapons. Ian held his gun as he saw Charlie doing it. Double-handed, across his left shoulder barrel pointed up and away from his face.

They approached Bud's Blazer. Both men headed towards the drivers side of the rig. Ian stayed just as Charlie had instructed him, about three paces back.

Charlie looked into the back hatchback window of the Blazer, he saw nothing. He then proceeded slowly up to the drivers side window . . . there was nobody home. Charlie could see on the ground what had to have been Bud's footprints, rapidly melting away on the muddy road-side. They headed from his rig straight ahead for about ten feet and then off to the right, disappearing into the marshy grass embankment below . . . Charlie knew what lay below – a creek that could swell-up pretty good on days like this.

Charlie's heart began pounding . . . he tried his best not to over-alarm Ian . . . but what he saw was prints that went towards the embankment but none that returned.

"Ian, you stay right here at the Blazer. Keep your gun in hand and keep your ears open – cause if I need your help . . . I may need it quick, you understand? If I fire a series of shots . . . you come help, you got it? Normally, I wouldn't even think about potentially endangering a civilian like yourself, but this ain't no typical situation. Oh yeah, and I did deputize you all legal like . . ." The two men smiled very uneasy smiles at each other . . . Charlie then nodded at Ian while looking into his eyes to see if he could count on him. Ian took a deep breath then nodded back to Charlie that he was ready.

"All right then," was Charlie's last words as he left to follow the foot prints that lead ahead and into the tall grass and short thicket of barbed black-berry vines.

Charlie moved onward off of the roadside and into the edge of the sloped embankment. He then made his way down the small slope . . . Charlie looked all around until he spotted a massive amount of rain-washed blood ahead maybe twenty feet. As he approached he noticed that there was a vast amount of blood in an area of mashed down grass. He walked up to the tiny trampled clearing – then a large pit welled up in his stomach as he spotted Bud's twelve gauge pump shotgun laying amidst rain-washed blood which covered most of its cold steel barrel . . . Charlie then additionally spotted three spent shells that laid scattered near the weapon. There were clothing fragments amidst all the bloody trampled ground. The clothing pieces were easily identifiable . . . Too easy! They were from Bud's uniform.

Charlie felt a cold grisly rush run up his spine. The hair on the back of his neck literally stood on end . . . Charlie gasped for air as he thought his heart was going to explode from his chest. He then started hyperventilating as he franticly began looking around in every direction for . . . a body . . . or, the attacker, be it animal or otherwise.

After catching his breath; and after recovering what was left of his nearly shattered nerves – Charlie proceeded further down to the creek below.

Upon reaching the creek, what he saw next caused Charlie to experience something that no amount of police training could have prepared him for – he stood frozen like a statue for a very long moment utterly terror-stricken!

Now with tears flowing from his eyes at a volume that nearly matched the intensity of the rain that fell on his face . . . Charlie with hands trembling, managed to raise his pistol towards the heavens. He was held steadfast in a vice-grip of total shock, grief stricken beyond measure. Charlie bellowed out a yell; a proclamation of his intense anguish and rage, as he squeezed off six rounds from his Glock 9mm semi-automatic pistol.

CHAPTER 24

Vendetta

IAN RUSHED DOWN the small hillside to join Charlie. Upon catching up to Charlie what Ian saw next he couldn't believe. A second later he bent over and began throwing up the coffee and doughnuts that he'd finished consuming not a couple hours before.

Charlie had just reached down into the shallow creak and retrieved by the hair; the completely severed head of Sheriff Bud O'Brien.

Bud's bug-eyed pale as a ghost face had a horrific grimaced expression on it – one that the words terror-stricken wouldn't even begin to describe.

Trembling uncontrollably from both fear and anger . . . Charlie stood there for a long moment just holding and staring glassy-eyed at the head, the only recovered remains of his best friend. He had no words, he'd cried until there were no more tears he could shed. There was an eerie silence all about them; none of the familiar sounds from small wilderness creatures could be heard. After what seemed an eternity but was less than a minute, Charlie finally spoke in a blank monotone lifeless sounding voice – Ian managed to upright himself; he too was trembling from the sheer horror and tragedy of it all.

"I . . . I looked . . . no sign of his body, this is all that's left . . . his shotguns laying up yonder – pick it up for me and put it in the back of the Blazer . . ."

Ian looked over into Charlie's blank face, "Charlie, I'm so . . . Sorry!"

Charlie then stood up straight and a new expression over came his face, one of scary intensity . . . he took a deep breath.

"Yeah, sorry . . . I know you are Ian . . . he was a good man, the best! He weren't just my boss, but my best friend . . . I tell you this . . . whoever or whatever did this is as good as dead! If you . . . if after all this, you don't want to get the fuck as far away from this area as you can . . . I could use your help. But just so we're clear . . . I ain't looking to do nothing short of hunting this thing down and killing it. And if it turn out to be human . . . I ain't looking to make no arrest, if you get my meaning! Now if you can live with that, so be it . . . otherwise, I'll see you get paid fair. You've more than earned your keep! Mind you I'm gonna tag and bag Bud's head . . . I'm gonna keep it for a short time on ice in an old chest-style freezer I use for game, that's in my garage. It locks and I've the only key. I need to keep this quiet for a short time . . . don't say nothing to your lady friend the television reporter."

Ian looked at Charlie totally stunned, while thinking to himself . . . *What the hell . . . ? How could he know?*

"That's right Ian . . . I know all about your rendezvous last night with her. Never forget you're in a small town . . . My town! I trust you didn't tell her much . . . anyway, when you put the shotgun in the back of the Blazer grab the jumper cables. The battery is gonna be dead as hell . . . we'll jump-start the Blazer – you drive it back to my place. People are used to seeing Bud's rig at my place, hell, sometimes for a few days in a row. Biggest problem will be Jenny, she's gonna be wondering why he don't show up or at least call in . . . but I'll deal with her when it's time to. Ian, all I want from you is . . . all I'm asking is if you decide to help me; keep this strictly just between us for the next twenty-four to thirty-six hours tops. That's our best chance to get this thing that done this and killed them hikers too, that I'm sure of . . . I know them forensic fellows are good about placing time-of-death and such – you let me worry about that. If things go south, I'll take all the blame . . . but don't worry too much . . . the Coroner's a friend, and he owes me. Owes me big time for keeping my mouth shut about what I know regarding a certain indiscretion he had about a year back with a lady of ill repute. Why, if word was to get to his wife about it . . . well, you can guess the rest. Anyway, I need time to hunt this thing down that did this to Bud and that young couple . . . what-ever the hell it is. I can't afford to spend the next couple days answering questions and filling out paperwork about Bud's death . . . Ian, even though the rains got them pretty washed away; I saw more of them weird huge tracks up by the side of the road in the mud. They were heading across the road. My guess is no doubt what you're thinking too . . . we follow the direction of them tracks which head in the general direction of the falls, and we find at least traces of the rest of Bud. That cave behind the falls is no doubt this things den . . . but, we're not going up there till later today . . . and when we go, we're going prepared!"

Ian knew Charlie was right. If they were going to get this thing they needed to move unobstructed by the media, and they needed to move quickly before the thing moved on or, something . . . What had Ian amazed was how Charlie could think so clearly, so methodically. All the while holding the head of his dead best friend. Ian figured whether he was ethnic stereotyping, profiling or whatever. Charlie's sudden unwavering resolve to do what he figured must be done regardless of consequences had to spring from the Indian in him.

Charlie and Ian began walking up the embankment back to the cars, Ian paused and grabbed up the shotgun. He couldn't bring himself to look at Bud's dangling head . . . Charlie did an exceptional job of keeping it together; as he held the grizzly head away from his body, blood dripping from its neck.

Ian finally broke, he had to ask, "Charlie, how can you stay so calm, my God man."

Charlie replied, "I will mourn his loss for the rest of my life! But the time for tears is over. What I can't figure is this . . . Bud pumped three rounds of extra-heavy load from his scatter-gun either at or into whatever it was. Now Bud he's a . . . he was an avid hunter, a dead shot. Never known him to shoot at anything and not bring it down."

Ian stared straight into Charlie's eyes . . . If this had happened even a week ago in his life, Ian would have taken the money and got the hell out of Dodge. But something in him had changed. Ian really liked Bud – he liked him a lot . . . and he felt about the same for Charlie as well. There was that; and the compelling intrigue which held Ian spellbound though be it horrifying . . . . Ian was certain about one thing, no mere human was responsible. They would be looking for something much more terrifying. And because it liked the taste of human flesh, it would need to be taken down!

Ian cleared his throat and spoke, "I'm in Charlie – I'm in all the way!"

Charlie nodded accepting Ian's word.

"Charlie . . ." Ian said with inflection that indicated a question was forthcoming. "Charlie, you do realize you're now . . . I mean this makes you acting Sheriff . . . right?"

Charlie didn't respond to what Ian just said. He just stared looking intently all around in every direction with a blank hollow expression on his face.

The two men got moving again, heading up the embankment. They soon arrived back to the Blazer and Charlie's car.

Charlie walked over to his car. He opened its trunk and pulled out an extra heavy duty garbage bag. Charlie always kept a box of the bags for various uses such as picking up road kill or such. He never dreamed in his worst nightmare he'd ever be using one for this. He placed the head in the bag and tied it off tight! Charlie then placed the bagged head in his trunk, closed it and walked back to Ian who was leaning over the hood of Bud's Blazer.

"Ian, move out of the way I'm gonna bring my car around to the front of the Blazer and jump-start it."

Ian stood up and moved out of the way. He went to the rear of the Blazer and opened up the back. Right away he spotted the jumper cables which were exactly where Charlie said they'd be. He laid the shotgun down in the back of the rig then grabbed the cables and closed the Blazer's hatch-back. Suddenly Ian felt flush and faint. His knees began to buckle, he began wiping away both rain and sweat from his forehead. For a brief moment Ian thought he was going down. He was suffering effects of the sudden realization of the gravity of the situation – which until now had seemed surreal to him; like he was watching more than actually participating in all that had and was happening. Ian now felt trapped in some horrifying dream, a nightmare from which he couldn't awaken. But he was sincere when he'd told Charlie that he was in all the way. His commitment was both to Charlie as well as to himself.

CHAPTER 25

The Plan

IAN AND CHARLIE pulled their vehicles into Charlie's driveway. His home was located in the middle of a block of older but nicely maintained houses. Charlie then instructed Ian to drive around the block and half-way up the alley. To park the Blazer behind his garage that was located behind his house.

As soon as Ian pulled out of his driveway; without hesitation Charlie grabbed the garbage bag from his trunk and proceeded directly to his garage and unlocked it. He entered and walked briskly over to his chest-style freezer. Charlie then deposited the garbage bag containing the head of his deceased best friend into the freezer. He then turned without looking back and exited the garage. Charlie locked the garage door and proceeded to the porch of his house. He shed no tears, but was having great difficulty suppressing the anger that was welling up in him like a tea-kettle that is rapidly reaching its boiling point.

After doing as instructed Ian rejoined Charlie at the front door . . . Charlie retrieved his keys, unlocked and opened the door.

They entered his small but very nicely kept and neatly furnished two-bedroom house, nobody was home. Charlie's wife was at work and his son Jeremy was at school.

"Take a load off . . ." Charlie pointed to the love-seat located adjacent to his couch . . . Ian sat down.

Charlie sat himself on the couch and took a deep breath . . .

"Ian, I've had a chance to re-think things and realize that what I've asked of you is more than I should ask of anyone. What I'm saying is if this goes south, even though I will try and take any rap all on myself . . . They, I mean a sharp district attorney theoretically could still go after you for aiding and abetting, suppressing evidence, interfering with disclosure of an investigation or something like that, I'm no lawyer. Mind you, I don't think it will ever come to anything like that . . . but still . . . ?"

Ian with a very sober expression on his face shook his head indicating he realized the legal risks were real.

"Charlie, I know why you're doing what you're doing . . . and I agree that keeping the press out of the loop and not getting totally bogged down with paperwork and answering questions regarding Bud's death; would take away valuable time that needs to be spent solving this. Besides, I have no family. No other place to be . . . Charlie it's you who has a lot to lose, not me. Anyway, if worst case scenario was to happen . . . hell, they got to feed us three squares a day right?" Ian smiled at Charlie.

Charlie chuckled for a brief couple of seconds, "Yeah, three squares."

Charlie then got dead serious, "As far as what I have to lose. Well, Bud was same as family. To my people nothing, and I mean nothing, is more important than family. I am a law officer that has served his community for a considerable number of years. Never had any run-ins with the law when I was young . . . Bud was my best friend. No judge or jury in the country would come down on me too hard . . . you neither I don't figure, unless you used to be John Dillinger or something?" Charlie flashed a slight grin attempting to lighten the mood just a bit.

Ian returned the grin and replied, "No, I have no priors, no rap-sheet either . . . Charlie I understand everything very well. I meant it when I said that I'm in. And just so you know . . . I respect that you're in charge, this is your investigation, you're the boss!"

Charlie was impressed by Ian's commitment. The two men were bonded cohesively, ready to do what must be done.

Charlie let out a sigh of relief and slapped his knees with the palms of both his hands. "All right Ian . . . We're gonna see this through . . . I've got a plan . . ."

Ian leaned forward in the love seat.

"Tell me Charlie, how do you think we should approach this? We're gonna go back up to the cave at the falls . . . Maybe the other parts of the Ape Caves as well?"

Charlie shook his head yes, "Yeah of course . . . We'll stake out the falls tonight, this thing seems to be nocturnal. But before that we're gonna go up onto the reservation. I want to speak to the wisest of the tribal elders; find out what he may know. Ian one thing I haven't asked you is . . . You're an expert in weird animals and such. What do you think we're gonna be hunting? Me personally I think it's a large rouge wolf!"

Ian smiled and nodded in agreement, "Charlie based on what we've seen . . . tracks and bite marks. I agree with you! Canis lupus, the gray wolf. It's the only animal, the only territorial apex predator that I can think of that has the bite capability to do the damage we've seen. I think I read that a wolf has a bite strength of up to fifteen-hundred pounds per square inch. Enough to snap a two-by-four in half. Nothing else, no other animal could have bit through Bud's neck like that; or inflicted the damage to the heavy bones of those two hikers. Only thing is the bite radius, so big, too big! And those tracks though they look mostly canine, they are just too large and too different – strangely configured."

Charlie an avid hunter who figured he knew every animal type in the area, rubbed his chin, while he listened intently to Ian. He was ready to defer to Ian's obvious expertise.

"Well, I don't know too much about bite radius. But I do know tracks . . . and you're right – too big and not shaped right . . . Ian you study the very unusual or thought to not exist anymore, animals, right?"

Ian looked curiously at Charlie, wondering where he was about to go with his question.

"Yeah, but ninety-nine out of a hundred times the animal or whatever, is easily explainable . . . usually cases of mistaken identity or such. But yeah, I like to keep an open mind."

Charlie was relieved that Ian chose to say open mind . . .

"Ian when I was a kid raised by my Grandfather on the reservation. He told me many stories of my people. Some were facts. But, some were supernatural stories mainly told I figured to make a point. Now as you may or may not know; stories of shape-shifting into an animal spirit during a persons vision quest are common among the Indian nations . . . and the French folk around here . . . well, the old-timers, when I was young . . . I heard them speak of something they called a Loupe-Garou, a man-wolf. Mind you I ain't saying I buy into any of it; but just suppose for a minute there's something to it . . . ?"

Charlie paused for a minute to check to see how Ian was receiving what he was saying. Ian seemed to be not astonished. Even still Charlie didn't want Ian to think he was some backward local yokel superstitious Indian.

"Okay, Ian forget that last part, I got a bit carried away – but just suppose for a minute there is a member of my people up on the reservation, which you know borders the falls. Well, what if there is a crazy person that really thinks they are some kind of beast. Especially maybe when they are additionally stoned out of their minds on drugs like meth, peyote or mushrooms. Maybe a person like that might act out like the animal they think possess them or they think they turn into; such as a wolf or bear . . . a cougar, whatever. Maybe a complete psycho might even use a weapon like a saw or sword; thinking it was their teeth – I know, it's a pretty far out theory!"

Ian looked Charlie direct into his eyes . . . Ian was amazed that Charlie also was at least contemplating extreme possibilities.

"Charlie you'd make a good Crypto-Zoologist. That's what it's called, what I do . . . I study things that most people immediately dismiss as impossible – I ask the question that few people are willing to ask. Which is basically, what if . . . ? Anyway, what you're talking about is called Lycanthropy . . . that's a disease of the mind where a person truly believes they become a wolf!"

Ian could tell by the expression on Charlie's face that now he really had his thinking-cap on.

"Ian just suppose that someone's so obsessed about pretending to be a wolf, or even actually thinks he is due to some delusion . . . Perhaps a person like that might fashion some kind of animal-like paws that he wears on his feet or Shoes. Shoes that were made to intentionally leave what looks like weird animal tracks . . . You know something like the idiots that make phony plywood Big Foot prints and go around stamping them into the ground!"

Ian shook his head in agreement to the theory – that it was certainly something to consider.

Ian couldn't help himself . . . Charlie had cracked the window regarding entertaining the idea of supernatural consideration. Ian decided to slam that door open.

"Charlie don't think for one second that I dismiss any of your thoughts regarding possibly looking at this from all angles. Regardless of how remote the possibility. Fact is I've been considering some of the same kinds of things myself."

Ian paused, hoping that Charlie was ready to listen and consider what he was about to say, even as wild as it was going to be . . . Charlie was in fact ready to hear about anything Ian had to say – after all, Ian heard him out regarding his thoughts. Ideas that if he would have expressed to most folks; they would either have thought he was kidding, or would have tried to have him committed.

"Charlie, I'll go you one further . . . What if, we are dealing with something that is part of something that has been around since the dawn of time. Something that perhaps science may never explain or accept. Something that the majority of the cultures of the world at one time long ago accepted as a reality. Charlie I'm talking about the possibility of a werewolf – a wolf-man. Crazy as it sounds that would explain many things. For example . . . it would explain much of the Big Foot phenomena . . . I mean why no dead Sasquatch has ever been recovered. Legend has it that if a werewolf is killed it reverts back to its human state . . . So all that would be recovered is just another dead person. I mean missing persons show up time to time found dead in the forest, right, it happens . . . And if you think about it, the classic wolf-man would pretty much fit most persons description of a Big Foot – tall, hairy and scary . . . Now I know this is really thin, but listen . . . What if at least some of the stories you heard as a kid about shape-shifting was true. And just suppose that the degree of a shape shifter to change into a beast is based somewhat on the cycles of the Moon. I mean what if in this case the fuller the Moon the more wolf-like the person can morph to . . . ? As crazy as the idea is, that would explain why people who claim they have seen a Big Foot; their descriptions vary so much. In my field I was inclined for years to believe that if Big Foot exists it must be a offshoot of Gigantopithecus. A ten foot ape that the fossil record indicates went extinct around a half million years ago . . . but some people think may have survived in the dense forests like around here. Maybe the shape-shifter not only becomes more wolf-like the fuller the Moon. Maybe the fullness of the Moon effects its size and strength – It draws its power so to speak from the Moon. Maybe the person that becomes the wolf their behavior is cyclical, by months or years even. What I'm saying is, maybe they can sometimes go for years without reverting to the beast that must kill. Now I'm just making wild speculations regarding things. I don't even know or have a clear theory of . . . but, just maybe this person, this werewolf, has been around for a very, very long time!"

CHAPTER 26

The Reservation

AFTER A LONG punishing drive up old gravel logging roads. Roads that had them challenging one rain-filled muddy pot-hole after another. Charlie and Ian finally reached their destination. Which was located several miles further up in the hills, and to the east of little Merwin and the Harmony Falls area.

During the car ride up – Charlie had informed Ian, that both he and his wife Elaine, had grown up on reservation land. Not far from where they were now; and that his Grandfather was the tribal elder he'd spoke of. He was Chief of the Lewis River Chapter of the Cowlitz Indian Tribal Council.

Ian noticed right from the start that the sparse housing on this reservation could best be described as dismal at best – no fancy giant Indian Casino's around here . . . just old run down trailers; and the occasional scrawny canine mutt that ran barking and chasing their car as they slowly made their way up the road . . . nobody seemed to be around. *They must all be inside their shacks and tee-pee's on account of the rain* . . . Ian mused.

As they proceeded . . . Ian noticed up ahead there was a half-way decent looking building. It sat alone serving as some kind of focal point located at the tail end of the dead-end main gravel road. Ian thought it appropriate that this was a dead-end road. Because that about summed up what he saw all around him. Nothing more than the dead-end of what might have once been a flourishing little community.

The only spark of commercial life was a one-pump old run-down gas station. There were a few other near skeletal remnants of buildings, symbols of what once was. Clear indication that some commerce did at one time take placc on this small main strip.

Ian noticed that one of the old dilapidated buildings appeared to have housed a *Native American Crafts and Gift Shop* – at least that was what the sign above the door proclaimed. By the looks of the buildings present condition and soap-covered windows, it had closed; gone out of business many Moons ago.

Upon reaching the end of the short dead end road. They came upon the one decent looking structure. A pre-fabricated metal pole building. The building had a colorful though severely faded sign painted above the entrance that read: *Tribal Council Hall & Cultural Center.*

Charlie pulled his car up to the building, parked and turned off his motor . . . he just sat there for a moment. He felt he should educate Ian just a bit about this tiny township and its inhabitants. Charlie took a deep breath, then let out a small sigh before he began . . .

"Ian, obviously this place ain't much to look at. At one time it wasn't near this bad. But anyone worth their salt up and got the hell out of here when they were old enough to get . . . but a few have hung on, mostly dregs. You know, the typical drunks and junkies . . . except for old timers, elders like my Grandfather. They stay mostly because they feel it's their duty to try and preserve our culture, I guess . . . I'm related to most folks up here . . . Bud and me, we're the only law ever comes around . . . well, just me now . . . It ain't big enough to support no tribal police. Anyhow, we never come up here lest we have to. But unfortunately, occasionally we catch wind that someone's cooking meth . . . So, we got to come up here and bust someone who's running a meth-lab. And then tear their place down and burn it up – deadly chemicals you probably know, seep into the woodwork and such."

Charlie paused for a second as Ian shook his head in agreement.

"Anyhow, we got to get involved when someone's cooking drugs up here, cause meth has a nasty habit of making its way down the mountain to our neck of the woods. Thankfully, heroin's generally the drug of choice up here. Most of the junkies these parts shoot smack . . . cheap Mexican brown heroin they get from migrant tree planters that come up here to deal. Now, I say thankfully, only cause heroin addicts generally don't cause too much trouble to the few decent folk in these parts. Generally, they just get themselves hopped-up and go to sleep. Mind you, we still have to deal with that occasional call to haul-off someone that's over-dosed . . . but, most folks up here just die slow quiet deaths . . . either from old age, or liver disease."

Charlie paused for a moment collecting his thoughts.

Ian just sat silent with a blank expression on his face. He was deeply saddened and speechless regarding the very disheartening bleak existence these people endure. Ian was instantly embarrassed that he'd allowed himself to sink so low into depression and self pity. He thought to himself what problem did he have by comparison to this once great and proud people. Ian's admiration of Charlie had begun increasing ten-fold – as he began realizing that this man who sat beside him had risen himself from such adversity; to become a man to respect. A man passionately filled with a true sense of honor, duty and absolute loyalty to his deceased friend – Ian was humbled . . .

Charlie took another deep breath and began speaking once more.

"Ian you're going to meet the man, the reason we're up here in the first place. My Grandfather, Charlie *Lone Wolf* Skamochawa . . . he's ninety years old, but don't let his age or his appearance fool you, he's as sharp as a tack!"

Charlie saw Ian crack a small grin, to which he replied, "Yeah, you guessed it. I was partly named after him . . . my Grandfather's a great man. He's the Chief of what little remains of my people. The eldest male of a long line of descending Chiefs before him. Kind of like royalty is passed down generation after generation from the same bloodline in England and such places. Anyway, Grandfather always seems to know exactly what's going on around these parts . . . I don't know how he gets his information. Most of the time he just sits doing what he does inside this building. Some up here believe that in addition to being Chief, he's also a medicine man. They say he has visions, and that's how he knows things. I've heard stories from some of the old-timer's up here about how my Grandfather has some kind of sixth sense or some such nonsense. Now I'm not saying I buy into any of that . . . but I can tell you this . . . If something out of the ordinary's going on around these woods, he'll know about it! Anyway, he's always here at the *Culture Center* this time of day, which by the way is getting away from us fast!"

Ian looked at his watch, it was almost three in the afternoon.

Charlie looked at Ian and nodded – indicating they should get moving. They both exited Charlie's car and headed up the couple of steps that led to the front door of the building.

CHAPTER 27

Wisdom

THE BUILDING WAS nearly as sparse on the inside as it was on the outside.

There were a couple rows of chairs located in the middle of the room. And a small glass case to the right, up against the wall that housed a few trinkets and artifacts. Ian enthusiastically approached the case but immediately noted at a glance that there was nothing much to look at – a couple of moccasins, a hand-made baby rattle, some feathers, a few beaded necklaces and bracelets. The back side of the case that once was devised to be able to lock, was broken.

Ian was suddenly once again saddened by his thoughts. He figured that if there ever had been anything on display of intrinsic value it probably was stolen long ago by someone for booze or drugs. Ian then turned to face a small podium at the opposite end of the room from where they'd entered. Sitting alone in a chair next to the podium was an old, long silver haired man. He was all dressed up in traditional Native American attire. His outfit was one you might expect to see him wearing; if he were in a parade or some tourist attraction.

At first the old man's outfit seemed strange to Ian. But then he realized that it made perfect sense. This place serves or rather served as a cultural center among other uses.The old man just couldn't let go of memories of better times.

Charlie walked quietly across the room over to his Grandfather, who sat in a chair with his head slumped over. He was lightly snoring . . .

"Grandfather!" Charlie spoke in a rather loud voice. His Grandfather awakened and lifted his head. Immediately he recognized his Grandson.

"Charlie . . . Me resting old eyes . . . You walk quiet, that good! Not easy sneak up on Indian . . ."

Charlie replied, "That's true Grandfather, unless it's another Indian doing the sneaking . . ." Charlie and his Grandfather laughed.

Charlie's Grandfather looked across the room at Ian.

"He with you Charlie . . . ?"

"Yes, that's right Grandfather . . . His name is Ian McDermott, he's my Deputy . . . Grandfather, Bud's dead. He was killed last night by some animal or perhaps murdered by a crazy-man . . . maybe you have information that might help us find what killed Bud . . . Grandfather I'm Sheriff now, you understand?"

Charlie's Grandfather shook his head, he understood.

"Sheriff Bud good friend our people . . . I will burn ten feathers . . . I will pray to great spirit he have good afterlife . . . That man, why not dress like you?" Charlie's Grandfather asked Charlie, loud enough for Ian to hear as well.

"Well, he's new, we haven't had a chance to order him a uniform yet . . ."

"Hmm law-man good job for good man . . . Like my Charlie . . ." Charlie's Grandfather looked at Charlie and smiled a big smile. Ian could see the great pride Charlie's Grandfather had for his Grandson.

Charlie figured telling his Grandfather any more about Ian would just confuse him. He knew his Grandfather had great respect for the law. He would be more inclined to share information in the presence of Ian; if he believed Ian was a law-man like himself . . . *I'm not really lying to Grandfather. I did sort of deputize Ian* . . . Charlie thought to himself.

Ian figured that Charlie had his reasons for telling the old man he was a Sheriff Deputy; Charlie didn't do random. There was always a solid reason behind his actions. Ian prepared himself to play the role of pseudo law-man. The truth was he was beginning to somewhat feel the part.

Ian crossed the room to join Charlie and his Grandfather.

"Grandfather, I'd like to introduce you to my friend, Deputy – Ian McDermott."

Ian couldn't help but be a little touched by being introduced as Charlie's friend . . . even if it was just for the sake of easing any tension. Tension the old man might have while being asked questions in the presence of a stranger.

Charlie's Grandfather smiled and graciously extended his right hand. Ian shook the old mans hand that felt to him like caressing thin paper.

"Me name Charlie Skamochawa. Me ninety years old. Me eldest of people on reservation . . . Some call me Chief. But me thinks Day of Chief's long past . . . Me father and him father before; they Chief's of great nation . . . Now people grow weak like old body."

Charlie Skamochawa paused while looking into the eyes of both men who stood before him. He then relaxed back into his chair, smiled and motioned for Charlie and Ian to grab themselves chairs to sit down and have council with him.

"Sit close, we will talk the talk of serious men . . . You will ask, what kill great law-man Bud O'Brien . . . You will ask, how hunt such thing . . . My Grandson – know this . . . What you seek walks as spirit and as man . . . Spirit world not believed by men, is truth! – know this . . . What you hunt, hunts you!"

Ian and Charlie each grabbed themselves a chair. They began carrying their seats across the room to sit close to Charlie's

Grandfather – who was a little hard of hearing. Once Ian and Charlie seated themselves, Charlie was first to speak.

"Grandfather, enough already . . . you can stop with the Geronimo meets Hollywood routine . . ."

Ian was totally confused by Charlie's statement.

"Okay, but tell me the truth Mr. McDermott, isn't that how you expected me to speak . . . ?"

Ian was completely caught off guard. He didn't know how to reply to the question just posed to him.

Both Charlie and his Grandfather began laughing – Charlie then explained the joke.

"Ian, my Grandfather is an educated man. Because he runs this little cultural center that rarely but sometimes still gets a tourist visitor; he feels he should speak the way the white man sees us – backward and uneducated. Then all at once he speaks like any other American citizen. To make his point I guess. Is that about right Grandfather?"

Charlie's Grandfather didn't answer he just smiled – Charlie continued.

"Ian, my Grandfather, he was the first person in our tribe to achieve a grade equivalency honorary High School diploma. He reads more books and magazines than any person I've ever known. Grandfather has collected books over much of his lifetime. But most of them are nearly worn-out ones donated to the tribe by Schools and Library's. You know when they upgrade, buy new copy's and such. Bud got that hooked up for him. Grandfather's got a book or two on about any subject you can think of. He loans them out to anyone who asks. It's the closest thing to a library they got around here. Grandfather keeps his books in the back storage room of this building. Bud, me and a volunteer contractor built this building a few years ago. In the back next to the little office; there's a half-bathroom with a shower. Grandfather sleeps in a bed we put in for him back there. Bud got all the building materials donated for the project from a Kelso hardware store and lumberyard. They gave us all we needed including the metal siding and roofing you see. Hell, he even got a direct T.V. satellite dish thrown in to boot. I pay the small fee to get the service. Not many up these parts got T.V. so some of the locals drop over time to time to watch. Ian, I tell you nobody could get people to dig-deep and donate to a good cause better than Bud."

Charlie bowed his head down for a moment – after a couple long seconds he raised his head back up. He glanced first at Ian, than looked directly at his Grandfather.

"Grandfather, do you still watch CNN and Jerry Springer every day?"

"Yes, it makes life here on the reservation, not seem so bad!"

All three men laughed.

Charlie then figured time was wasting and he'd better get directly to why he and Ian were there.

"Grandfather . . . you know what goes on around these woods better than any man alive. Tell me straight – what the hell killed Bud and them lost hikers . . . ? What kind of animal am I . . . what is it that me and Ian here, what exactly is it we're hunting . . . ?"

Charlie's Grandfather took a deep breath and put both hands on his knees. He scooted forward just a bit in his chair. And then got a sudden very serious look on his face.

"It was said to me by my father when I was a boy; just as he was told by his father before him and on back as far as any man knows . . . That what you seek is neither animal nor man, but is both. It was said that it changes from man into beast at will. It was said that its power comes from the Moon. Why the man becomes the beast no one could say. Why the man surrenders to the beast within, only during certain months and certain years, this too no one could say. It was first called *Sasquatch* by my people . . . Which means hairy man-beast. It was the white-man who misunderstood the meaning and changed that to mean ape-beast. It is no ape-beast like the pictures show in my books. It was said by my ancestors that the beast is a man who is possessed by the spirit of a wolf! I do not know who the man-wolf is . . . but I believe it comes from an old family . . . perhaps Indian, perhaps white-man. There are many white-men who live in nearby towns. Many are decedents of French fur-trappers and hunters that settled in these mountains. It was said that it cannot die either by natural death nor can it be killed easily. It was said to my ancestors by Frenchmen fur-traders. There are ways to kill this man-wolf they called Loupe-Garou. It was said to my people that the man cursed by the demon wolf-spirit is immortal, except to fire and silver. And if its head be separated from its body . . . This was told to me by my father . . . This was told to my father by his father; just as it had been told by our people for many generations before my Grandfather's time. These stories were told not as a tale to be told, but as truths . . . this is all I know of these things!"

Both Charlie and Ian just sat there. Neither could think of anything to say or any further questions to ask regarding what they'd just heard.

After an uncomfortable silent moment first Charlie, then Ian stood up from their chairs. Charlie after collecting his thoughts, spoke.

"All right then, good information, we'll keep it all in mind . . ."

Charlie smiling, leaned forward and shook his Grandfather's hand.

His Grandfather then turned towards Ian, smiled and extended his right hand. Ian responded with equally polite enthusiasm as he began shaking the old mans hand.

With Ian's right hand still held within his own; Charlie's Grandfather spoke once again, this time directly to Ian.

"You did not used to be a law-man . . . Are you not the great hunter who found the ugly fish – the one thought to be long gone from this world . . . ? You will need your skills, and more, for what you and my Grandson are to hunt!"

Ian was startled which caused him to abruptly retract his hand from their shaking.

"Uh, that's right! But how'd you know?"

Charlie's Grandfather smiled a large smile.

"You're name and face is on the cover. The cover of one of my favorite old National Geographic magazines!"

Ian with a look of astonishment on his face gazed over at Charlie . . . Charlie just stood there grinning while shaking his head. His Grandfather never ceased to amaze him either.

After a momentary pause – all three men began to laugh . . .

CHAPTER 28

Preparation
Part I

CHARLIE AND IAN were in Charlie's car heading back towards town from the reservation. A few minutes had gone by with neither of them saying a word. Finally Ian could take the silence no longer.

"Charlie did you ever get in touch with Jenny with some sort of cover story about Bud not showing up to work? What if she's been trying to reach him?"

Charlie shrugged his shoulders, paused a moment, then replied . . .

"Don't worry too much about Jenny . . . I told her Bud had to go out of town for a couple of days unexpected like. Bud actually had been considering going to Seattle to meet with some lawyers of the family of those hikers, answer some questions and such. Surprisingly, she didn't ask me any further questions about it. Fortunately, I didn't have to lie more than I did. If this works out the way I'm hoping . . . those are tracks I should be able to cover. Jenny's a good egg. She's tight lipped when it comes to not answering many questions asked by out of town lawyers, law-man or whatever. That pretty much goes for most folks from around these parts. We keep things to ourselves. If we wanted the world to know our business, we wouldn't live secluded as we are up here in the mountains."

Ian shook his head in agreement that it was good Charlie didn't have to dig a potentially deeper hole for himself than he did. Ian also understood how the populous of the small township of Harmony Falls would probably be a very self-reliant group of people. Not likely keen on much interference from the outside world.

"Say Charlie, changing the subject . . . You said this morning that when we go on stake-out tonight you wanted us to be better prepared. After hearing what your Grandfather had to say and adding to that some wild theories I have of my own that I told you . . . just exactly how do you suggest we better prepare ourselves?"

Charlie had been giving that very topic much deliberation.

"Ian that's a sixty four silver dollar question – and I mean silver! I know a guy who lives just outside of town, Louis Batiste Charbonneau . . . Yeah, ole Charbonneau; he's both the best taxidermist in these hills, as well as a master gunsmith. Mind you I mean a real old-world type craftsmen. Anyway, here's my plan . . . Soon as we get back to town, we go to my wife's store. We collect-up as much silver as she's got in that jewelry case of hers. I'm gonna tell her everything! She'll believe us when we both tell her all of the facts as we know them . . . She's gonna lose it big time when I tell her about Bud, be ready for that. Ian, we're gonna take all that silver and have bullets made to fit that pop-gun of yours . . . Me, I'll keep my faith in my 9mm Glock; which I'm gonna load with hollow-tip splatter points. If it's of this natural world those splatter rounds of mine will drop it and good. And of course your weapon loaded with silver bullets would do the trick as well . . . especially, if it, well, is something else – you know, like you and my Grandfather think. Hopefully, you can pump enough silver into it to bring it down that way . . . We're not taking any unnecessary chances – I'd rather us play the role of backward superstitious fools about the silver bullet thing; then play the role of educated and enlightened dead men . . ."

Ian shook his head in absolute agreement.

"Plan for the worst and pray for the best. Isn't that about how Bud would have put it . . . ?" Ian asked already knowing the answer . . .

Charlie replied, "Yeah, he'd of said something just like that! We'll thank God for small favors. At least the rain stopped – looks like it's gonna be a nice clear night tonight. The Moons gonna be full. Now, that may or may not work in our favor, for whatever it is we're hunting. But assuming it has night-vision and can see plain and clear in pitch-darkness . . . at least maybe that evens up the score a bit by giving us bright moonlight to see by."

Preparation
Part II

Charlie pulled his car into a marked parking spot at the back-end of the building. He took a very large breath of air, then exhaled equally hard. Both Charlie and Ian sat there in the car a moment collecting their thoughts. Ian broke the silence.

"Charlie . . . Let's say for an instance that what we're gonna be dealing with actually does fit the general description of a werewolf . . . I mean if that's the case, then it's safe to assume that there may be more of these creatures lurking about. Not necessarily in these neck of the woods, I would guess they are mainly loners. But I'm just saying . . . what if many of the old legends are true? It seems to be a commonly held belief that if you're attacked and bitten by a werewolf but don't die, you become infected. Infected I guess would best describe it. Anyhow, you then will become a werewolf yourself."

Charlie looked intently over at Ian.

"Ian, if that's right . . . how'd it all get started in the first place? Where did the first werewolf come from?"

Ian thought for a second then replied, "Maybe there's something to your ancestors belief in animal spirit guides and shape-shifting. Maybe if a person's spirit was say the wolf and then coincidentally he was bitten by one, it somehow created some kind of aberrant, incipient new species . . . Hell, I really don't have any idea. I'm getting too far out there with speculation. It's just impossible to say. Kind of like which came first the chicken or the egg?"

Charlie could wait no further.

"Lets go in and face the music . . . This should be interesting if nothing else. Elaine is gonna either buy into some or all of what we tell her, or she'll be making a call to have us put in straight jackets and a padded cell!"

Ian raised his eyebrows, took a deep breath and let out a sigh while he nodded a small nod of agreement. The two men exited the car.

Elaine smiled a huge smile the second she spotted Charlie and Ian enter the store.

Her smile was cut short when she noticed the bleak expressions on both men's faces.

Elaine spoke first, "Hi boys, you both look like you just saw a Ghost! You want something to eat? I've got some freshly made chicken and jo-jo's getting ready to come up."

Both men's expressions didn't change as they approached her.

"What, Charlie . . . My God, nothings happed to Jeremy . . . ?"

Charlie shook his head no assuring her that wasn't it. "No Elaine, Jeremy is fine! But we do need to talk. Let's go to your office in the back . . . Jackie can cover for a few minutes, right?"

"Yes, of course, she came in a few minutes early. I was going to leave for the day in about twenty minutes . . . What's going on?"

Charlie motioned for Ian to follow himself and his wife to the back room. Ian followed.

The three stood there silently in Elaine's office for a brief moment. Then Elaine spoke.

"Okay Charlie, what in God's names got you so . . ."

Charlie grabbed a chair and motioned for her to sit down. Charlie and Ian remained standing.

"Elaine, honey, I don't know exactly how to tell you all that I have to. So I'm just gonna do it best I can."

Elaine softened the look on her face. She could tell that something was wrong – Seriously wrong! Before Charlie could utter another word . . .

"Oh my God no – it's Bud isn't it?"

Elaine had always been very perceptive, almost psychic at times Charlie used to say.

Charlie bowed his head slightly. "Yeah . . . Bud's . . . Honey . . . Bud's – dead!"

Elaine gasped for air . . . She then put both hands on the cheeks of her face . . . She began looking around the room anywhere except into either men's eyes . . . desperately fighting back tears that began flowing without her even making a crying sound.

Elaine, after an eternal moment of seconds, managed to gather herself. She looked up deep into Charlie's eyes.

"How . . . ? How'd it happen?"

Charlie looked over at Ian for a second. Then he looked back into his wife's eyes.

"Bud went after whatever animal killed them hikers and scared the hell out of Jeremy and Katie . . . He went late last night without telling me about it . . . Anyway, the thing, the animal . . . it attacked and killed him . . . Ian and I found . . . we found what was left of him up near the falls turn-off."

Elaine looked with disbelief at Charlie, "No . . . No mere animal could kill Bud O'Brien . . . No . . . It had to be something more . . . There's something more to it – tell me!"

Once again Charlie looked over at Ian before he spoke.

"Elaine, whatever it was that killed Bud . . . it left nothing more of him than his . . . his head! We found more of them weird tracks that I told you about around where we found . . . I tell you, I've never seen or heard of anything like this before . . . Elaine, I don't know exactly how to put this but . . . Grandfather he said . . . well, Ian and me too I guess, we think this thing is some kind of a . . ."

Elaine interrupted with a very cold matter-of-fact expression on her face.

"Monster! . . . You all think it's some kind of a monster, just like Jeremy said . . . Charlie you know our boy wouldn't have made something like that up . . . and I believe you all may be right!"

That was the single largest piece of evidence in Charlie's mind to support the idea of some kind of monster for the lack of a better explanation. He knew as well as Elaine it wasn't in his sons make-up to create fantastic stories. Even still, both men were surprised by what Elaine had just said – but they both shook their heads in agreement.

Elaine Continued . . .

"Nothing short of a monster could have done that to Bud . . . He's . . . he was the best damn hunter and backwoodsmen ever known since Daniel Boone . . . Charlie you know as well as me about the stories of a monster living in these mountains . . . tales we were told as kids. I never thought of them as just stories and neither I figure did you! Charlie Redtail you are not just my husband. And you're not just a law-man for this town neither. You're first and last a Cowlitz Indian Brave. And I am the wife of a proud man . . . You hunt down and kill that thing that done this to Bud. Just make certain my love that after it's done – you come back to me in one piece!"

Elaine then looked over at Ian, "That goes for both of you!"

Ian couldn't help but get choked up just listening to the pride that this fine women had in their people. Not only was it apparent to him that she passionately loved Charlie with all her heart . . . But she loved their heritage, who they were as well.

Charlie was a little choked up himself by the words that came from his wife. He cleared his throat and spoke.

"Listen honey, we need to take some things from your jewelry case. Things I, things I won't be bringing back!"

Elaine looked deep into Charlie's eyes, she then spoke in a very calm almost monotone voice. "Of course, after how Jeremy described that thing, and now . . . Bud . . . you'll be needing silver!"

Both Charlie and Ian looked at Elaine with confused expressions on their faces.

"Charlie, I know you have a hard time believing in such things; but I had another one of my, you know, visions . . . That thing, it's a monster – just take it! Take all of the silver in the case. Now go . . . Mind you Charlie Redtail you have Charbonneau make you as many bullets from it as he can!"

Neither Charlie nor Ian could believe how she seemed to be able to read their minds. What was even more astonishing to them – Was her conviction to the idea that they would be facing a monster; not a murderous lunatic or some vicious rogue animal such as a cougar, bear or wolf. A notion they had only considered to be a remote possibility.

CHAPTER 29

Craftsmen

"HERE WE ARE . . . old Charbonneau's place . . . This half crazy Cajun lives in a small cabin just up this gravel driveway. Your gonna meet a true old world master craftsmen . . . That is if he don't shoot us both for trespassing. He's getting up there in years and his eyes aren't so good." Charlie exclaimed as he made a left turn off of the main road just a couple miles west of town.

Ian then spoke, "What if he's not home . . . ?"

Charlie replied, "He'll be home this time of day . . . He runs his little business of ammunitions-smithing and stuffing furry animals, out behind his cabin in a small shed . . . he'll be home!"

Ian looked over anxiously at Charlie as the two men drove up the long gravel driveway. Charlie spotted Charbonneau's old beat-up Ford pickup truck parked in front of his cabin.

"See there, I told you he'd be here . . ." Charlie proclaimed, all the while being secretly greatly relieved that he'd guessed correctly. Ian let out a sigh of relief as he smiled at Charlie.

Charlie pulled his car up right behind the old truck. He put the car in park, turned off the ignition, and slumped back into his seat. He looked over at Ian . . .

"All right . . . Ian you let me do all the talking . . . Some of these old-timers they get awful leery of strangers."

Ian smiled and nodded in agreement. Charlie continued.

"Okay Ian grab that bag and let's go talk to the old Frenchy . . ."

The two men climbed out of Charlie's car. They walked up to the front door of the old pioneer looking dilapidated age-grayed cedar cabin.

Charlie knocked a couple times on the door, nobody answered . . . Charlie then waved his hand motioning for Ian to follow him elsewhere.

"Ian, lets go out back to his shed. That's where he works his magic!"

Ian followed Charlie around to the back of the cabin – to a good sized outbuilding. Through the door's window they could see Charbonneau busy pulling something from a small brick smelter located at the opposite end of the building. Charbonneau then turned and was banging away on some metal that lay across an anvil . . .

Charbonneau caught the two men looking in at him out of the corner of his eye. In one deft motion he spun around and grabbed-up his double barrel ten gauge shotgun and pointed it straight at their heads as they looked in the window.

"Who go dare . . . ?' The old man yelled.

"It's me Charlie Redtail and a friend of mine," Charlie replied quickly.

"Oh, Charlie dat you . . . ? Okay, okay . . . You co-monde inside visit wit me, yeah?"

Charlie opened the door – Charbonneau had already set his shotgun down. He'd leaned it back in the corner that he kept it.

"Charlie, what tan I do yer fer, eh?"

"Louis . . . my friend Ian here and me we got a job for you. But mind you it's a rush job! Now, I'm gonna have to owe you on it . . . but you know my credits good right?"

"Yah, yah, you credit, she's good . . ."

Charlie continued, "Okay then . . . we got a bag of silver jewelry . . . You can keep the turquoise stones for a tip for doing us this big favor. Anyway, we need the silver melted down and bullets made from it to fit this gun . . ."

Ian had already un-strapped his concealed pistol from his ankle holster . . . He handed both his gun and the small paper bag that was filled with Indian jewelry to Charbonneau.

"Beretta . . . Ah, dat nice gun, oui?" Charbonneau remarked as he took the weapon Ian handed him.

Charbonneau looked inside the paper bag as he handed Ian's gun back to him.

"Louis know size . . . Trente-deux cartridge . . . Plenty silver for maybe cinq bullet . . . De stones Louis keep, no charge you fer make de bullets! You hunt an kill de Loupe-Garou? I Charbonneau never see, but have heard de tales of de beast. I hear tell of the man-beast since I boy by some de old time Injuns, like you Grandfather. He tell you too, no?"

Stunned, Ian and Charlie looked momentarily at each other . . . They were beginning to wonder if everyone knew what they were up to. Ian was additionally made uneasy by the multitude of small furry stuffed mummies – corporeal remains of critters which stood ominously in suspended rigor. Posed in life-like postures, the woodland creatures were everywhere you looked throughout the shed. All of which seemed to be staring directly at him, watching his every move.

Perhaps it was because of the sincerity on Charbonneau's face when he asked the question . . . But for whatever reason, at that very moment Charlie just couldn't bring himself to lie.

"Yes Louis, that's right. We're going to hunt and kill the Loupe-Garou . . ."

Charbonneau took the bag of silver jewelry and dumped it out on his work-bench.

He appeared to be examining the metal as he bit into some of the pieces – Charbonneau then retrieved a small brown glass jar from a drawer in his work-bench that was labeled *Aqua Regina.* He opened the jar and poured from it a yellowish semi-transparent liquid down onto some of the jewelry pieces. A small swirl-cloud of vapor and small bubbles began forming in a few seconds as the liquid boiled and danced on the surface of the silver.

"Dis good silver! Louis can do it . . . come back de trois hour will have done!"

Charlie looked over at Ian. The two men smiled at each other. Ian new immediately that Charlie was right. They were definitely in the presence of a true craftsmen.

Charlie and Ian both thanked Charbonneau. They then turned and walked out of the shed leaving him to do his work. Once Charlie and Ian returned to the car. They just stood there looking at each other speechless for one protracted uncomfortable silent moment – Charlie finally spoke up.

"Ian, we're gonna go back to my house . . . I'm gonna get my thirty-aught-six. There should be pretty good visibility tonight if the sky remains clear; what with the full Moon and all. Anyway, if we get lucky, maybe we can take this thing down from a distance. That is unless you want to wait until we see the whites of its eyes? Mind you, I'll still be packing my Glock, for close encounters of the worst kind!"

Ian looked for a fleeting second down at the ground and then back at Charlie . . . Suddenly the thought of seeing whatever the hell they were going up against – up close and personal; crept vividly into his minds eye. Without further hesitation Ian replied . . .

"Hell yes, lets go get your rifle!"

That said, Charlie and Ian climbed into the car. Charlie turned the car around. They drove the long gravel driveway until it reached the main road, then turned onto the main road heading east back towards town.

CHAPTER 30

French Connection
Part I

CHARLIE AND IAN had just reached Harmony Falls town-ship – when they were abruptly passed by an old Dodge truck that sped past them on their left. Just after passing them, the truck then swerved back into the right lane just ahead of them. The old Dodge began picking up speed. The truck had two men in the cab and three baying hounds riding in its back. The dogs continued to bellow out loud and shrill as the truck sped away.

"Charlie, aren't you going to pull those guy's over and? Give him a ticket or something? He's driving like he's pretty drunk!"

Charlie didn't seem concerned, "Nah, that's just old John Eagle driving one of our local colorful Frenchies . . . Old John ain't drunk, just a bad driver. Hell, he ain't even got a driver's license. And his truck hasn't had new license tabs in twenty years I'd guess . . . Now, John Eagle he's second only to my Grandfather as a tribal elder . . . The man's a relic. I'm not about to run him in. Looked like he was haling Jean-Chastel around. He does that time to time . . . Anyway, we got much bigger concerns facing us today than writing up an Indian for driving without a license, taxing around one of our crazy in-bred Cajuns! Chastel must of got a ride to town to pick up some supplies. He don't buy much, and not often. He lives nearly self sufficient. Hunts and fishes for what he needs. He's a hermit type like most of the Frenchies around these parts. Keeps to himself. He lives on reservation land a few miles up mountain from the falls and Ape Caves . . . It's said his great great Grandfather was given land by my people as a dowry. And, that he's the descendant of a French trapper that married the daughter of a Chief. Bud and I figured he must be a bastard. His father must have screwed one of the whores that come around once in a while chasing local loggers for their paychecks. Cause neither of us knew of his mother, or of his father for that matter. His father and all his family before him; well it's said that family bury their dead way up in the mountains. Believe me, if you wanted to bury a body up in those hills. Well, there's a whole lot of dense forest and nearly impassable terrain up there to do it in. Places that you could plant someone that would never be found. Everyone round here knows Jean-Chastel Gevaudan is a poacher, just no way to prove it. My Grandfather told me a few years back that he once spoke to Gevaudan for a long spell . . . He told me that Gevaudan had extensive knowledge of our ancestors and the old ways of our people. Once Bud told me he had a run-in with Jean-Chastel. This happened before I was Deputy. Chastel got drunk and disorderly at Gracie's bar; Bud got called in to make him leave. Bud told me Chastel held a grudge against him for that. Bud used to jokingly refer to Jean-Chastel Gevaudan as the red-skinned Frenchman!"

Charlie laughed a small laugh . . . Ian looked over at Charlie . . .

"Gevaudan . . . huh, you don't say? Charlie that name happens to be the name of a province in France . . . Nothing uncommon about that. Lot's of Europeans took their names from their ancestral roots like provinces, towns and such . . . But I need to use a computer. I need to access the internet to check my fuzzy memory. I need to check on something I once read about a long time ago . . . back in college . . . at U.C.L.A."

Charlie glanced over at Ian. "Southern California man, huh? You don't look much like the surfer type!"

Ian replied, "No, not much of a surfer . . . I tried it once on vacation in Hawaii – damn near drowned!"

Both men laughed . . .

Ian then got serious as he looked intensely back at Charlie.

"Charlie you've got a computer with internet connection at your house don't you?" That morning, Ian had seen a computer sitting on top of a small desk in Charlie's kitchen.

"Yeah, we're not that backward up here . . . It's mainly my wife's. She uses it mostly for keeping her books and staying in touch with family and friends through that *Facebook* thing. I mainly use the computer at the office; but we want to stay clear of Jenny if you know what I mean . . . but yeah, no problem, we've got one. What are you wanting to look up?"

Ian didn't want to say too much until he had a chance to check his facts.

"Well, it's just something about that guy Jean-Chastel Gevaudan . . . His name, I've heard that name before. I believe there was an outbreak of unexplainable animal attacks in France a few hundred years ago . . . in the general area of Gevaudan . . ."

Charlie glanced over at Ian as he drove up the street towards his house – Charlie looked confused as he raised his voice a bit.

"A few hundred years ago! – huh?"

Charlie pulled into the driveway of his house. Both men exited the car and proceeded into the house.

French Connection Part II

Charlie led Ian straight into the kitchen to his wife's computer. "Go ahead Ian, there's no password protection, so just sit down and go for it!"

Ian did just that. He began by *Google*-ing *Strange phenomena Gevaudan, France* . . . That brought up exactly what he was looking for – what he had only fragmented fuzzy memory of. Charlie was looking over Ian's shoulder staring at the computer screen. He was still more than a little confused, but intrigued non-the-less.

Ian glanced back at Charlie flashing him a sly smile. One that underscored that he was very satisfied with himself.

"All right, here we go . . . Charlie can you see the screen okay?"

Charlie shook his head yes, as he replied, "Yeah Ian, I can see just fine . . . You just selected: *Wikipedia . . . The Beast of Gevaudan!*"

Ian took a deep breath while the page loaded . . .

"Yeah, that's right!" Ian replied while exhaling . . .

"Okay, here we are!" Ian began speed skim-reading the page – Charlie was trying to do the same. But he was having some difficulty due to his disadvantaged distance from the screen.

"Charlie, in a nut shell what this is all about is this . . . There was a series of brutal animal attacks that occurred around the area of Gevaudan France back in the seventeen hundreds. Maybe as many as two hundred people were killed by some kind of beast that was later described as a very strange huge wolf-like creature. Now here's where it gets really weird. The beast was finally brought down by a master hunter. One who was contracted by King Louis the fifteenth of France to hunt it down and kill it. The beast had been shot many times before by other hunters, but with little or no effect to the creature. Many of the hunters were killed by the beast during their efforts . . . And so the rumors that it was a werewolf began to prevail across the countryside. So the King appointed a master hunter who decided he was going to take no chances much like you and I this afternoon . . . He had silver bullets made . . . And in his successful hunt, shot the creature twice, once through the heart which apparently killed it – I say apparently, because it gets even stranger. Oh yeah, and as far as our master hunter goes. Well, unfortunately for him it was said he was savagely bitten by the beast prior to getting his second kill shot off."

Ian paused for effect as he spun himself around in the swivel chair to face Charlie. "Now Charlie, get this . . . The name of the hunter was . . . Jean-Chastel . . . Isn't that the same name as your local crazy Cajun as you call him . . . ?"

Ian already new that was the guys name. He'd heard Charlie say it plain and simple.

Charlie took a step closer to the computer. He had to read the screen himself. After doing so he just stood there without speaking for a long moment, staring at the computer monitor as if he were mesmerized by the words . . . Charlie finally broke his silence. "Yeah, that's his name . . . Holy shit! . . . Ian . . . Of course this could all be coincidence! I mean of course it is . . . Hell, you said yourself that lots of immigrants took their last names from the towns and provinces they came from . . . and Jean-Chastel . . . That has to be a really common Frenchy name don't you think? Besides, if there was anything here, I mean anything to this . . . he would have changed his name or something, wouldn't he?"

Ian reluctantly nodded in agreement, but with little conviction . . .

"Yeah, I think the name is common enough . . . But why would he bother changing his name? I mean who would believe anything like this would ever be more than coincidence. Anything else would be unbelievable! What I'm even suggesting here any rational person would say is impossible! But impossible or not, I want to check out something else . . ." Ian began key stroking the computer key board once again. Charlie watched Ian go back to *Google* to check something via search engine.

Ian typed in . . . *Jean-Chastel – Beast of Gevaudan* . . . The page loaded in seconds. "All right . . . Charlie it says here Jean-Chastel recovered from the wounds he sustained while killing the beast. It says he was paid handsomely by the King of France for killing the creature and ending the rain of terror. Oh, and by the way it says here that the beast didn't look like any typical wolf but was wolf-like. It was said to have had many very strange features. But nothing really credible was recorded regarding what those strange features were exactly. This is bizarre . . . The very night the wolf-like creature was killed. Its body was reported as probably stolen . . . Anyway, it mysteriously disappeared without a trace. It says here it went missing sometime in the night while being transported by wagon. It was being sent to Paris to be stuffed and preserved by a master taxidermist. It was supposed to have been eventually sent on from there to be put on display at the Royal Museum in Versailles. Oh, you got to love this . . . The night the beasts body disappeared – it was said to have been a full moon! Hmm, maybe it wasn't quite as dead as they thought?"

Ian paused to catch his breath. He needed a moment to fully absorb what he'd read and was telling Charlie . . . Ian resumed reading. He continued to pause now and again, to summarize to Charlie what he'd read.

"Okay, this is interesting . . . It says here that Jean-Chastel used the money the King gave him for killing the beast to buy passage on a ship bound for the America's. The last known records are sketchy. There is pretty clear evidence to support that he became a mountain-man . . . A fur-trapper who spent some years in and around Quebec. It says from there he was thought to have migrated west and then south . . . And get this . . . though not substantiated . . . It is commonly believed by most historians that Jean-Chastel followed trade routes that eventually led him to settle near a predominantly French pioneer settlement. Located in the foothills near the Colombia River in what is now Southwest Washington State.

Ian needed to catch his breath – he once again swiveled his chair around to look up at Charlie. Ian was curious to see if this was as interesting and disturbing to Charlie as it was to him. Ian could see by the expression on Charlie's face that it was. Ian then stood up to look eye to eye with Charlie.

"Granted much if not most of what happened to Jean-Chastel after he left the ship is pure conjecture . . . I mean records show that he made the journey to North America all right. Records show clearly that he disembarked near what is now Nova Scotia. But beyond that . . . this is all speculative. Just best guesses by historians."

Without saying a word Charlie left the kitchen, leaving Ian alone just standing there. Ian stepped from the kitchen into the living room. There he just stood attempting to make sense of the facts and theories; anything that might be useful.

When Charlie returned to Ian, he no longer was wearing his uniform – he was dressed in camouflage hunting gear from head to toe! "Okay, Ian I'm gonna grab my rifle and put it in the car . . . You all done with the computer?" Ian nodded that he was.

"I figure we've got another couple of hours to kill . . . That's enough time for us to drop by Gracie's and grab a beer or a stiff drink. Whatever's your poison, is on me. Confidentially Ian . . . I used to have a tiny bit of a drinking problem – sort of a mean drunk you might say when I'd be hitting the *Wild Turkey* . . . It wasn't anything serious mind you . . . I wasn't, you know, the stereotype raging alcoholic Indian that can't hold his fire-water or nothing like that!"

Charlie smirked slightly. Bearing a thin grin as he looked at Ian to check what reaction those last words might invoke. Ian stood stoic, emotionless . . . He was the last person in the world to be judgmental regarding any form of alcoholism. One thing Ian could spot a mile away was denial and rationalization – when it came to those aspects of the illness he was a practiced master!

Yeah, it takes one to know one . . . Ian thought to himself.

Charlie continued, "I guess I never really climbed up all the way onto the wagon so to speak, not like Elaine wanted me to anyway . . . I still enjoy a nice cold beer or two now and again. Hey, since I never climbed all the way onto the wagon . . . I guess I can't fall off it!"

Charlie laughed. Ian smiled and began laughing as well. After a few moments of enjoying his own levity . . . Charlie stopped laughing and became serious once again.

"I did mostly give up the hard stuff when I became Bud's Deputy . . . had to . . . That was Bud's one demand of me. But Bud's no longer around, and under the circumstances . . . hell, a shot or two don't sound too bad – hair of the dog?"

As perceptive as Charlie was – Ian was guessing that Charlie must have noticed the slight shaking of his hands while he was typing. That, and perspiration which had begun welling up on his forehead due to stress-accelerated detoxification. Ian thought to himself – *Charlie no-doubt can smell the alcohol sweating out of me like dander falls from a mangy dog . . . Yeah, he's put two and two together sure as shit – takes one to know one . . .*

Ian hadn't woke-up this morning with much of a hang-over to speak of. Nothing more than he was used to dealing with daily. But he was beginning to suffer a bit more of the afternoon DT's than was typical. "Yeah Charlie, hair of the dog . . . not a bad idea!" Ian replied trying not to sound to eager or desperate, as he thought to himself – *Jack Daniel's, the cure for mange!*

CHAPTER 31

Liquid Courage

CHARLIE AND IAN set at a corner booth . . . They'd been sitting in their chairs for a little over an hour. Both men had for the last half-hour forgone with their usual drinks; in lieu of several shots of distilled nectar from the blue agave cactus.

Charlie held his shot high – he said out loud for all the bar patrons to hear. "Here's to Bud O'Brien! The best god-damn man I ever knew and the best friend I ever had . . . !"

Ian motioned his hand downward signaling Charlie to bring it down a couple of notches – before he unnecessarily brought on more attention that might arouse any suspicions regarding Bud's absence.

Ian stood up from his chair. He staggered ever so slightly as he began straightening his shirt and re-tucking it into his jeans.

"What do you think Charlie . . . should we get out to old Charbonneau's place to pick up the package?" Ian looked around to see if anyone was listening to him. Nobody cared – they were all off in their own worlds.

Before Charlie could answer Ian. He was distracted by who just entered the bar. Charlie looked up at Ian. Then with an exaggerated shift of his eyes and simultaneous half turn of his head in the direction of the door. Charlie signaled Ian to turn and have a look.

Ian did just that. His heart sank into the pit of his stomach. It was her . . . Marsha Steward. She briskly walked across the room straight up to their table. Ian set back down.

"Hello boys!" Marsha said with sly enthusiasm.

Charlie spoke first, "Ma'am . . ."

Ian then spoke, "Hi Marsha, would you like to have a seat?"

"No . . . no, I just saw the Deputy's car out front. I thought maybe I'd find you here . . . Ian, I noticed your car and trailer were still parked at your camp-site . . . So, I knocked on your trailer . . . to say goodbye. We're leaving . . . not much more to report on around here. You know, now that the bodies have been discovered – is there . . . ? So how come you're still hanging around?" Marsha all the while stood looking directly at Ian.

"No reason for me to be hanging around any longer either . . . I'm just saying my goodbye's to Charlie here . . . Guess I'm getting a bit of a late start to get moving . . . I'll probably pull up stakes either tonight or tomorrow morning."

Ian sounded convincing. But Marsha still looked at him with suspicious eyes.

"Where's that big handsome Sheriff?" Marsha asked rather casually.

Charlie spoke up, "Uh, Bud's up in Seattle for a couple days on departmental business."

Marsha left that topic alone. "Well, Ian, it was very nice meeting you . . . Here let me give you my card – call me so we can meet and have coffee or something sometime."

Marsha dug into here purse and retrieved her business card. She handed it to Ian, "All right then . . . Bye!"

Marsha turned and walked slowly back across the room. Without hesitation she exited through the side door she'd come in through.

Marsha walked briskly over to her stations van up to the drivers window. She motioned for Tom to role down his window – He promptly did.

"Change of plans . . . I tell you something's still cooking around here. I can feel it. We're going to move the van up the way just a bit. We'll park out of site. My guess is those two, they're going to rendezvous with the Sheriff back up the mountain. That is once they've loaded up with liquid courage! Tom, it's not hunting season yet is it?" Tom shook his head no.

"Well, the deputy, he's all dressed up like Rambo. Like he's ready to hunt, something!"

Back inside the bar Charlie looked over at Ian. "Well, thank God for small favors. At least we've got her out of our hair . . ."

I wonder? – Ian thought to himself.

Charlie stood up. "Let's get going . . . We're losing daylight."

Ian got up from his chair. Charlie laid down enough money to cover their tab. Ian put down some cash for a tip. The two men walked from the bar to Charlie's car.

CHAPTER 32

Silver Bullets

IAN STAYED IN the car while Charlie walked up to the front door. They had spotted Charbonneau looking out the window at them as they pulled up his driveway.

Ian watched the cabin door open. He saw Charbonneau hand Charlie a small brown paper bag. Ian watched the two exchange some pleasantries. Then Charlie turned and walked back to the car.

Charlie climbed back into the driver seat and handed the small bag to Ian.

"Charbonneau was able to make three bullets. He said the purity of the silver is excellent and these will be powerful and accurate. I laughed when he said that. I told him they wouldn't be any more accurate than the marksman who fires them . . . I hope your handy with that pop-gun of yours . . ."

Ian smiled a small reluctant smile as he looked intently at the bullets in the bag.

"Yeah, well, I'm no Dirty Harry, when it comes to handguns, but I'm okay!"

Charlie pulled his car around. They exited the long driveway back onto the main road.

A few minutes later they were driving through town; heading east towards the mountains.

Charlie decided mostly for Ian's sake that he should speak. Ending an almost ten minute uncomfortable silence.

"Well . . . Ian, here's what I figure we should do first. First let's head up to the falls . . . Maybe if we're lucky, well if you can call it luck . . . we'll discover some more . . . evidence."

Ian knew by what Charlie had just said, that he meant more of Bud's remains. The thought was just too grizzly for him to call a spade a spade.

"Ian, something else you should know about Jean-Chastel . . . A couple years back Bud caught wind that Chastel might be the guy who was peddling moonshine to some of the unfortunates up at the reservation. Bud question a few of them. But nobody would drop dime on the guy. They no doubt didn't want to lose their source. But more than that. Bud said they seemed scared to death to even talk about it at all. Bud figured Chastel probably was the moon-shiner. The guy had to get a little money somehow. But he never could prove it. If Chastel was running a still. It was nowhere around his cabin. Probably had it hidden way up in the hills. Anyway, Bud did some checking on Chastel. You know, Police records, public records, you name it. Nothing came back on the guy. And I mean nothing at all! There are no records that he even exists. The man's a ghost, a total recluse who lives completely off of the grid. He don't own any vehicle. Occasionally, like you seen today. Chastel will bum a ride into town from someone up on the rez . . . But Christ, just to do that . . . He's got to walk several miles up and down hill and dell. And I mean through some god-damn dense forest and steep-ass ravines. Just to get to anyone who has a car or truck."

Ian couldn't help being fascinated regarding Jean-Chastel Gevaudan. How someone, anyone, could live completely by their own rules – totally outside the entrapments of modern society to him was incredible – that was unless you were an immortal savage werewolf!

Charlie took a deep breath. His mood seemed to suddenly change to that of dead seriousness.

"Ian, if your crazy theory is even part right . . . If Chastel is our guy. Well, that would make things simple!"

Ian looked at Charlie confused. "How so?"

It was starting to get dark, Charlie switched on his headlights. He then glanced over at Ian. A forced grin had replaced Charlie's normal pleasant smile, his eyes looked wild. Charlie's sudden change of expression made the hair on Ian's neck stand on in. Charlie then spoke in an overly-calm voice.

"It's easy to disappear someone who's already invisible!"

Charlie grew quiet again as they approached the stretch of road that his son Jeremy and Katie had crashed his bike – and Bud had been killed.

Ian didn't know him that well – but what little Ian did know of Charlie; he knew this was not typically his demeanor. Charlie was getting more intense, more single minded by the minute. Singularly intent on utterly destroying whatever had attempted to attack his son and Katie. And had attacked Rob Richards, killed that hiker-couple, and . . . his best friend, Bud.

For some reason and Ian could not for the life of him understand this – he was no longer afraid. Even as absurd as it seemed when he'd run it over and over in his mind. Ian could not get Jean-Chastel Gevaudan out of his mind. It was much more then the pseudo-facts – Ian just somehow felt the connection.

"Charlie . . . what if this guy Jean-Chastel – what if he was named, or named himself, after the Jean-Chastel of the seventeen hundreds in France we were reading about? What if he's just some crazy serial killer type who's obsessed with emulating people in the name of that whole *Beast of Gevaudan* thing he read about . . . Or, maybe he's even some distant relative of that guy and it plays into his delusion – and due to his lycanthropic mental illness he puts on some animal skin suit when he goes out on killing sprees. That would explain quite a bit of it, right? Shit maybe he's even a cannibal!"

Charlie swerved just a little as he took his eyes off of the road as he glanced over at Ian. He then grunted a low deep response.

"Yeah, maybe . . . ?"

Charlie glanced up at his rearview mirror, "But we got another concern right now."

That caught Ian off guard breaking his concentration. "What, what other concern?"

Charlie shook his head in disgust, "We're being followed by your lady-friend!"

Ian looked over at Charlie. "My lady-friend . . . ?"

Charlie took a deep breath. He then nodded with exaggeration as he again glanced for a second back into his rearview mirror . . .

"Have a look for yourself!"

Ian twisted his body in his seat as far around as he could. He then turned his head the same direction to afford a good vantage point to look back at the roadway behind them . . .

Ian replied the moment he made out what was behind them – the KATW Channel thirteen news van. "Oh shit, you're kidding me!"

CHAPTER 33

Moon Rises Harmony Falls

CHARLIE TOOK A left off of the main road. He and Ian were now on the long bumpy gravel road that led up to the falls. Charlie glanced over at Ian, then focused back on his driving as he spoke, "They saw us turn . . . They'll catch up with us in just minutes, so here's the plan. Soon as we get up to the little parking area we're gonna grab the guns and flashlights and head up towards the falls before they get here. That means we've got to move fast! We sure as shit don't want them dogging us up at the falls."

Ian nodded in agreement while he replied, "Yeah, good idea! They'll think twice before wanting to head up through the thick trees and briars all the way to the falls in the dark – especially trying to pack their equipment!"

Charlie was glad Ian was on the same page, he continued . . .

"That's right . . . they probably won't attempt getting up to the falls by themselves. But if we give them any chance to follow us, mark my words they'd make the climb. Getting in our way every step. And maybe frightening off what-ever the fuck we're hunting. That lady reporter she's got guts I'll give her that. Well, like I said we're gonna move fast! We ain't gonna give them no easy opportunity to follow!"

Charlie and Ian continued for the next ten minutes bouncing around up the old logging road. Until they reached the small clearing that served as a parking area at little Merwin, the small lake created by Harmony Falls.

Charlie parked his car. Turned off his ignition and lights. He then pushed the button to pop open the trunk. "All right, lets get moving. Ian grab the rifle out of the trunk . . . And there's duck tape and a couple of flashlights back there grab them too! I'm gonna use the tape to lash a flashlight to my rifle."

Ian nearly leapt from the car. He bounded to the rear of the vehicle and grabbed-up everything Charlie had asked him to retrieve.

Ian handed the rifle, one of the flashlights and the role of tape to Charlie.

Charlie briefly set the flashlight and tape onto the hood of his car. He then positioned the rifle with its stock against the ground holding it with his knees barrel towards the sky. He rapidly retrieved the flashlight and tape from the hood and swiftly lashed the flashlight onto the underside barrel of his rifle. Without further delay; Charlie took the lead and the two men headed into the dense thicket heading towards the falls. Just before disappearing into the woods. Both men heard the distant sound of a vehicle approaching. Ian turned and looked back. They'd already put around fifty yards between where they were and Charlie's car . . . Ian could see rapidly approaching headlights. The lights were dancing up and down in the tall trees alongside the gravel road – as the vehicle made its way to the parking area. Marsha Steward and her cameraman driver Tom Iverson, had arrived.

An eerie, strong wind suddenly began blewing. Trees, bushes and tall grass began whipping to and fro – making it more difficult to trudge through the low hanging fir and alder tree limbs . . . tangles of vine maple and multitudes of rain-water soaked limbs and foliage. All of which continuously slapped them in their faces and all over soaking them head to foot.

Ian mused . . . *It might as well be pouring down rain – wouldn't be getting any wetter!*

Charlie and Ian kept moving forward quickly, as quietly as they could . . . Charlie looked back over his shoulder at Ian and spoke in little more than a whisper. "Ian, the wind is blowing from the North . . . That's good! We will be up-wind, throwing off our scent. The noise from the trees will make it more difficult for us to be heard.

Ian thought to himself . . . *Yeah, but harder for us to hear as well.*

Charlie and Ian were nearly coming out of the dense woods back alongside the lake-bank near the falls, when Charlie switched his rifle-mounted flashlight off. He motioned for Ian to extinguish his battery operated torch as well. Charlie then knelt down on one knee. Ian followed suit. Both men remained hidden by cover as they gazed up at the elevated position of the falls – which was less than forty feet from where they knelt. From their present position which was facing side-on to the falls. They could see that somehow the massive boulder had been returned to its place of origin. Completely closing off the falls-side entrance to the cave.

Charlie spoke very quietly. "Okay, plan B . . . There's an animal trail just to the right of the falls created by herds of elk making their way from up in the mountains down to this watering hole . . . Hikers use it all the time in the summer . . . The trail goes about three miles up into the hills. Then it opens to a large clearing . . . Just beyond the clearing about a quarter mile further up, the forest gets real dense. Never been logged, old growth forest. That's where Jean-Chastel's cabin is . . . shall we?"

Ian shook his head yes . . . The two men arose from kneeling – switched their flashlights back on and proceeded towards the trail.

Primarily due to the combination of adreneline and all the walking he'd done over the last couple of days. Ian was doing a good job of keeping up with Charlie. Somehow miraculously, he wasn't even getting out of breath; as they traversed up the trail which was beginning to present itself as a fairly steep incline.

Charlie looked back over his shoulder and showed the first glimpse in hours of his usually jovial self as he softly spoke, “You’re doing pretty good for a white guy!”

Ian was equally quiet with his reply, “Are we there yet?”

CHAPTER 34

Cabin Fever

CHARLIE AND IAN crouched low amidst a thicket of bushes and black berry briars. In the moonlight they could clearly see Jean-Chastel's small log cabin. There was smoke billowing from the cabin chimney. At this elevation there was small patches of snow on the ground. It wasn't freezing out, but nearly.

Charlie looked over at Ian and spoke very quietly almost in a whisper, "What time do you have?"

Ian glanced at his watch and replied in an equally quiet voice . . .

"It's quarter till ten."

Charlie stood up straight and spoke in an almost normal volume . . .

"All right . . . enough of this creeping around. We're gonna walk right up there and announce our presence. Mind you, have that silver pea-shooter of yours drawn and ready! Ian despite what I've said . . . if he's our man, I'll make the arrest if possible!"

Ian had figured all along that Charlie was the kind of man that would at least try to do the right thing. Not that Charlie wasn't capable of taking a life; Ian knew with clarity that Charlie was quite capable should it become necessary. It was himself that Ian worried about. *Can I do this – can I shoot to kill should it come down to it . . .* ? Ian had asked himself that question over and over during the hike to the cabin.

Both men walked briskly but very cautiously with guns ready, up to the front of the cabin.

Charlie spoke once again, this time in little more than a whisper...

"Okay, Ian listen up . . . I want you to keep very low and quiet as you make your way to the back of the cabin. Once your in place back there. Stay clear of the back door and keep your head down. When I announce my presence at the front – you be ready if he decides to bolt out the back. If he does bolt out the back . . . don't try and be no hero. Shout at him to freeze. But if he doesn't stop of his own accord; don't do anything stupid that could get yourself hurt, he's a big guy. And likely as not he may be armed with a shotgun or something, you understand? Ian, all those wild stories and theories we been talking about . . . if this is the man we're after, that's all he is, a man nothing more . . . Just a crazy lunatic! Hell, maybe Chastel really does think he's some kind of animal or something, I can buy that – mind you that don't make him any less dangerous. A crazy can be the worst monster you can imagine . . . So, if you see him, shout out your position and I'll come running. When your ready. I'm gonna give you about two minutes to get into position. Then I'm going up and announcing myself – got it?"

Ian nodded his head yes, as he thought to himself . . . *Just a man . . . Of course Charlie's right . . . Chastel is just a crazy, a "big" crazy Cajun, nothing more!*

Ian took a deep breath filling his lungs to capacity . . . He then let his breath out slowly in an attempt to help gather his composure and steady himself. Ian, shaking just a little from both the cold and his nerves; retrieved his pistol from his ankle holster. He'd already loaded it with three silver bullets during their drive up to the lake.

Ian crouched over low. He began making his way towards the back of the cabin; moving slowly and as silently as he could.

Behind the cabin were two small wooden outbuildings. From where Ian stood one appeared to be a shed. And one smelled to be an outhouse. The shed door was closed but not locked. Ian went over to it. He quietly opened the door and shinned his flashlight in; taking caution to not expose his light beyond the confines of the shed. Ian was horrified by what he saw as hundreds of flies flew directly at his face. Instantly a stench beyond putridity completely over-came his senses. Ian gagged. He bent over at the waist and began succumbing to uncontrollable heaving – but somehow after an eternal instance of convulsing he managed to hold back further reflux of sputum and soured acidic throat burning stomach content which had nearly filled his throat and mouth. *Zero residual presence* – Ian thought to himself as he successfully managed to swallow his mouthful and suppress his instinct to scream-out from terror educed panic. He nearly lost his balance as he stumbled from wobbly knees as he slowly backpedaled from the shed door. Ian managed to maintain enough presence of mind to switch off his flashlight, as he continued to back away from the shed. He began to shake all over from shock and nerves. He took a deep breath and reached down deep within himself and managed to summon a semblance of composure. It was now too late to rely on anything that could pass for courage. Ian's brain had switched to auto-pilot. He was now on survival mode pure and simple. *Fight or flight* – Ian mused. He knew all about that natural instinct in animals, humans too. Only problem was, the choice had been made. Ian thought to himself… *Too late to run, the plane's already left the proverbial runway!* Ian positioned himself just off to the side of the back door of the cabin. Shaking from shattered nerves and the cold; he crouched down and waited at the back of the cabin, alone, in the full moonlit night.

Charlie now had positioned himself just to the left of the cabins front door. Rifle leveled chest-high at the doorway. He began speaking loud, clear and in a forceful voice.

"Jean-Chastel . . . This is the Harmony County Sheriff's Department . . . We need you to come on out with your hands empty, held high in plain sight . . . We got some questions to ask you . . . Now don't get no idea of bolting out the back. We got a dozen men positioned all around your place . . . You're completely surrounded! You got less than a minute to come on out . . . Or, we're coming in! You got that Chastel . . . ?"

Hearing Charlie yell-out those words caused a twisting cramping knot to well-up within Ian's stomach . . . *A dozen men surrounding the place, yeah right!* Ian thought to himself. His heart pounded harder and harder. Ian's sweating palms made gripping his pistol with any confidence increasingly difficult.

In less than thirty seconds the cabin door burst opened . . . Jean-Chastel stood there completely naked, empty handed in the doorway.

The cabin was dimly lighted by a couple of oil lamps. The only thing within the cabin Charlie could make out clearly was a very large head and claws in tact; bear-skin rug laying on the floor in the center of the cabin.

Jean-Chastel just stood there motionless in the opened doorway as Charlie moved to position himself directly in front of him.

As Chastel stood there motionless in the bright moonlight. Charlie couldn't help but notice the exceptionally endowed Chastel was not circumcised.

Before Charlie could think of what to ask or even say, Chastel spoke, "So Charlie Redtail . . . You think you're going to what, arrest me? You think you're pitiful jail can hold Jean-Chastel do you . . . ?"

Chastel began to laugh maniacally as he began to . . . Change!

Charlie couldn't say a word, he was beyond terrified . . . he was nearly hypnotized by what was happening right before his eyes!

Jean-Chastel began to quiver and shake . . . His stomach began convulsing and undulating in a way that was beyond any grand-mal seizure. Hair began springing up and out of his every pore. Every muscle and bone in Chastel's body began pulsating, growing . . . Altering . . . Changing into . . . Something else . . . Humanoid, but not human.

Chastel's jaw began elongating. Charlie could hear its bones, cartlidge muscles and tendons pop and creek as the transformation dramatically increased. This thing before him; its nose and jaw became that of an enormous canidae. Its bloody teeth began falling out of his mouth as they were replaced by protruding fangs. It's fangs continued to grow and grow as the monster retracted its lips snarling and growling in rage . . . Its eyes no longer resembled human eyes. They had become yellow translucent mirror – like orbs with garnet-red blood filled veins . . . The fingers of its hands rapidly transformed to long spindly protrusions which supported claws that were like massive dark spikes. Its ears enlarged ten times over as they grew to become canine-like . . . Thick dark bristly hair now covered its entire body. Chastel continued to morph and enlarge into the beast that stood over seven feet tall directly in front of Charlie. It then rose-up onto the balls of its humanoid feet making it even appear larger. Then its last recognizable aspect of humanity transformed to become enormous paws with massive pads like that of a giant wolf!

Charlie fired a shot from his rifle. His shot struck point-blank. The splatter-point bullet struck with tremendous force the center of the creatures chest. The impact knocked the monster backward a couple feet . . . Blood spewed from the wound, some of which splattered across Charlie's face. But to Charlie's utter horror, beyond that there was little if no other effect. The massive beast just let out a blood-curdling howl as it stepped forward and grabbed Charlie's rifle by the barrel and ripped it from his grasp, tossing it aside.

Ian heard the shot. Without hesitation he came running from the backside of the cabin to its front. Within seconds Ian spotted for himself the horrific spectacle that was unfolding at the cabins front door.

The creature lashed out at Charlie. With one swipe from its massive right claw. The beast sent Charlie flying backward six feet where he landed on his back. There was blood pouring through the long gashes of the front of Charlie's shredded camouflage shirt. Ian was momentarily frozen with fear seeing Charlie laying there completely sprawled out, nearly unconscious from a single blow from the, monster!

Then seeing that Charlie was all but done in. Ian drew upon some internal strength that he'd never known he possessed. In one deft motion he turned towards the beast aiming his pistol steady dead on at the creatures head and shouted. "Jean-Chastel . . . Jean-Chastel of Gevaudan, France . . . Slayer of the Beast of Gevaudan I know who . . . I know what you are . . . My, my gun is loaded with silver bullets!"

Before Ian could utter another word or squeeze off a round – the beast leaped ten feet from where it had stood . . . Upon landing, it ran incredibly fast as a biped. But then it bent forward onto its front claws. As a quadruped it instantly further accelerated to a gallop that would have overtaken even the swiftest race-horse. The massive beast crossed the clearing in seconds then disappeared into the dense forest.

Ian began running towards Charlie, but before he reached him; Charlie had already managed to get back up onto his feet.

With help from Ian, Charlie managed to remove his shirt . . . Ian was glad to see that that the bleeding made the wounds appear to be much worse than they actually were. Fortunately for Charlie, his puncture resistant *Kevlar* hunting shirt had offered some protection from the deadly swipe he'd taken from the beasts razor sharp claw. Charlie took the remains of his shredded shirt and tied some large pieces together and then wrapped and tied the rags around himself serving as field dressing for his chest.

Ian could hardly believe the physical and mental toughness that Charlie had. He undoubtedly was in extreme pain but hardly showed it.

Charlie walked over to his rifle and grabbed it up from the ground. He looked back over at Ian . . . Charlie almost sounded in good humor when he spoke. "Well, you don't need to say I told you so!"

Ian could not believe his ears. He just shook his head in utter amazement of . . . . everything!

"Charlie . . . Out back there's a shed that's filled with . . . Bones, and . . . what looks like some of what's left of . . . Bud."

Charlie didn't act or sound surprised when he replied . . .

"That figures . . . He shut down his den back at the falls . . . Probably removed anything he kept there . . . Too many people know about it . . . Too many of us have left our scents there . . . He's gonna find him a new den . . . Probably just keeping the remains here till he does . . . He surely never counted on anyone figuring him to be a . . . . Okay, I'll say it . . . a werewolf! . . . Hey – which way did it head anyway?"

Suddenly Ian processed that the direction the beast raced off was down mountain . . . down towards . . . "Marsha!" Ian shouted as both men looked at each other then began rushing towards the trail to the falls as fast as they could move.

CHAPTER 35

Vanity

"TOM ARE YOU ready – are we ready to shoot . . . ?"

Tom Iverson shook his head yes and gave Marsha a big thumbs up . . . He expertly held the television camera with one hand as he balanced it on his shoulder. Tom called out to Marsha, "Ready . . . three, two, one . . . go!"

"This is on the spot investigative reporter Marsha Stewerd coming to you from Little Merwin Lake, Harmony Falls, Washington . . . This is the location where just two days ago the bodies of Roger and Stephanie Warner formerly of Bellevue, Washington, were discovered in a cave located behind the falls approximately two hundred yards from this very spot. We are waiting at this parking area to hear any new developments from local law enforcement which are here canvassing the area for reasons we as yet do not know. We are here set up to hopefully get an on the spot interview with them upon their return to their car which is parked in this very lot. Which has become their temporary base of operations. This is Marsha Steward for KATW channel thirteen news reporting to you from Little Merwin Lake, Washington."

Tom relaxed the small television camera from off of his shoulder. He switched off the camera light and set the camera back into the van and lit a cigarette.

Marsha looked at him with some disgust, "Okay, we'll do a couple more takes in a few minutes – that is of course once you've finished with your smoke break."

Tom rolled his eyes at Marsha – "Marsha, exactly what do you think we're going to accomplish up here in the middle of the forest in the dark. I don't want to end up on the menu of some bear or whatever ate those hikers if you get my drift!"

"Tom, just finish your damn cigarette and next time try and keep the camera steady!"

"Sorry! My hands were a little shaky, only cause its fucking freezing up here!"

Marsha looked at Tom, she shook her head with disdain . . .

"It's bad attitudes like that . . . lack of cooperation from support people like yourself – that keep me from moving to a larger market like L.A., or New York. Now come on, lets do this thing at least a couple more times. And this next time please keep the camera at tight close-up on my face; stop focusing on my boobs!"

Tom tossed his half smoked cigarette onto the ground. He grabbed the camera from the van and switched on its light. They both moved over to their previously designated marks.

"Okay, once again from the top – ready . . . three, two, one . . . go!"

Tom did what he always did . . . he momentarily closed both of his eyes to relax them before re-opening the one that looks into the view-finder. But this time when he re-opened his eye, there was nothing to view . . . No Marsha Steward.

It had happened so fast and there was no sound . . . She had been decapitated with one powerful swipe from the beast.

Tom opened both eyes and looked up from the camera. Marsha's headless body stood there directly in front of him. He hadn't seen her in the view-finder because like instructed he was focused in close and tight on her face.

"Fuck! Fuck me!! . . . . Fuck me!!!" Tom screamed to the top of his lungs . . .

Marsha's body finally collapsed slowly then fell to the ground like a frozen statue that just melted.

It was then that Tom saw what had loped his bosses head from her shoulders. He tried with all his might to scream once again but no sound came. He leaped into the vans side slide-open door. He quickly slammed the sliding door closed and locked it. Tom fell twice inside the van as he scrambled to lock the driver and passengers doors. He lunged himself to the very back of the van and locked the back doors. Then it began . . . It started with the deafening horrible scratching sound of claws on metal. Like fingernails on a black-board but a thousand times louder. The van began rocking violently but only for a moment. Tom was traumatized to the point of catatonic deliria. The beast began smashing into the van. Creating enormous dents into its thin metal siding with every smashing blow. The sliding door buckled, windows were shattering – another strike and it would be all over . . . It would have him! But just when Tom had almost blacked out from terror the attack on the van stopped as abruptly as it had begun.

Tom heard Ian yelling out Marsha's name . . . Charlie and Ian were running towards the van as fast as their winded bodies would carry them.

When they drew close they could see the devastation inflicted on the van . . . Then they saw Marsha's body and her head which had rolled over next to Charlie's car.

Ian was first to reach Marsha's body. Under any other circumstances throughout his life he would have lost his lunch . . . But he'd seen so much over the last couple of days and this night; that though he was shocked and appalled by what lay by his feet. He didn't feel sickened by the site.

Charlie shinned his flashlight through the spider-webbed front window of the van. He spotted Tom Iverson curled up. He was rocking back and forth in a fetal position. Tom had the look on his face of someone who fit the cliché of having seen the proverbial ghost. Only both Charlie and Ian knew what Tom had actually seen was much, much worse!

Charlie and Ian were able though with considerable difficulty to get the heavily smashed-in sliding door open far enough to literally drag Tom from the van.

Charlie asked Tom to describe what had happened but Tom either wouldn't or couldn't utter a word.

Charlie had Ian open the trunk of his car and get a blanket out. Ian wrapped the blanket around Tom who was in deep shock. Ian tucked Tom's head down and managed to guide him into the back seat. Charlie and Ian without a seconds hesitation got in Charlie's car as well. Charlie fired it up and spun a ninety degree power-turn. His tires were spinning and throwing gravel and dirt. Once headed down the dirt road which led to the main road below, Charlie as quickly as he could accelerated up to better than fifty miles-an-hour. They bounced around violently as they bounded over the heavily pot-holed logging road, but Charlie didn't let off the gas. All four tires were squealing as he turned right onto the main road. Charlie then switched on his cop-lights and promptly further accelerated to better than eighty.

The three men were now racing towards town. Up to this point no-one had spoke a word . . . Ian finally broke the silence.

"Charlie, sorry, I wasn't thinking – I should be driving, you're in no condition . . ."

Charlie glanced for a second over at Ian. He began to cough a few shallow coughs.

"Nobody drives this baby but me," Ian and Charlie laughed small laughs. Charlie coughed a couple more times. The last time he coughed, a small amount of blood collected in the corner of his mouth. Tasting it – Charlie checked himself in the rearview mirror, he saw the blood.

Ian oblivious to Charlie's coughing up blood, turned to check on Tom, who still was silent. He just set there in the back seat rocking forward and backward as he stared straight ahead with a far-off look in his eyes.

Ian then turned his head back towards Charlie. "Charlie . . . Cameraman Tom, he don't look too good . . . I think Elvis has left the building if you get my drift!"

Charlie spoke up, "Yeah, seeing . . . going through what he did – his boss wasn't the only one to lose their head!"

Ian bowed his head, tears began to well-up in the corner of his eyes.

"Anyhow – Doc's gonna be pissed about being woke up, again! But I guess I better get our camera guy looked at . . ."

Ian replied without hesitation, "Yeah, it would be a good idea to get yourself checked out as well! Get them cuts properly sterilized and bandaged up!" Ian hadn't a clue of how right he was about Charlie needing medical attention.

Charlie shook his head in agreement. He then felt compelled to ask a question that he figured Ian could answer as well as any man . . . Any man, that was except maybe his Grandfather or Jean-Chastel himself.

"Ian . . . I guess what we seen tonight fits the bill that Chastel is what about anyone who seen what we did would call . . . Well, hell, would call a werewolf! A real monster! The stuff we been told all our lives is nothing but superstitious nonsense. That said . . . What I remember from movies I used to watch as a kid about such things – don't you got to be bitten by a werewolf and live to become one? I mean I don't have to worry about these here scratches do I?"

That very thought had already crossed Ian's mind . . . He thought hard for just a moment before answering. "Charlie, my guess is nobody except maybe Jean-Chastel could answer that with absolute certainty. But so far, it seems most of what we've seen seems to fit within most of the common legends and beliefs about the subject. So I'm gonna go out on a limb and say – I doubt if you can be infected without being either bitten or maybe direct blood transfer. The infection, if you can call it that; I think it transmits through saliva or blood. I really think you're okay!"

Ian looked over at Charlie – in an attempt to affect additional reassurance winked at him . . . But the truth was; Ian really had no idea. Charlie's guess was as good as his!

Ian spoke back up. "Charlie, I think we should let Doc Matthews in on all of this . . . He may be able to shed some light from a scientific point of view. And he might be able to lend some idea as to how you should deal with Bud's head. So you don't spend your next twenty Christmases in Walla Walla, if you get my meaning!"

Charlie sighed, but then shook his head in agreement.

They were now getting close to town. Ian shared another thought.

"Say Charlie, if you can hold on for a few more minutes before we go to see Doc Matthews . . . swing by my campsite. I've got a drawing pad and some colored pencils in my trailer. I want to sketch, well, best I can – while the image is fresh in my mind. What I, what we saw . . . Sort of map-out the look of the thing to show the Doc.

Charlie once again nodded in agreement, "Yeah, Ian that's a good idea, I mean if you can draw?"

Ian paused before answering, "Well, I'm no Michael Angelo. But I can draw a little – you know had some art in High School . . . It comes in handy in my line of work, drawing a little that is."

The three men drove into Harmony Falls township. Charlie did as Ian asked. He first drove Ian to his trailer. Ian jumped out of the car and was back in less than a minute, with sketch pad and a box of colored pencils in hand.

Charlie then drove the short distance to Doc Matthews'. Charlie and Ian climbed out of the car. They managed to get Tom out of the back seat and onto his feet. He still said nothing.

Charlie and Ian helped Tom along by keeping their hands under his arm-pits to steady him a bit. The three men walked up to Doc's office front door. Charlie pushed the button on the intercom . . . Doc Matthews answered in a few seconds – with a very irritated tone in his voice.

"Who is it, what do you want?"

"Doc it's me Charlie. Hey, I got a man in deep shock down here. And well, I guess I could use some looking at myself."

There was no response . . . But not one minute passed before the front door opened. Doc Matthews stood there in pajamas, robe and slippers.

"Okay, don't just stand there. Get on in here and lets have a look . . . Come on now, cold as hell out tonight. I can't heat the whole damn town!"

The three men walked in. Charlie and Ian continued to support and steady Tom.

Doc Matthews took one look at Charlie who stood there bleeding through his make-shift bandaged chest.

Charlie spoke up, "Doc this here's a big city television cameraman, his name's Tom Iverson. His boss-lady got killed tonight right in front of him . . . He's in shock or something."

Doc Matthews looked disgustedly at Charlie. "Oh really, shock, is that your considered medical opinion? Well, regardless, he's gonna be okay – you, I'm not so certain . . ."

Doc Matthews began unwinding the make-shift bandages from Charlie. Once removed he looked closely at the wounds.

"Hmm, aside from getting some disinfectant on these here cuts. They look like they'll be okay once bandaged up, proper that is. But that's not what's got me concerned . . . It's this purple-blue and yellow looking bruising around your side right here," Doc Matthews lightly touched Charlie's ribs. Charlie flinched from sudden pain.

"Charlie, follow me to the room in the back. I got an X-ray machine back there, we're gonna get a picture to know for sure . . . But, I'll bet dollars to doughnuts you got at least one if not a couple broken ribs. Maybe by the look of your eyes you even got a little internal bleeding going on. But you're breathing seems pretty good. Too deep and regular to be a punctured or collapsed lung I should think."

Doc Matthews and Charlie went back to the small X-ray room. Tom Iverson had laid down on an exam table. Ian kept periodically looking over checking on him. Ian was both unnerved and concerned about the way Tom looked like a pale-faced nearly motionless zombie. He eerily resembled to Ian; that of a rigor-mortis stiffened cadaver with lips drawn tight as a drum. And his eyes . . . Ian couldn't help notice that Tom's eyes never seemed to blink – as he lay on his back staring aimlessly at the ceiling.

Between the occasional checking on Tom – Ian continued with a project that he'd started shortly after the three men had come inside Doc's office. He was busy working on a sketch. A drawing of something that if Ian hadn't seen for himself, he would have thought came from a Hollywood movie, a "B" movie at that.

After what now had become a solid hour of power-sketching between periodic glances over at Tom . . . Ian completed his rendering of the most terrifying thing he'd ever seen.

Ian mused as he gazed at his completed sketch-art . . . *I never claimed to be an artist . . . This is no prize-winner . . . But essentially, this is what it looked like to me!*

The Beast of Harmony Falls

Doc Matthews and Charlie came walking into the room. Doc spoke to Ian, "Yep, it was just as I suspected . . . Charlie here's got two cracked ribs! He's gonna be feeling them real good when he wakes up in the morning. As you can see I went ahead and patched him up proper in the other room after taking the X-rays – he'll live . . . Okay, now let's have a look at your quiet friend here."

Doc walked over to the examing table Tom was laying down on. He flashed a small pin flash-light into Tom's eyes. He then looked up at Charlie.

"Okay, maybe you'd make a decent Doctor after all . . . cause you're right. This mans in deep almost catatonic shock! I'll give him a sedative – best you take him home with you Charlie and have that lovely wife of yours nurse him for at least a day or two. He's in no shape to travel tonight. Unless maybe that television station he works for sends someone to fetch him. Then I suppose he could fare the trip okay enough."

Charlie spoke up, "Yeah, well, Doc they're gonna have to pick him up even if he gets feeling like himself. His van's too smashed-up to drive. I'll take him home with me tonight like you said. Tomorrow I've got a lot of calls to make . . . paperwork up the ass to fill out. Things to explain to a lot of folks including his people; that's gonna be one hell of a conversation! I've got to tell them their star reporter has been killed on the job. And her cameraman driver has been scared to the point that he can't even speak! How bout we switch jobs Doc . . . ?"

Doc Matthews laughed while shaking his head indicating no-way! He then asked, "What the hell happened anyhow? That pretty reporter everyone in towns been yapping about, you say she's, dead?"

Ian stepped over to Charlie who was now sitting in a chair near the exam table Tom was on. Ian opened up his sketch-pad and showed Charlie his drawing. Charlie smiled a half-smile. He looked up at Ian. "Hell Ian, that ain't half bad. That looks pretty much dead on. Except when I saw it up close . . . it didn't look like no comic book monster like your drawing here!"

Ian and Charlie laughed at Charlie's observation; but only for a breif moment. Both men knew too well what was happening was no laughing matter.

Doc Matthews tried to see what Ian had shown Charlie, but from his vantage point he couldn't. "All right, what's all the secrecy . . . ? What're you two jokers looking at?"

Ian looked Charlie straight in the eyes, "Well, do we show him? . . . do we tell him?"

Charlie held his right side with his left hand . . . Doc had given him a couple of pain pills – but they hadn't kicked in yet. And the pain was increasing by the minute. With his right hand Charlie made a bowing gesture, indicating to Ian to tell Doc, all of it!

The Telling

Ian looked deep into Charlie's eyes. An effort to double check that telling Doc what he was about to was in fact okay . . . It was.

Ian motioned for Doc Matthews to take a seat after he'd carried into the room a couple extra chairs. Tom continued to lay on the exam table staring up at the ceiling. He remained almost motionless except for the unsteady shallow raising and lowering of his chest as he breathed.

Ian also needed to take a seat just to tell the tale. After everyone present but Tom was seated, Ian took a deep breath and began.

"Okay, Doc what I'm about to tell you is going to sound nothing short of crazy! But please keep an open mind and hear me out."

Doc Matthews shook his head yes, indicating that he wanted to hear what this was supposedly all about.

"Okay then . . . without going into each and every little detail that would take the rest of the night to cover. Suffice it to say in a nutshell it's like this . . . The local man that got all tore-up and is in the hospital in Portland and those hikers that got killed . . . and . . . Sheriff Bud

O'Brien he lost his life because of it as well. They were all attacked by a . . . well, for lack of a better word . . . Monster!"

Doc Matthews turned his attention from Ian over to Charlie. Charlie bowed his head while nodding in agreement to what Ian was saying.

Doc Matthews looked back at Ian, "Bud! . . . Bud, dead . . . ? All right, I can take a joke as good as the next guy . . . but right now – what in the hell is going on?"

Neither men even flinched at the accusation that they were pulling his leg. Doc ran his fingers through what little hair he had left on the top of his head.

"Hold your horses – you two are just going to sit here and tell me that Bud and that young couple was killed by a monster! Hell-fire and brimstone . . . Rob Richards was going on about Big Foot attacking him. Now don't tell me you two are saying Big Foot's running around attacking and killing people, you two high on something? . . . I sure as shit hope so . . . I sure as shit hope you're not even suggesting. You're serious, Bud's dead? – God almighty!"

Doc just shook his head back and forth. He had a slight grin on his face as if he was waiting for the punch line of the joke.

Ian thought hard about how he was going to present the rest of it . . . There simply was no way to tell it and not sound like both he and Charlie were, nuts! With that, Ian decided to just go for it and deal with damage control after the fact.

"Well, to call a spade a spade so to speak – the monster we're speaking of is both a man as well as a wolf-like beast."

Doc Matthews looked from Ian to Charlie and back at Ian . . . Looking for any sign that they were anything less than completely serious. Doc didn't know Ian, but he knew Charlie. Whatever they were talking about . . . Charlie believed every word that was coming from Ian's mouth.

"Wait just a minute . . . Wolf-beast? Are you trying to tell me . . . now let me get this straight. No, no don't tell me . . . this is going too far – you don't expect me to believe for an instant . . . that you've been chasing around after some kind of . . . Werewolf . . . ?"

Both Ian and Charlie looked directly at Doc Matthews while shaking their heads yes! All three men then turned simultaneously to look at Tom; who had managed to grunt barely loud enough to be heard. Hearing Doc's reaction to what Ian had been saying Tom had tears streaming from the corners of his eyes. He gasped for air over and over. Trying with all his might to summon the strength necessary to communicate. To make Doc understand a fraction of the nightmare vision that held his severed psyche in gridlock. After what appeared to Ian, Charlie and Doc to be several excruciatingly painful and exhaustive attempts; Tom finally managed to summon what little was left of his severely bent mind, just enough to scream. *"Were . . . Werewolf!"*

He was then over-come by what Doc Matthews would later describe as a grand-mal seizure followed by a massive coronary. After twenty minutes of non-stop CPR administered by Doc Matthews until Doc was nearly to a point of collapsing himself. He looked for a second over at Charlie who stood next to him at the exam table. Charlie shook his head back and forth indicating that Doc had made a valiant effort; but that it was time to stop. Doc nodded in agreement then glanced up at the clock and noted the time. The now unnaturally blue-tone wide eyed rigid body of Tom Iverson KATW channel 13 news cameraman lay lifeless.

Ian thought to himself while pacing back and forth . . . *Regardless of what Doc chooses to write in his report as the actual cause of this mans death. The plain and simple truth was – Tom had been scared to death!*

CHAPTER 36

WITHOUT SPEAKING A word Doc Matthews momentarily left Charlie and Ian. He returned less than a minute later with a white cotton sheet that he placed over the body covering the face of Tom Iverson.

Doc's entire mood had changed. He sat down and motioned for both Ian and Charlie to do the same. Then suddenly to both Charlie and Ian's surprise Doc spoke very calmly, "All right, it's clear to me that this television cameraman had been severely traumatized by something . . . Something he'd seen. And due to the nature of his work he's no doubt seen his share of terrible things. Yet something frightened this man to the point of – well, he must have seen something beyond that of say normal human experience to put him in such a state as he was when you brought him to me. I should have taken that more seriously than I did, for that I'm sorry! As for the rest of what you were telling me, I don't know what I believe. But it's clear to me that you two believe it. And I've known Charlie all his life – he's not the sort to make up fantastic stories. So I guess you two are at least telling me the truth based on what you believe you saw. And something with powerful claws tore through Charlie's protective clothing, gashed him up and broke his ribs. You say that shirt you were wearing, its fabric was Kevlar?"

Charlie nodded yes, "Hmm, your wounds, are very similar to some of the wounds I saw on Rob Richards. Okay, I'm willing to accept that there is some kind of rogue beast out there."

Charlie then began to go into detail about how he'd found Bud's, head. And how he'd stored the head in his freezer chest and the reasons why. Charlie then asked Doc for advice on how he and Ian should proceed; based on the presumption that everything they'd told him was fact. As the hours past . . . Doc was becoming more and more convinced that what he was being told by both Charlie and Ian was even as fantastic as it sounded, the truth.

"Doc I'm telling you straight. I saw Jean-Chastel turn into a, well hell a werewolf best describes it, right before my eyes! Ian didn't see him make the change. But Ian saw him after he'd changed into what he did!"

Ian spoke up without hesitation with a very excited almost out of breath sound resonating in his voice. "What I saw, it was no normal animal! Don't even suggest that it could have been a bear reared up on its hind legs or nothing like that. I saw it plain as I see you now. The sky was clear and the Moon was full, plenty of light. I'm telling you Doc . . . This thing mostly resembles a wolf, but it can stand and walk upright like a man. It even looked to me like it probably has an opposable appendage like a thumb of sorts. My bet is it can grasp objects. Oh, and when it struck Charlie . . . I mean it sent him flying like he was a rag doll. What are you Charlie, about six one or two . . . ? I'm guessing two-twenty, two-twenty five . . . ?"

Charlie replied, "Yeah, that's about right."

Ian jumped in, "Doc, the thing towered over Charlie . . . It's huge! I mean it must have been nearly eight feet tall and it's got to be . . . I mean by the look of it . . . and the depth of its tracks that we saw . . . It's very heavy! God knows what it weighs. And when it finally took off running . . . it took off on two legs. But after a few yards it dropped down onto all fours. I tell you when it hit all fours, it took off like a bat out of hell. I'd guess it was moving at thirty-five maybe forty miles-an-hour when it hit full stride!"

Doc rubbed his chin, took a deep breath then interjected.

"Why you figure . . . I mean if this beast was a big as you say it was . . . Why'd it take off running . . . I mean couldn't it have easily killed you both . . . ?"

Ian thought about that question for a couple seconds . . . Charlie didn't reply. He was waiting to hear what Ian was going to say in response to that very good question.

"Doc, it's like we've been trying to tell you . . . It's both beast and a man. No doubt even in its beast form it retains at least some human intelligence. It heard me clearly state that my gun was loaded with silver bullets!"

Doc Matthews smiled and shook his head, before replying to Ian's decleration of having his gun loaded with silver bullets.

"Silver bullets! – are you serious?"

Charlie finally could sit on the sidelines no longer.

"That's right Doc . . . we had old Charbonneau the gunsmith make us up some silver bullets for Ian's pistol. And damn good thing we did . . . cause I figure if we hadn't . . . if that thing hadn't ran at the thought of getting shot with silver – well, we wouldn't be here talking to you about it now. Cause one more thing you should know. I shot the thing point-blank in the center of its chest with my rifle. My rifle was loaded to bring down an elephant. And all it did was piss the thing off! You know me Doc. I'm handy as hell with a rifle – I don't miss, especially point blank. And where I found Bud's . . . head . . . His shotgun was on the ground surrounded by prints in the mud of the thing . . . along with three spent shotgun shells strewn about. You tell me Doc, you've been hunting dozens of times with Bud – you ever known Bud O'Brien to shoot at any animal and not bring it down dead-bang! Let alone after firing three times with heavy load buckshot?"

Doc Matthews just set there with an expression of concern on his face. One that nearly mirrored the depth of conviction to their story that was equally shared by Charlie and Ian. Doc had point of fact been convinced, nearly anyway.

Doc slapped his knees with the palms of his hands. He stood up, took a long deep breath, then spoke, "Okay . . . fellows you didn't hear this from me. But as far as dealing with the fact that you froze Bud's head, and drove Bud's Blazer to Charlie's house . . . I recommend you drive the Blazer back up to Little Merwin. Park it near that television van. Now aside from dental records . . . Well, fire does one hell of a job of making it difficult if not impossible to tell whether something has been tampered with, frozen, or otherwise. Also, from what I know about that hermit Jean-Chastel . . . I'd bet dollars to doughnuts there aren't any dental records to concern yourself with as far as dealing with his remains if you get my drift. Now that's all I have to say about any of this . . . You two need to get back up there and finish this thing before he sets out to finish you! You represent a real threat to him. You believe you know what he is. You know where he lives and maybe how to deal with him . . . he knows this too! So that makes you a priority target! Chastel's either gonna pull up stakes and high-tail it out of here. Or, he's gonna stand his ground. If he eliminates you and the evidence, he's pretty much home free. But like I said before . . . I'm not telling you or suggesting that you do anything, nothing at all – you heard none of this from me. I've got my own worries with reporting this television mans death. By the way, I'll need at least one of your signatures as witnesses on the death certificate . . . but we'll concern ourselves with all that later. You two get going . . . sunrise is suppose to be at 5:40 am – you're gonna want to be up there before first light. It's already too light from the full Moon to offer much cover. But maybe if you're lucky you can sneak back up to his place and catch him off guard. He probably figures he hurt Charlie more than he did. Maybe he figures he scared the hell out of both of you so he's got some time. He might figure you guys won't be coming back his way for a while. Who knows, like I said, you might get lucky! If he's anything like you say . . . he's probably very nocturnal. Hell, he's got to sleep sometime! God almighty – it hasn't even sunk in with me that Bud got himself killed. Let alone by some kind of monster! Charlie you got a beautiful wife and fine young boy to get back to. Ian, you seem like a likeable sort. Both of you take caution, and come back in one piece!"

Ian finally summoned the courage to hand over to Doc his notepad with the drawing he'd made of the beast.

Doc took the notebook, opened it up and started looking at Ian's sketch. Surprising to both Charlie and Ian – Doc had nothing smart-alecky to say about it. In fact he seemed intrigued by the drawing but said nothing regarding . . . Doc continued . . .

"By the way Charlie, there's a couple reasons beyond what you've told me; that even as crazy as this all sounds, I am finding myself believing at least some of it. Jeremy and his gal friend Katie . . . they both gave pretty much the same description of that thing as you two . . . and there's more! I read in the newspaper this morning that Rob Richards up and disappeared from that Portland hospital. The article said he was bedded in a room by himself on the six floor. A nurse making her midnight rounds found the window in his room busted out. A search of the parking lot below showed no sign that he'd jumped. They did spot some rain-smeared bloody paw prints around the glass from the shattered window. The prints were thought to have come from a very large dog that had stepped on the broken glass. The sixth floor hall-way security camera tapes were reviewed . . . Rob didn't leave by way of the front door if you get my meaning."

Charlie and Ian looked back and forth at each other . . . Ian began shaking his head as he thought to himself. *That's right, Rob Richards was bitten! Christ, him disappearing like that would have been useful information to have known earlier.*

Doc continued, "Charlie, that kid of yours has got a good head on his shoulders. Make sure you two return with yours!"

CHAPTER 37

Incineration
3:00 am

CHARLIE AND IAN had just left Doc Matthews. Charlie was driving back to his house to retrieve his former bosses Chevy Blazer and . . . head.

Ian stayed in the car while Charlie went into the house to fetch the keys to the Blazer. No lights came on within the house and he was back out in less than a minute. Ian guessed that Charlie managed to not wake his wife or son. Charlie went and got a gas can from his garage. Ian noticed by the way Charlie was lugging the can it must have been full. Charlie set the gas can in the backend of the Blazer. Then Charlie returned to his garage and completed the grizzly task of retrieving the frozen head of the former Bud O'Brien from the freezer chest. He placed the black plastic bagged head into the trunk of his car.

Ian almost leaped out of the car when he saw Charlie open the trunk to place the head within. Charlie then walked over to Ian and handed him the keys to the Blazer. Ian agreed to drive the Blazer and follow Charlie back up to Little Merwin.

Both men climbed into their vehicles. Ian drove the Blazer from behind Charlies garage around the block. He met up with Charlie in the front of his home. Ian then noticed Elaine was watching the two men from the front window, as they pulled away from the house.

Once again Ian was amazed by Elaine Redtail. Who he now surmised must have at least a notion as to what they were up to. Either by what Charlie might have told her during the very brief time he was inside the house . . . Or, somehow like other things . . . she just knew.

Little Merwin Lake – 4:30 am

Charlie and Ian arrived at Little Merwin. The Moonlit night was beginning to give way to the forthcoming daylight.

Charlie climbed out of his car and walked briskly up to Ian who was still seated in the Blazer. Ian opened the drivers door, hoped out of the Blazer and joined Charlie. Both men just stood leaning up against the Blazer. A couple seconds passed while Charlie further contemplated their next move.

"Ian here's how I see it. Now if you spot any holes in my plan don't be shy. I want to hear bout it – okay?"

Ian smiled at Charlie with a reassuring smile and nodded gesturing a resounding yes . . . indicating clear, that he'd speak out with any disagreement or suggestion of alternative ideas if need be.

"All right . . . I say we splash gas all over inside both the van and the Blazer – we torch them big time! We carry the gas can up to Chastel's cabin and do the same up there. I haven't got all the details worked out. We're gonna have to play some of this as it comes. First I'm gonna move my car far away from the van and Blazer – don't want my car going up in flames leaving us stuck up here with no ride home."

Ian could see by the way Charlie was carrying himself that his side was hurting him bad. He could also see Charlie was one tough son-of-a-bitch by the way he didn't make anything of it.

Charlie decided that he'd leave his rifle in his car. He'd just carry his Glock shoulder holstered so he could carry other things like gas or the head of his dead best friend.

Charlie continued, "On the drive up here I did a lot of figuring. At first I thought we should torch Buds head inside his Blazer . . . But that didn't fit into the story I'm working on. One that later will explain certain things, and be a believable story. Anyway, I figure I'll pack Buds head up to Chastel's and place it in that shed with his other parts. Well, and other folks parts as well I reckon. But anyway, we'll then torch that shed. They'll be able to identify Bud's skull by dental records. And that's good. That's what we want, to pin this where it belongs . . . all on Chastel. It's good and bad that it's not raining and windy. The rain masks scent and makes moving around without being heard much easier. But at least we won't get too soaked. We're gonna still get plenty wet from the wet branches and such that we got to make our way through."

Ian didn't really comprehend the whole picture . . . But regardless he felt trusting Charlie was as good an idea as not. Ian replied . . .

"Okay, all right Charlie . . . sounds right, that's our plan then."

Charlie fetched the gas can from the Blazer – then set Bud's head far away from both the Blazer and the van. Charlie heavily dowsed both vehicles inside and out with gas. He then created a trail of gas on the ground that branched out to both vehicles. Charlie took the gas can and set it far away from danger, over next to Buds head. Then after what seemed an eternity of final contemplation focused on details . . . but was in reality less than a minute. Charlie glanced one last time over at Ian. Ian nodded yes; once again showing his solidarity regarding the plan. Charlie then lit a match and tossed it onto the gas trail . . . within seconds both vehicles were raging infernos.

Charlie walked as fast as he could and picked up both the gas can and the bag containing Buds head. Ian caught up to Charlie in seconds. Charlie held out the bag just to see if Ian would without thinking instinctually reach to take it. Ian looked at Charlie with disgust knowing that Charlie was just trying a bit of levity to ease the tension. Ian then reached over and took from Charlie's other hand the now less than half-full six gallon plastic gas can.

As Charlie and Ian looked intently around the scene . . . Both men suddenly realized the remains of Marsha Steward was nowhere in site. Without speaking of it – they both surmised to themselves that her head and torso had most likely been hauled-off by Chastel . . . to likely serve later as his breakfast, lunch or dinner.

Both men knew they needed to put serious distance between themselves and the burning vehicles as quickly as possible. Charlie and Ian started heading towards the falls and the pathway which led up the mountain; at a pace that was just short of jogging.

This time they didn't bother bringing flashlights. The unwanted truth was it would be daylight before they could reach the cabin even if they could maintain their present pace; which both men knew they couldn't!

CHAPTER 38

Harsh

CHARLIE AND IAN reached Harmony Falls . . . Ian looked over at Charlie who was holding onto his side and breathing hard and shallow.

"Charlie, lets take a quick breather before we head on up the trail."

Charlie looked at Ian who appeared to be fit and ready to continue. He immediately realized Ian was just thinking of him.

"Nah, Ian, it's okay. I appreaciate the thought. But we've got to get up there before Chastel has had time to high-tail it on out of here. Ha! . . . high-tail . . . that's a good one, get it, tail . . . ?" Charlie managed a small laugh. Ian smiled both at Charlie's comment, as well as his unrelenting determination.

Ian reached over to Charlie and took hold of the bag containing Buds head. Charlie held firm to the bag for a couple of seconds. Then after seeing that Ian was determined to relieve him from the burden of his load. Charlie let go of the bag. He stood there for a moment looking at Ian who now was carrying in one hand the half-filled gas can – and Bud's head in the other.

"Ian you sure you can handle all that? We've still got a good hike on our hands from here to Chastel's cabin – all uphill from here."

Ian smiled at Charlie, "I'll make it, no worries! I'll set the load down, rest my arms now and again as I need to."

The truth was Ian didn't know if could make it that far with that much load or not. But he was determined to give it his all!

Just then Charlie and Ian were mildly startled by hearing two explosions that happened in succession. The noise came from way back in the direction of the parking area. Both men knew the explosions were the *grand finale* of Bud's Blazer and the van that they'd torched not ten minutes previously.

Ian looked at Charlie, "That wasn't all that loud, was it? You don't figure Chastel could have heard that from way up the mountain . . . could he?"

Charlie shook his head no as he replied, "Not likely, even if he's got some kind of heightened hearing . . . too much forest and up and down terrain between here and there to muffle the sound . . . at least I hope!"

The two men started up the trail heading to the cabin. Charlie led the way. His pace was now considerably slower than what was typical for him. Ian knew it was due to the level of pain Charlie was in. And for Ian's benefit as well.

Charlie glanced back over his shoulder towards Ian.

"Maybe Chastel can only make the change at night . . . ?"

Ian didn't answer right away. After several long seconds of contemplation he replied, "Well, if werewolf-ism stays consistent with most of the legends from not only central Europe; but all around the world. Including as you know native Americans. Though the stories vary a lot culture to culture. Most agree on one thing. The classic shape-shifter can make the change at will, day or night. Though I believe based on what I've heard and read; its powers are directly linked, they are associated with the cycles of the Moon. So, if I had to make a wild guess. I'd say our guy can make the change into the beast anytime. But I'm guessing his powers and strength are less during the day than at night. And are greater when the Moon is full or nearly full, than other times of the lunar cycle. The reason I believe in the idea that the shape-shifter can change anytime. If you think about it. It's always nighttime somewhere. The Moon is always out somewhere in the world. But again, this is only speculation. Hey I know – we could always ask Chastel!"

Charlie didn't look back. Ian saw him shake his head back and forth and herd him chuckle a shallow laugh as he replied.

"Yeah, you can do the asking . . ."

Charlie and Ian continued their trek up the pathway for nearly an hour. They finally came upon the open clearling. They stayed near the tree-line and kept as low as they could. They kept moving forward and uphill until they could see it. There it was, Chastel's cabin. Smoke was pouring from the Chimney.

Charlie and Ian crouched down onto their knees staring at the cabin which was around a hundred yards from their position. Ian was relieved to finally be able to once again set his load down. His arms ached severely from carrying the gas can and bagged head non-stop for the last half mile.

As they contemplated their next move, their luck along with the weather, changed. The early morning sky grew dark as charcoal gray clouds suddenly came rolling in from seemingly nowhere. The storm clouds were now directly above them and filled the sky for as far as they could see in every direction. Thunder started to roar. There were a couple flashes of lightening off in the distance. Then all at once the heavens opened up with near golf-ball sized hail-stones. Charlie and Ian were being bombarded; they pulled their jackets over their heads, and moved under an enormous fir tree thats canopy offered some protection. Then to their great relief the hail began to lessen. Unfortunately, the reprieve only lasted for a couple of minutes before the weather switched from hail stones to torrential rain mixed with snow. The temperature in minutes went from tolerably cold, to near freezing – as a great north wind swept across the mountain side. Old growth fir trees, giant monoliths that had withstood for decades all that mother nature could unleash. Began succumbing to the great winds. The typical forest sounds of birds and small furry creatures ceased to be audible. All Charlie and Ian could hear was the near deafening sound of the roaring wind and massive trees whose branches whipped wildly. Ian couldn't help but flinch now and again from the occasional massive cracking and snapping sounds created by storm defeated branches that periodically would crash down onto the forest floor. Both men were drenched head to toe.

Charlie's long gray streaked ebony hair which he wore pulled-back in a pony-tail had come undone from the strong winds. Even heavy soaked – his hair blew in every direction. Large strands relentlessly would stick across his face; forcing him to continuously wipe icy water and hair from his eyes. Ian began to shiver uncontrollably. But Charlie could see clear enough that Ian was beginning to succumb to the severity of the near freezing effects created by the storm. Charlie spoke with just enough volume for Ian to hear him above the whipping wind and pounding snowy-rain. Both men strained to hold their heads up just to look at each other to communicate. Their eyes stung from the sideways blowing snow and rain as it hammered their faces and made numb their exposed hands.

Charlie knew making a move on Chastel was either now or never!

CHAPTER 39

All In

CHARLIE STOOD THREE quarters upright and motioned for Ian to follow. Ian picked up his two loads and stood crouched over as both men proceeded stealth-fully towards Chastel's cabin.

Once the two men were within fifty yards of the cabin Charlie motioned for Ian to come close to him. Charlie leaned up against a large fir tree and clenched his side. He was breathing rapidly with short choppy breaths.

Ian could see by the look on Charlie's face, and by the way he was now holding himself even tighter than before; that Charlie was more than just in pain – he was in trouble! Charlie spoke to Ian in just above a whisper. "Ian, I wish I could tell you otherwise. But this is gonna be largely up to you now. I'm pretty much spent. If you don't want to go through with this . . . hell, I'd be the last man on Earth to fault you for it. Tell ya the truth my side feels like it's about to burst open and spill my guts out. It's just about to double me over. I can't even hold a weapon with a steady hand, let alone fire one."

Ian looked deep into Charlie's eyes. He then saw blood was forming around the hand Charlie held his side with. The gashes that Doc had taped-up were opening up again. Ian remembered Doc had said *the x-rays showed a couple cracked ribs.* And though he didn't think likely, he didn't completely rule out that there could be some possible organ damage as well. One thing Ian knew for certain, Charlie was tough, double tough! And for Charlie to admit to succumbing to pain – that was all Ian needed to hear to immagine just how bad Charlie was hurting.

Ian very quietly replied, "Charlie, if you can hold on a while longer . . . I figure we didn't come all this way not to see this thing through. As I'm sure you know, I'm no hero. But god-damn-it . . . that thing attacked and killed those hikers and Bud. Hell, it damn near killed your son and his girlfriend. It probably turned that local fellow who was hospitalized into a monster too. So for their sake, and anyone else that thing has or will slaughter or infect with the curse of the beast. We're gonna finish this thing or die trying. Should the worst happen . . . I can accept that. But after all we know, all we've seen with our own eyes – things that nobody will ever believe. Hell, even if somehow we could prove Chastel's the killer, keeping the whole werewolf thing out of it. What jail cell could ever hold him? Even if he got the death penalty. It could never successfully be carried out! Christ the only capital punishment that would work would be decapitation, possibly total incineration, or death by a firing squad using silver bullets! Nah, the only way I see it . . . we've got to put a stop to Chastel here and now ourselves. Or, he will go on and on for generations killing and infecting! But don't worry too much . . . cause just between you and me . . . I've got no intentions on dieing here today. I'm, we're, gonna put that thing down and for good! All I ask Charlie is we form a pact. If Chastel does attack us and one of us, you know, was to get bitten and lives through it . . ."

Charlie looked deep into Ian's eyes . . . Charlie nodded his head, yes. It wasn't necessary for Ian to complete that sentence. He understood and agreed.

Leaning there against the tree trying his best to catch his breath. Charlie who over the last couple days had grown to really like Ian; now additionally had tremendous respect for him as well. Up until that moment. Charlie had largely felt that Ian though likeable and capable; was predominantly a passionless man. One who was drowning in self-pity and giving up on himself and the world. All be it for reasons Charlie could understand. Charlie could easily see himself climbing into a bottle and losing his reason to live, if he was to lose Elaine and Jeremy; like Ian had lost his wife and daughter to such a senseless tragedy.

What Charlie saw in Ian as he looked deep into his eyes, was a man who had undergone a total reclamation. Ian was now as Charlie had imagined him to have been not so long ago. A confident, courageous, focused man of purpose and conviction. Somehow through the course of recent horrific events; Ian had managed to salvage himself.

Charlie thought to himself how pressure and situations of great stress effect people different. *Some bluff . . . Some fold . . . Some raise!* Ian had just gone . . . *All in!*

CHAPTER 40

Surprise

SPEAKING IN LITTLE more than a whisper . . .

"So what's the plan . . . ?" Ian asked Charlie as they both looked up ahead at Chastel's cabin. Smoke was pouring from the chimney. It billowed in every direction from the strong wind. The ever changing storm had once again transformed – from its former existence represented as near forty mile-an-hour sideways blowing wind and torrential rain mixed with snow. Now to blizzard-like snow-fall. The temperature continued to drop.

Charlie gasped for air, "Ian, you're in charge now!"

Ian knew he had to think of something and by the looks of the way Charlie was now shivering . . . the sooner the better!

"Okay . . . All right, Charlie you follow behind me up to say around thirty feet or so in front of the Cabin. Then lay down on your gut facing the cabin. That way you can rest your pistol on the ground. You're gonna cover me. Your gun might not be lethal to him. But I'm guessing it don't do him no good neither. It probably will sure as shit sting like a son-of-a-bitch if you open up on him. Something like you or I getting shot with pellets. Now, I'm gonna get close. I'm not gonna knock or anything. I'm going straight in and fast. Maybe, if I'm lucky, I can catch him by surprise! I'll open fire on him on site. If it takes silver to bring him down – hell, I don't want to miss, I've only got three silver bullets. We might only get the one chance if you know what I mean!"

Charlie was now shivering uncontrollably. He managed to shake his head in agreement with the plan.

Ian picked up the gas can and the black plastic garbage bag. He and Charlie began the final march towards the cabin. The bag Ian carried was starting to make crunching crackling sounds with each step he took. The bag along with its prior partially thawed grizzly contents was beginning to re-freeze. They bowed their heads attempting to protect their faces from the blowing frigid snow. Steamy vapors now more visible than before created by the plummeting cold and their heavy breathing from fatigue – exited their mouths and noses with each breath.

Ian with Charlie close behind, slowly began their final assault on the hillside leading to the cabins front. As they walked up the hill due to the snow – they now had to high-lift their knees with every step as they trudged ahead. The snow was accumulating in depth by the moment. By the looks of the clouds in the sky above them and all around, it wasn't going to be letting up anytime soon. Ian glanced back over his shoulder at Charlie, whose face was nearly covered with ice and snow. Tiny icicles hung from the bangs of his long hair. Ian was beginning to worry that especially due to Charlie's weakened condition; frost bite and hypothermia could very soon become a real threat. Perhaps as great a threat as the one they would soon be facing up ahead in the cabin. They were completely exposed, and not just to the harshness of the elements. They now stood out boldly in contrast to the newly formed white world that encompassed them.

Most of their hopes for a stealthy approach had now been eradicated by the storm. The only thing remaining in their favor was the noise created by the wind and snow. That at least offered them some hope that they still might be able to successfully launch a surprise assault.

Charlie and Ian now stood hunched-over around thirty feet from Chastel's cabin. Charlie looked into Ian's eyes then nodded he was ready. He then proceeded to unsheathe his pistol from his shoulder holster. Charlie then chambered a round and made ready his weapon. He then dropped to his knees and proceeded to lay belly down onto the frigid snowy ground. Charlie held his Glock with both hands, aimed at the cabin's front door just as Ian had planned.

Without hesitation Ian set down his loads. He bent over and retrieved from his ankle holster his thirty-two. Ian made double certain it was primed and ready. His first three rounds, pure silver.

Ian glanced over at Charlie, "Okay, let's do this!"

Ian started towards the cabin. He made sure to stay just over to the side far enough to allow Charlie a clean shot in the direction of the doorway.

Ian picked up his pace. His heart was now pounding so hard it felt as though any moment it might burst through his chest. But he kept on moving faster and faster. When he'd reached just a few feet from the cabin – Ian turned his body sideways, ran and slammed his right shoulder into the front door with everything he had. The door broke-away from its hinges upon impact. It didn't offer anywhere near the resistance he'd figured on. Ian crashed into the one-room dwelling, slipped on the bear-skin rug – and fell smack onto his back in the center of the room. Upon impact Ian's head flopped back and struck the solid wood floor; his pistol slipped his grasp and slid across the room. Ian was completely stunned, barely conscious and couldn't move. He gasped with all his might for air, but none would come. The wind had been completely knocked out of him. Ian laid momentarily helpless, barely conscious. He was acutely aware with empirical clarity of one thing. If Chastel was in the room or nearby . . . if found in his present dazed condition and weaponless, he would be a dead man!

After a few seconds had passed, which to Ian seemed like an eternity – with great difficulty Ian finally managed to re-inflate his lungs. His breath came back to him, first in short painful sips; then moments later he was able to take-in a full chest expanding, gasping gulp of air.

Ian finally was able to turn over, place both hands on the floor and lumber himself up onto his left knee. He then straightened himself up, recovered his balance and raised himself the rest of the way up onto his feet and quickly retrieved his pistol. Ian walked to the threshold of the front door-way and gave Charlie a thumbs up, indicating that he was okay. He then waved his left hand repeatedly towards himself, signaling Charlie to join him inside the cabin.

CHAPTER 41

Mark of the Beast

IAN NOTICED THAT Charlie had troubles of his own standing up. But once on his feet Charlie seemed to be better from the rest.

In mere moments Charlie joined Ian inside the cabin. Ian was holding his pistol in his right hand and was panning his eyes and his gun all around the room.

Charlie paused in the doorway to check out the remains of Ian's frontal assault. The door-frame was completely busted into fragments. The door itself was completely in tact, but it now laid predominately on the floor, barely hanging onto its twisted beyond repair lower hinge.

Charlie spoke in a quiet voice, "Nice entrance, Ian . . . Subtle!"

Ian couldn't help but chuckle just a little – at the thought of what he must have looked like when he burst through the door and fell flat on his back!

He then looked directly at Charlie and replied, but not to Charlie's last comment.

"Well, it's nice to see you're still among the living."

Ian then pointed to a number of icy mud-covered old tin coffee cans. The cans were sitting dripping muddy water and snow atop an old hand-crafted table that set up against the cabin-wall. The cans hadn't been there long; they were still mostly covered with snow.

"Charlie, check out all those dirty, snow-covered coffee cans. Hey, and what's that, is that money in them?"

Ian exclaimed in a near normal volume – temporarily forgetting to keep his voice down low.

Not a second after the words escaped Ian's lips – the cabin back door flew open, and in bounded Jean-Chastel Gevaudan. He was carrying a shovel in his right hand and in his left hand and arm, he carried four more mud and snow covered coffee-cans. One can, he held with his left hand, the other three cans he held pressure-pinned, cradled against his large chest.

Upon seeing his unwanted guests. Chastel immediately dropped the coffee cans and began moving swiftly, straight for Ian.

"So you think you can challenge me . . . Me! . . . Who has feasted on man for centuries . . . Know well who kills you . . . I, Jean-Chastel, subjugate legionnaire of Samyaza!"

Chastel then raised his shovel and swung at Ian's head. Ian managed to duck and leap backwards as he fired one round at Chastel. One round which missed its target badly. Chastel's mighty swing of his shovel just missed Ian's skull by inches. Charlie who was around ten feet from Chastel leveled his pistol at Chastels face and squeezed. His first shot struck Chastel in the side of his forehead. Blood and bone fragments sprayed the wall behind. Not a second passed before Charlie lowered his weapon slightly. Still holding his pistol with both hands, Charlie squeezed-off two more rounds in rapid succession. Both were marksman targeted heart-stoppers. Chastel realled backwards from the concussive impact. Ian was momentarily stunned. His mind hadn't caught up with all that occurred in what had been less than thirty seconds.

Ian looked at Charlie . . . nerve charged adrenaline surged through him. Ian began shaking as he stood looking down at Chastel – who not a second earlier had dropped onto his knees, and then onto the floor face down just a few feet from him.

"Charlie, you got him . . . you got him good! It must not take silver if you get him in the head. Doesn't take silver if you blow its brains out, I guess!"

Charlie kept his gun pointed at Chastel as he slowly approached the body.

Ian went over to the table to have a closer look inside the coffee cans.

"My God . . . Charlie, there's hundreds and hundreds of dollars in these cans. Some of the money looks old . . . real old!"

Charlie was now standing over Chastel's body, watching for any signs of movement, as he replied, "Yeah, well that makes sense. He runs a still . . . sells shine to folks, mostly dregs on the rez. He's been doing odd jobs, accepting only cash for hell, who knows how long – century's maybe? He doesn't put his money in banks, that would create a paper trail. He buries his money in cans in the backyard and such. He was probably digging up his loot, getting ready to split. You know, needed some traveling money to make good his escape!"

Ian shook his head in agreement, "Yeah, in this economy . . . I guess even a monster needs money to travel now-a-days!"

Both men laughed a nervous laugh at Ian's levity.

Charlie looked for a moment directly at Ian, who was picking up the cans that Chastel had dropped onto the floor. Ian set the cans onto the table alongside the others. He then started emptying the contents of the tin-cans onto the table, to count the loot.

"Hey Charlie, I wonder if there are more of these money cans still buried around out back?"

Before Charlie could answer. He was startled to the point of near heart-attack. Charlie let out a very uncharacteristic screaming yell while simultaneously looking down at his ankle; which had one nano-second earlier suddenly felt like it was being squeezed by a vice. Ian instantly jumped nearly out of his skin at Charlie's shriek. He lost all concentration on the filthy green-backs that he was stacking into neat piles of likewise denominations as he spun-around to see what had Charlie so spooked. Then in an instant Ian saw what Charlie was seeing. Chastel was not dead, not by a long shot. He was making the change, and making it fast!

The hand that held Charlie pinned by his ankle was no longer a human hand. It was now something else entirely. Hairy, clawed, and thickly muscular. Chastel was rapidly bursting through his clothing. He was getting larger and hairier by the second. His body was morphing, making the change into the beast faster than either could comprehend.

With no more then a second of hesitation . . . Ian stepped around Charlie to get a clear shot at the thing that held Charlie tight within its grasp. Suddenly Chastel raised his head from its face-down to the floor position . . . he let out a piercing howl! Ian fired two silver-bullet rounds at point blank range into the back of Chastel's head. Bone, blood and brains spewed, flowing in every direction around Ian and Charlie's feet. Charlie managed to kick his ankle free from the beasts grip. Both men stared at a scar-like marking on the palm of the claw that was slowly reconfiguring into the hand of a man. The marking appeared to be shaped like a five pointed star. Ian recognized the symbol from what he'd read on the subject of werewolves – he took a deep breath then spoke.

"That star-shaped scar on Chastel's hand . . . I believe that's referred to as the "*Mark of the Beast!*" A five-pointed star like that, or pentagram . . . in Carpathian and Gypsy folklore, well, a mark like that on the body is supposed to mean that person has been cursed; it means that person is possessed by a demon. I tell you Charlie . . . even in my line of work, I never much believed in any of that sort of thing. But my eyes have been opened. And my mind . . . my mind has been blown, wide-open! Never again am I gonna just summarily dismiss the possibility, well hell, of just about anything! You and I know that the legends were all pretty much true regarding werewolves. That said . . . think about it – what else could be real?"

Charlie raised his eyebrows and shook his head in agreement. He then picked-up the shovel that Chastel had only moments ago tried to pummel Ian's brains from his skull with.

Charlie took a deep breath then exclaimed almost shouting.

"This is to be certain!"

He spun the shovel within his hands around until the shovels head was positioned in such a manor necessary for use as a wood-be ax. Charlie then elevated the shovel well above his head and in one deft motion swung it down; plummeting the edge of the shovel mightily to the back of Chastel's neck. Charlie instantly had completely decapated the beast-man.

"That was for Bud, you son-of-a-bitch!" Is all Charlie spoke for the next several seconds as he dropped the shovel to the floor. Suddenly becoming out of breath and breathing shallow, Charlie clutched-hold of his side. The adrenaline serge was wearing thin and fast; he was rapidly once again succumbing to the pain and trauma of his wounds.

Then right before their astonished eyes, Chastel began a rapid transformation – but this time in full reverse . . . from the beast, back to his former human self.

Ian wasn't all that undone by what had occurred. It was almost like the supernatural, had become natural. Gore and horror had become the norm over the last couple of days. And somehow at the moment this seemed to him to be little more than just another days work.

Ian knew it would take perhaps years of studying all the facts and filling in the blanks with suppositions and conjecture; to even begin to comprehend let alone explain the very existence of this enigma that was the man-monster: Jean-Chastel Gevaudan.

Ian thought to himself – *Samyaza, Chastel said Samyaza . . . Where have I heard that word before? – well, now's not the time to be thinking about . . . We have much more pressing issues that are gonna require explanations – especially the decapitation of Gevaudan!*

Ian understood with crystal clarity that now was the time for men of action to take action! To take any and all steps necessary to keep the two of them from spending the rest of their lives in prison. Or, perhaps worse . . . on – *death row!*

Ian looked over at Charlie . . . It was though the two men were sharing the same thoughts.

Charlie nodded it was time to finish this thing.

Both men exited the cabin. Ian went back to where he'd set down the black plastic bagged head of Bud O'Brien; he picked it up and hurried back to the cabin.

Charlie took the bagged head of his dead best friend from Ian – he then began walking towards the shed out back of the cabin. When he got to the shed without hesitation he opened the door – the stench and flies overwhelmed him, he began to gag. Charlie could take a lot but this was more than he could bare. Quickly, without stepping inside the shed; which was full of corporial remains. Charlie with outstretched arms, turned the bag upside down and let Bud's head drop and role around until it came to rest on top of the other rotting body parts. Charlie then tossed the plastic bag into the shed; closed its door, and hastened his pace to get back to re-join Ian. Charlie could have gone through the cabins back door. But that would have meant he'd of had to step-over Chastel's dead body. And he'd been told as a young boy by his Grandfather that was bad medicine. So he chose to walk around the side of the cabin to re-join Ian.

The storm had nearly passed. The wind was no longer blowing hard and the snow had stopped all together. Both Ian and Charlie thought to themselves. *Thank God for Small favors!*

The moment Charlie reunited with Ian, without saying a word, Charlie went back into the cabin. He fumbled through a couple of drawers in its wood-be kitchen until he found a knife to his liking. Charlie then went over to the lifeless remains of Chastel's head. He probed the knife around inside the head until he managed to dig-out Ian's two silver bullets, then put the two heavily disfigured silver slugs into his pants pocket. Charlie then pulled out his Glock, and at close range, he fired two shots into the back of Chastel's head; in the general angel as the entrée wounds made from Ian's rounds.

Ian flinched at hearing each shot fired; while he was out back dosing the shed with gas. After splashing gas all about the inside of the shed, Ian lit a match and set the shed ablaze. He then with gas can in hand marched around the cabin and re-joined Charlie.

Ian stood in the front doorway of the small pioneer-style cabin as he watched Charlie throw one after the other of Chastel's three glass hurricane oil lamps at the cabins inside walls. The lamps let out a loud crashing crackling sound as the glass globes and bases shattered from the forceful collisions; splashing the lantern glass and its previously contained oil across the walls and all over the floor inside the cabin. Charlie then motioned for Ian to come inside and empty the rest of the gas from the can he held all around inside the cabin. Ian did just that, the two of them were convinced that a blaze created by this much accelerant should no-doubt totally consume the place, leaving very little forensic evidence behind.

Once both men stood a couple feet outside the cabins front doorway, Charlie looked directly into Ian's eyes and spoke, "You got some matches left I hope!" Ian, shook his head yes.

Charlie took a deep breath . . . "All right then Ian, strike one up and torch this fucker!"

Ian threw the empty gas can into the cabin, it landed right next to the torso of Chastel. He then retrieved a match from his coat pocked. Struck it, and tossed it inside the cabin. Both men leaped and ran backwards as far as they could get from the cabin . . . In less than a second the entire inside of the cabin became transformed into an explosive raging inferno!

CHAPTER 42

The Story

CHARLIE TURNED TO Ian. "Okay . . . Ian, it happened like this! Acting as my deputy you and I came up here after getting a distress call for help from Bud. Bud said he had strong evidence the murderer was Chastel. But, by the time we arrived to the parking lot at Little Merwin we found Buds rig and the T.V. peoples van had been torched. On Bud's theory we came up here to question Chastel . . . Chastel had been busy torching his shed. You know, torching the remains of his victims that he'd put in the shed, including Bud's. When we caught up to him he'd already dug up cash to help with his get-a-away. He was inside his cabin, front door open. He'd been busy dousing the place with gas and lamp-oil. And he was about to light the place up. He must have figured that by torching his cabin he'd get rid of any other incriminating evidence. While still inside the cabin he must have spotted me near the entrance. You were behind me. Ian that bear skin rug, that will help explain some of the sightings of the beast. And further the story of his overall craziness. You see, I'll say Chastel was wearing what looked like a bear-skin rug pulled all around him. The head of the bear set on top of his head like a hat. Anyway, Chastel then struck a match and tossed it over his shoulder which started his cabin to burn. He then picked up the shovel that he'd been using to dig up his money. He then came at me. I shouted at him to stop, drop the shovel and all that. He didn't. I drew my weapon and fired several shots. I'll let them determine the number of shots from ballistics, if it even comes to that. Anyway, I'll say I believe that I hit him in the chest and maybe near the back of his head as he was spun-around from the impact of the chest shot. How many times and exactly where I shot him I can't be certain. It all happened so fast. Ian, I dug-out your silver slugs. And shot him in the holes your bullets made. Now my gun is a much larger caliber than yours so that should cover that well. And the fire will make determining most things very difficult. I'm intentionally gonna stay vague and inconclusive on certain aspects of my story. They get very suspicious if you've got a clear answer for every little detail. Anyway, now here's where my story does get a bit thin . . . but that's okay. These things rarely if ever make total inside the box sense. Anyway, we both saw Chastel get sent backward spinning around from the impact of my shots. He staggered around inside the blazing cabin and appeared to me to . . . though, I can't be certain. Now this is important . . . Ian, I saw this part, you didn't. It looked to me like he fell backward onto his shovel. I'll let them try and prove otherwise. You know, how it managed to decapitate him. The amount of impact that it would take, angles and all that . . . one things for sure. Stranger things have happened. Oh, and Ian . . . . don't get too concerned. The thing they want more than anything, is for the bad guy to have been caught. What they won't admit to but is nevertheless the truth. Even better, the perpetrator faced ultimate justice. Closure is what they all want. It's what they need! Especially the victims family's. They need to assign blame to hopefully a real bogeyman, a monster if you will. You know we have that covered. More than anything . . . they want all this to just go away. We have that covered as well. Ian believe me . . . the powers to be will want to case-close this as fast as possible, that I assure you! You and I will be the only ones who will ever know the whole truth. But think about this. What would be less believable. Our lie, our cover story . . . Or, the actual truth. Don't bother answering, we both know the answer to that. Ian, this story – it's the only way. At the end of the day – the guilty person was caught and judged the only way possible."

Ian, who had his head bowed during most of Charlie's little speech . . . raised his head and looked Charlie square in the eyes. Ian confidently shook his head in agreement to all that Charlie had said.

"Charlie of course you're right. You're story is basically identical to what I was going to suggest. Absolute truth in this case would land us both either on cell-block "C" or in the nut house. And like you said . . . what really matters is the guilty person was caught. And on behalf of Bud, and all the victims – justice was served best as possible. That's our story front to back. Anything beyond that goes with me to the grave – you have my word!"

Charlie looked deep into Ian's eyes. Charlie knew Ian spoke the truth.

"Say Ian . . . what was it that Chastel called himself . . . ? Something like a legionaire for Samy-something . . . ?"

Ian paused for just a second before replying, "Charlie, I think he said – Samyaza . . . I believe that's the name of a demon. A fallen angel cast from heaven for raping human women. Whereby creating giants and beast-like creatures called nephilim. To be cursed by the *mark of the beast* must have something to do with demonic possession. What's especially frightening to think about is . . . well, if werewolves exist. Then it makes a certain amount of sense that many other legends dismissed as myths may have their basis in fact. Maybe werewolves, vampires and all sorts of things that go bump in the night. Maybe much of it is real. Maybe werewolf-ism and vampire-ism spreads like an infection, through bites and such. But not so much as an infectious disease as we understand it. But that's how the demon transmits, takes possession. What's that the Bible says – I am Legion, for we are many?"

Charlie listened intently to what Ian was saying. It was unnerving just how logical it sounded based on what he'd seen for himself.

Ian spoke up once more, "The good news is . . . if demons and I guess Satan too for that matter, does exist. Then so must the angels . . . And that would mean so does God! I think it's time we both consider getting a little more religious!"

Charlie shook his head in agreement to that. Then he spoke up, "Well, right now all I want is to get the hell . . . the heck, that is . . . down off this mountain . . . and I may need some help. I've got a whole other mountain to climb when I get back to my office. A mountain of paperwork to fill out. I've got to tell Jenny why Bud never went up north to that meeting and tell her a believable version of how he got killed. Then I've a number of agencies and people to contact. Not to mention call an emergency council meeting to appear before. I suppose they'll make me Sheriff official like. It's not like they've many other choices. And I've got to arrange to have a burial ceremony for Bud – And it's gonna be a hero's ceremony! He gave his life going after Chastel. The fact is, we never would have got him if he hadn't."

Ian bowed his head and nodded in agreement.

"Ian, I don't suppose you want to stick around for a couple days for Bud's ceremony do you . . . ?"

Ian smiled, then shook his head no.

"Nah, I figured not . . . probably best you get the hell out of these parts soon as you can anyhow. That way the majority of the story-telling will come from me. It won't be much. Regardless of the few inconsistencies that might raise some eyebrows regarding my, our story. There's enough evidence burning in that shed of Chastel's to convict anyone. Like I said before – they'll file this case-closed as fast as they can. Odds are you won't even be contacted. I'll just have you fill-out your statement of the facts when we get back to the station."

The two men continued to just stand there for another long moment watching the cabin burn. It was the first time all day they'd felt warm. The cabin was now totally consumed by flames. It would with no-doubt burn right to the ground.

After they both had their fill of gazing at the flames . . . Ian was the first to turn away from the cabin. He spoke while shaking his head, “It’s amazing how fire cleanses just about everything – let’s get out of here!”

CHAPTER 43

The Descent

AT ABOUT HALF way down the trail that led to Little Merwin and Harmony Falls. Charlie's side began hurting him so badly he could no longer keep going on his own. Charlie had to swallow his pride and ask Ian to help him walk. Ian was glad to help his friend, but knew it had to be very serious for his proud friend to actually require his help to walk.

The wind was no longer much of a factor, but it had started raining again. An icy-cold rain. It was still only a few degrees above freezing. The snow on the trail was melting fast – and it was muddy and slippery, difficult traveling, especially down-hill.

Ian took Charlie's left arm and put it around his neck for support. The two men continued their trek down the mountain, occasionally stumbling and slipping. They even fell, once. Charlie laughed about it as they picked themselves up, totally covered in mud.

"Ian, too bad we don't have a helmet camera rolling. I'm sure we look funny enough for *America's Funniest Home Video* . . . or, at least it would be a hit video-short on *You Tube!*"

Ian admired how Charlie could make light of the situation, even when suffering as badly as he was.

Finally the two men reached the trails end, at the side of Harmony Falls. They had also reached an elevation that was below the snow-line.

Ian was now almost totally out of breath. But he managed to speak, "Okay, Charlie . . . not much further to your car . . . piece of cake now!"

Charlie didn't answer . . . he just nodded his head in agreement. Ian looked down at Charlie's right side . . . Charlie's clothing was now completely blood-soaked all around his wounds.

Charlie finally managed to speak, "Ian, you an me . . . we're friends, right . . . ?"

Without hesitation Ian replied, "Charlie Redtail, of that I'm certain . . . you and I are friends!"

"Good, then Ian, I can speak openly with you about something . . . ?"

"Of course you can Charlie . . ."

"Good . . . Ian my side hurts!"

Both men began laughing so hard they nearly fell over.

Ian and Charlie were finally able to hasten their pace. They had reached the semi-level lake-bank trail that led to the gravel parking area.

Once they reached the parking lot, they were amazed how utterly destroyed both Bud's Blazer and the television van were. Both vehicles had exploded and burnt-up to become charred skeletal remains of their former selves. Basically non-recognizable.

Charlie handed his keys to Ian the moment they reached his car. Ian helped Charlie get in. Ian started to strap Charlie's seat belts on – but the pressure from the shoulder strap proved too much for Charlie to bare. So he opted to ride without protection. Ian fired up Charlie's car and immediately began driving down the old bumpy gravel road heading from the parking lot towards the main road; taking it as easy as he could. Once on the main road Ian asked Charlie how to turn his cop-lights on. Ian switched them on and proceeded to speed his way back to town. Ian wanted to get Charlie to Doc Matthews as quickly as possible! Ian glanced over slightly towards Charlie.

"Hey Charlie, one thing's been bugging me. Do you think we should have grabbed at least some of that money? I mean, I didn't want it, much as I could use it. But you could have used it for, say Jeremy's college fund – or, it could have been donated to your tribe or something." Charlie smiled slightly.

"Nah, Ian. I didn't want any part of it, for the same reason as you. It's tainted, blood money. Bad karma, nothing good could come from it."

Ian smiled and shook his head in complete agreement.

CHAPTER 44

The Doctor is In

ONCE INSIDE DOC Matthews office. Doc took one long look at the very dirty blood soaked Charlie and began shaking his head.

"Okay, let me have a look at you . . ." Doc proclaimed with a little disgust in his voice. Doc helped Charlie get out of his shirt. He then began unwrapping the bandages that he'd skillfully put into place less than eight hours before.

"Ian, you see that bottle of antiseptic sitting over next to the sink . . . fetch that for me."

Ian immediately did as Doc Matthews requested. Doc then continued busily working on cleaning up the wounds.

"Well, you'll live . . . But sure as shit you've pushed yourself to the limit! Doesn't look like infections gonna be a problem, what you need more than anything is rest . . . Lots of rest! No more beating through the brush. Assuming of course that you two have finished with that unpleasant business that I don't want to know about . . ."

Doc spoke his last words with a very slight, sly grin. Charlie didn't answer he just nodded his head yes.

"Good! This town needs to get back to its same old boring way of life. I assume you'll be calling a meeting of the town council. Well, I'll be attending. Being the only Doctor, who runs the only medical facility this little burgs got, my vote carries some weight. You'll be our newly appointed Sheriff, or by God I'll threaten to pull up stakes for greener pastures! Not that you need my support. The people of this town, well hell, I'll say it. Charlie they loved Bud, but they love and respect you too! You're a damn good man – the only man for the job . . . that is, if you want it?"

Charlie didn't say anything . . . There was suddenly an uncomfortable silence. It was too quiet for Ian's comfort, so he broke the silence by speaking up, "Of course he wants it! He's one of the two best law-men I've ever known. You both know who the other one was. The people of this town should consider themselves lucky to have a man like Charlie be their Sheriff. A man I'm proud to call my friend!"

Doc Matthews had just finished gauze-wrapping Charlie back up – when Charlie spoke, "Well, I can't thank you enough, Doc. Ian, we need to make our way to the station and get started with reports and such . . ."

Doc Matthews smiled at Charlie, "Paying your bill will be thanks enough . . . Okay, Chief bleeds-a-lot, how bout you try and stay out of my office for a while, hmm?"

Charlie replied, "You got it Doc . . . say, here's an idea – how bout you send the bill for patching me up, that's twice now. How bout you send it to the town council for them to pay? Me being injured in the line of duty and all!"

Doc looked at Charlie with a startled expression on his face. Charlie then winked at him in plain view for Ian to see as well. Doc shook his head with a big grin on his face – all three men began laughing!

Charlie stood up. Ian helped him get his shirt back on.

Doc shook Charlie's hand, and then Ian's as well.

"Well, Ian . . . I don't suspect I'll be seeing you again, at least anytime soon. You take care of yourself!" Ian replied with a smile . . .

"You take care too, Doc. Who knows, our paths might cross again – stranger things have happened!"

Charlie smiled and shook his head in agreement to that. Charlie and Ian waved goodbye as they left Doc's clinic.

Ian climbed into the drivers side of Charlie's car after first helping Charlie get in. He began thinking to himself how fortunate this town was to have both Charlie Redtail and Doc Matthews looking after them. It was at that moment Ian's worries about any investigations into Chastel's death melted away. He knew how much this town needed a good Sheriff. Ian had seen for himself the lengths the locals would go to protect their little corner of the world. Charlie was right. As far as the world would care, justice had been served!

Served on a silver platter, Ian mused.

CHAPTER 45

The Office

JENNY WAS BUSY polishing her nails when Charlie and Ian walked through the door of the tiny Harmony Falls Sheriffs department.

Jenny spoke up first, "Charlie, have you read the paper? There's a weird story on the second page. Seems Astoria is dealing with some kind of vampire cult that's moved in and opened some underground club. They call themselves sanguinarians. They're becoming quite a problem for local law-enforcement there . . . some unexplained deaths and such. Kind of reminds me a little like what's been going on around here. Bodies have shown up totally drained of blood – that's called . . ."

Jenny looked down at the paper on her desk.

"They call that exsanguination . . . Weird!"

Jenny just shook her head in disgust. Charlie spoke with a very saddened tone to his voice, "Yeah, that's pretty weird! Hey, Jenny, I've got a lot to tell you . . . some really bad news. And I mean really bad news! I'll give you all the details later. Right now I've got a million things that I have to do. I'll tell you this much right now since you're sitting down."

Charlie's voice then cracked and genuine tears filled his eyes. Ian bowed his head.

"Bud went and got himself killed in the line of duty. Come to find out he didn't go up north to a meeting like he told me. He must have got side-tracked by some hunch, or tip, or something. Anyhow, he set out by himself to check on that hermit Chastel. He must have thought it was a weak tip; a long shot that didn't pose much danger is why he went without me and Ian. Anyway, unfortunately his hunch proved more correct than he was prepared for. That son-of-a-bitch mad mountain man, Jean-Chastel Gevaudan killed him! You know that guy – the one you always said gives you the creeps! He killed Bud. Ian and I went after him; and well, that ended badly for Chastel. But like I said I'll give you all the details later today. Right now I've got a million reports to get started on and people to contact."

Jenny started crying, though she did a good job of not falling to pieces altogether. After a few seconds she managed to speak.

"I always knew that man was no good . . . Didn't I always say it! He killed Bud, and you guys killed him . . . Well, good! Saves the taxpayers the money for a trial. Keeps some ass-hole of a city lawyer from maybe getting him off for being crazy! He's dead, good!"

At that moment Jenny noticed that Charlie was all bandaged up. "Oh my God, Charlie, are you hurt bad?"

Just then Ian spoke up, "Yeah, he's pretty cut-up . . . That madman cut Charlie up pretty bad! And get this – he cut him up with bear claws! Yeah, that crazy son-of-a-bitch was wearing a bear-skin, equipped with claws!"

Jenny took a deep breath and shook her head while she added . . .

"Well, thank God that lunatic is dead, is all I have to say about it! Oh, Mr. McDermott, I got a message for you. A guy, Matt Larsen called. He said the samples you sent him were badly contaminated. But he said the samples mostly looked like that of probably a dog . . . but it was mixed-up . . . No, that isn't exactly how he put it . . . Just a second, he made me write this part down."

Jenny picked up a note-pad from her desktop.

"He said, and I quote . . . The DNA was fused at the cellular level with elements of what resembled both human blood as well as that of Canis Familiaris, that means dog. Or, possibly, but not likely, that of Canis lupus . . . that means wolf." Jenny with note in hand, held it out towards Ian.

Ian smiled as he reached towards Jenny's note held hand and spoke while he accepted it. "Thank you, Jenny, thank you very much!"

Charlie then interjected, "All right, Ian follow me back to my office . . . I've got to get a signed statement from you about all that occurred."

Ian followed Charlie back to his office. The two men entered the office. Charlie closed the door.

Charlie then dug around in his desk until he found the right file-folder that contained the paperwork for Ian to make an official statement.

"Here Ian, take your time . . . What you write down needs to reflect in essence what we've already discussed. But it's okay . . . a good thing even, that our stories have small subtle differences. They won't sound rehearsed that way. So follow what we've discussed for the most part. But make sure you write in your words not mine. And try not to sound pre-recorded if you get my meaning!"

Ian understood perfectly what Charlie was saying. So with pen and paper in hand Ian began writing down his version of the last few days events. Events that climaxed with the death of the killer, Jean-Chastel Gevaudan. It took nearly two hours for Ian to get it all written down. During that time Charlie had been on the phone with the television network that Marsha Steward and Tom Iverson had worked for. He then notified all of the proper agencies including the County Coroners office, and State Police.

Ian did a beautiful job of describing certain things with clarity and keeping other things intentionally a little vague. The more Ian wrote the more he actually began believing it all happened exactly the way he was describing it. It was like all of the supernatural aspects ceased to have any relevance.

When Ian had completed his statement he immediately had Charlie check it over. When Charlie finished reading it. He just sat back in his chair and looked at Ian. Charlie had an expression on his face that reflected his near amazement.

"Hell, Ian . . . that's the best statement of the facts I've ever read. It's a damn masterpiece! That's exactly how it all happened, all of it! From your perspective that is. Don't change any of it, not a word! If ever questioned . . . Never deviate from what you have right here, of which I'll have copies. Ian, those are the facts! Anything else is, would have been impossible!"

Charlie then pushed-back and stood up from his chair. Without saying a word he left his office for just a couple of minutes. Upon returning, he handed Ian a plain white business-size envelope. Charlie then spoke, "Ian, here's a little petty cash to help cover some of your expenses like gas, meals and such. When you get settled somewhere; you just get me your address and I'll have a check for what we owe ya, plus a little extra bonus for all you been through."

Ian smiled, "Thanks! say, before you left the room, you said – those are the facts, anything else would have been impossible – well, that's what makes our story, even with its peculiarities believable . . . cause your right Charlie. Anything else would have been impossible!"

Charlie then took a deep breath, "Ian, I've been thinking about something . . . something I believe Bud would have wanted you to have."

"Oh, and what would that be?" Ian replied with more than casual curiosity expressed in the tone of his voice and look on his face.

"Come on, lets go for a short drive . . . I'll tell when we get in the car, while we're on our way. And by the way Ian, I'm feeling good enough to drive. I don't think I could stand being chauffeured around by you for even one more minute!"

Charlie paused after saying that for effect – it worked . . . both men laughed quietly.

CHAPTER 46

Hello

CHARLIE LIED . . . IAN wasn't angry about it, just confused. Once in the car Charlie decided that Ian had to wait to find out what he'd referred to as something Bud would have wanted him to have.

The only thing Charlie would say about the matter was Ian had to be patient. What Bud would want Ian to have was at Bud's place; and they were mere minutes from there.

When Charlie pulled his car into Bud's driveway, Charlie began asking Ian questions.

"Ian, you're all alone. No family, well except mine that is. There will always be a place at my table for you my friend – and you remember that especially around the holidays. But, anyway, what I'm getting at is all the traveling you do, basically you're all by your lonesome, right?"

Ian replied reluctantly, not sure where this was going . . .

"Yes . . ."

"Ian, I'm a pretty good judge of people . . . it goes with my job I guess. I'll bet you like animals, am I right?"

Once again Ian answered with as few words as possible . . .

"Yes . . ."

"They say people who like animals can generally be classified as either cat people, or dog people – my guess is you're a dog person, am I right?"

Ian started to laugh a nervous laugh. Later he'd feel silly that he didn't pick up on the clues. After all that was what he was best at. Still, at this moment he honestly had no idea what this was all about. This time he paused before answering, trying to read Charlie's face . . .

"Yeah, I guess I'd say I'm more of a dog guy, but cats are okay . . ."

That said, Charlie climbed out of the car and Ian did the same.

Charlie motioned for Ian to follow him. Charlie began walking to the back of the house. It was then that all the pieces suddenly fit. The moment Ian heard a dog barking at their presence.

There in the back of Bud's place was a very nice dog kennel that housed a beautiful young male German Shepherd – who stopped barking and began wagging its tail the second he recognized Charlie.

"Ian, allow me to introduce you to Scout . . . Scout, this is Ian. Scout is, was Bud's pride and joy. He's only around nine months old. He's the offspring of champions. The fact is this here dogs pappy was highly decorated. He gave his life protecting his dog handler-officer. Bud got him as a pup from some friends he had with the Vancouver K9 force, kennels. You know, dogs, bred, raised and trained to be Police dogs. Bud's been working with him, he's a good dog! I'd take him myself but the terms of my lease-to-own doesn't allow me to have a dog. It's a shame cause I know Jeremy would want him. But since that can't happen . . . I know Jeremy and especially Bud would want him to go to a good man. So I'm asking you, for Bud, and for the sake of this beautiful animal – couldn't you use a road companion that will serve you well as a guard dog?"

The two men entered the kennel . . . Scout went straight to Ian and began licking his hand. It was almost like he knew this was his one-shot! Then Scout put the close on . . . He set and extended his right paw to Ian. Ian's heart pounded, the truth was it was nearly love at first sight. Ian had always thought German Shepherd's were one of if not the finest looking dogs.

Charlie went and got some dog food from the small lock-up shed built within the kennel. He filled Scouts food dish. There still was plenty of water in the very large water dish.

"Here boy, you must be starving! He hasn't ate in nearly two days. Well, Bud always way over-fed him. So I guess a little fasting didn't hurt him more than cause him a grumbling belly."

Ian looked over at Charlie . . .

Charlie spoke once more, "Bud told me he got him cheap cause of his friends in the K9 kennels. But if he would have bought him traditional like. He'd of gone for around a thousand dollars or more. He's had all his shots and all of that."

Ian stepped back. He looked from Charlie back at Scout.

"Ah hell, why not . . . how bout it boy . . . ? You want to team up with the likes of me?"

It was as if Scout understood every word that came out of Ian's mouth. He wagged his tail and barked three times in rapid fire.

Charlie grabbed the remains of the fifty pound bag of dog food and dish. He found a smaller water dish and took that as well.

"These go with you Ian . . . compliments of me, Bud and Scout here . . ."

Ian smiled, "Well, Charlie, how bout you take me and Scout here back to my campsite. I need to pull up stakes and head down the road."

Charlie, Ian and Scout left the kennel. The three climbed into Charlie's car and away they headed to the *Firlane Resort RV Park.*

CHAPTER 47

Goodbye

CHARLIE PULLED INTO the resort. He drove straight over to Ian's Jeep and trailer. It was easy to spot, it was the only rig and trailer in the place.

The two men and Ian's new found companion just sat silently for a few minutes. Finally Charlie broke the silence.

"Well, Elaine's gonna be upset that you didn't stop by and say goodbye!"

Ian was nearly getting choked up. It hadn't been since he was in college that he had what could have passed as a good friend, let alone a best friend. But no friendship he'd ever had compared to the bond he shared with the man he sat next to.

"Yeah, well, I have enough gas to get me down the road." Charlie looked at Ian with a questioning look on his face . . .

"Down the road – where are you heading to anyway?"

Ian replied, "Well, I thought Astoria, Oregon, sounds interesting. What with that outbreak of vampire's and all."

Charlie just shook his head as both men laughed at that – all the while knowing that Ian spoke the truth.

Charlie then looked as though a light-bulb had just gone off inside his mind.

"That's it Ian . . . this is your calling – you know, paranormal investigations and such. You've always sort of fringed on it, right? Hey, how about I put in a call to the Astoria Police. Let them know what a fine job you did helping us with our difficult weird case. I'll tell them difficult and weird, is right down your alley – your area of expertise as it were."

Ian paused for a second, "Yeah, maybe it's time I reinvent myself just a bit. Change with the times and all that. What was it that television character from that X-files show used to say? Oh yeah, the truth is out there! Well, you and I know that the truth can be stranger than fiction!"

Charlie took a deep breath and replied, "Boy you got that right."

Ian smiled as he looked straight at Charlie, "Yeah Charlie, make that call if you want . . . we'll, I . . . I mean Scout and me, we better get a move on. I want to pull into Astoria before dark. You know, with them vampires and all!"

Both men laughed, but Charlie had a slightly concerned look on his face as he continued to listen to Ian.

"First a werewolf, now vampires . . . Lions and tigers and bears, oh my! Well, Charlie, after what we've been through – I'm not totally ruling out any extreme possibility. Probably its nothing more than club freaks. Or, some nut job running around with plastic fangs – some fruit case that's seen one to many Bela Lugosi movie . . . but still . . ."

Charlie looked directly at Ian, "Yeah, but still . . . well, you take care! Get yourself a silver crucifix, some garlic and maybe a wooden stake or two. You know, can't be too careful! Okay, Ghost Buster, you better get going!"

Ian shook his head in agreement to that. The two men said their good-byes. Ian and Scout climbed out of Charlie's car. Charlie pushed his trunk release button. Ian walked to the rear of the car, reached in and grabbed the bag of dog food and the dog bowls. Ian then shut the trunk and moved out of the way . . . Charlie backed his car up and began to leave. Charlie then suddenly stopped and rolled down his window, "Scout you take good care of my friend, Paranormal Investigator – Ian McDermott!"

Scout wagged his tail and barked three times.

Those words resonated in Ian's head . . . that was it! That was perfect! He would have new business cards made by some print shop as soon as possible. Maybe even get an online private investigators certification and license.

CHAPTER 48

Partings

IAN HOOKED HIS Jeep up to his trailer. He then unplugged it from all the utilities and went back inside to double check that everything had been properly put away making it travel ready.

"Well, Scout, looks like that's about it. Come on boy, lets go to the office and pay the bill, so we can get a move on."

The two headed over to the office. After paying, Ian asked Molly Turner the owner of the RV Park, directions.

"Molly, can you tell me the best way to get from here to Astoria, Oregon?"

Molly looked at Ian kind of funny – like everyone should know that.

"Say, you didn't have a dog when you arrived – did you?"

"No, I just picked him up today, as a matter of fact!"

Molly rubbed her right hand on her chin . . .

"Course I only seen him once . . . but that dog looks a lot like Sheriff Bud's!"

Ian smiled and replied, "Yeah, that's because he used to belong to Bud . . . He was given to me."

Molly looked at Ian somewhat suspiciously . . .

"A gift, huh, you don't say . . . ? Well, anyhow . . . the best way to go, is to head back to Woodland. Then go north on I-5 for about thirty miles I guess. Take the turn off to Longview. Head into Longview keeping your eyes peeled for Oregon Way. Cause you'll be making a left onto it. That will head you straight to the bridge that crosses the Columbia to Oregon. Once across the river, you'll be heading west up the Rainier hill. No more turns from that point. Just keep on that road for about I'd say seventy miles or so and you're there. From Astoria it's just minutes on down to the Oregon or Washington beaches, and lots of camp grounds and RV parks. Might be some good clam digging this time of year. That what you going for, clam digging?"

Ian smiled, "Oh, I suspect I'll be doing some digging around!"

Ian and Scout left the office and returned to the Jeep. They climbed in. Ian fired it up and the two of them headed out of the *Firlane Resort* turning west towards new horizons.

EPILOGUE

Part I

Three hours later

"WELL, BOY . . . LOOKS like we've made it, welcome to Astoria. I don't know about you, but I'll be glad to get out and stretch my legs. I'm getting a little hungry, you probably are too, huh boy? Say, since I've got a few coins in my pocket, since Charlie was so kind as to front me some – how bout I spring for some lunch at a restaurant. I know what you're thinking . . . I spend too much money eating out. Yeah, you're right. This will be the last time for a while. Say, later this evening we'll spot us a nice grocery store and stock up on some groceries. This is nice . . . it's been a long time since I've had anyone to talk to while on the road. You're not much of a conversationalist. But you're sure a good listener, aren't you fella?"

Ian petted Scouts head. Scout waged his tail and panted happily. They were bonding fast.

Ian and Scout were now heading through downtown Astoria.

"Look boy, there's a nice looking restaurant just up ahead. And by that I mean it looks nice enough for the likes of me. Not too expensive if you know what I mean. But no dive either. Scout it's called *Pigs-In-A-Blanket* . . . with a name like that it's gotta be good, right? You know, just like that jelly. With a name like *Smucker's* it's gotta be good! I always thought that was funny. Like the word *Smucker's* sounds good!"

Ian laughed at his levity . . . Scout barked his approval at the humor.

"Okay then boy . . . I'll tell you what. You're gonna stay in the Jeep. I'll crack a window for you. And when I come back. I'll have a little surprise for you. Maybe some bacon or sausage . . . how's that sound boy?" Scout barked once loudly as if he understood completely.

Ian pulled his Jeep and trailer into the far back of the restaurant parking lot. So not to block any traffic.

"All right then – you keep guard of all my worldly possessions. I won't be long. Hey, while I'm inside, maybe I'll get a good tip on a near-by camp ground or RV park that doesn't cost an arm and a leg. One that takes shaggy guests like yourself. Okay, There, the windows cracked. Looks like it's gonna start raining again anytime. It's pretty windy and cold so I know you won't get over-heated. I do hate to leave you just when we started getting to know one another. The worst part is you don't understand much, if any of what I'm saying. Well, if somehow you can understand – just know I will try and be fast. You be a good boy while I'm gone!"

Ian climbed out of his Jeep, then locked it's doors. He then walked across the parking lot and into the restaurant.

Once inside, Ian looked around until he spotted a sign that said seat yourself. He did just that and immediately picked up a menu and began looking it over.

Hmm . . . Breakfast served twenty four hours a day, nice! ***The "Gold Coast Special" breakfast . . . Two farm fresh eggs, your choice of either three slices of bacon or three sausage links, hash browns and toast of your choice: $8.99*** *– well now, that sounds perfect!*

Ian looked up from his menu and noticed his server was waiting with a smile on her face.

"Can I get you some coffee or something to drink? While you decide what you'll be having."

Ian noticed the pretty young womens name badge.

"Hello, Jennifer . . . I'll have a large tomato juice and the *Gold Coast Special* breakfast, for lunch that is."

Jennifer smiled, "Good choice . . . Sausage or bacon?"

Ian paused for a second.

"Uh, bacon!"

Jennifer continued, "What type of toast would you like?"

Ian thought about that one for a couple of seconds, "Sour dough!"

Jennifer smiled and made her notes on her order pad.

"Oh, and how would you like your eggs?"

Ian returned a smile to Jennifer, "Over hard, would be great! Say Jennifer, have you lived here in Astoria long?"

Jennifer looked at Ian with a slightly surprised look on her face as she replied, "No, sir . . . I've been staying, house sitting for my Aunt and Uncle for a couple months while they were traveling. But they just got back this week. I was living before, and will be returning to Seattle. I got this job about a month ago . . . you know seasonal help. And actually today's my last day. This job ending actually worked out perfect timing wise for me. Cause I just got a letter of acceptance a few days ago to the Nursing program at the University of Washington, in Seattle. That's where my parents live. Anyway, I've been working here and there for the last couple of years saving what I can for School. Oh, my gosh . . . I've practicly told you my life story!"

Jennifer began to blush.

Ian held up his hand gesturing that it was quite all right as he smiled.

"No, no it's good to hear your plans are working out for you. Say, one more question. What do you know about a new nightclub in town? I've heard it's sort of a place where . . . I don't know . . . kind of attracts, what's the word? goth people, and persons interested in say the occult and such like that. I'm doing some research, some investigation you might say, and . . ."

Jennifer looked at Ian. She rapidly surmised that he didn't exactly fit the profile of its patrons. She knew the place he was refering.

"You mean *The Morgue* . . . *?* That place is just a couple blocks from here. Down on the wharf, the water front, pier 13, I think. I've never been there. I mean I've been by it. I've never gone into the club. But I've heard stories . . . it's a real creepy spot. The cities been trying to shut it down ever since it opened last June. But, I hear the owner has deep pockets and has powerful lawyer's and all that. Anyway, he's been able to keep the place going. Even with all the local Church groups and the city council trying everything they can to shut the place down. You're right. The place attracks lots of goth's and you know, all those poser vampire types. Real freaks, some of them. I'm surprised there's enough people into that sort of thing in this little town to keep a place like that going. I mean maybe in Portland, or Seattle . . . but in little old Astoria? I've heard weirdo's come from miles to hang there. Well, I'm no one to judge, different strokes and all that. But that place is not my thing if you know what I mean . . . Not at all!"

Ian smiled and shook his head in agreement.

"Yeah, I hear that. Not my cup of tea either. It's just, well, like I said I'm doing a little research . . ."

Jennifer smiled, "What are you . . . some kind of private investigator, or undercover cop, or something?"

Ian took a deep breath, then offered up a sly expression on his face. He winked at Jennifer as he replied, "Yeah, something like that . . . say, do you know the name of the person who owns or runs the club?"

Jennifer giggled, "Yes I do . . . but it's going to cost you – In the form of a good tip that is. Good information doesn't come cheap around these parts!"

Ian laughed, "No, no I don't suppose it does. If the food here turns out to be half as pleasant as the conversation . . . you'll be well compensated!"

Jennifer laughed, "Good, cause a girls got to pay for her schooling somehow, right? His name is, and you're going to love this . . . I read in the paper that his name is Vladimir Drago Salizzar. But Molly said people just call him Salizzar. Now doesn't that sound just like out of a movie or something? I've never seen him myself. But a gal, Molly – who used to work here. She told me he's like out of this world good looking. Long black hair, dark eyes, and a perfect though a bit pale, complexion. She said he talks with some sort of Eastern European accent. She said he even . . . and get this . . ."

Jennifer paused to look around to make sure no other ears were listening; none were.

"He like wears eyeliner, red lip gloss and clear nail polish. But Molly said he didn't seem gay, maybe bisexual if anything like that! I mean how weird is that? Maybe in a big city. But around here – in a town of mostly loggers and fishermen. The guy wears make-up? No wonder nobody ever sees him during the day. Looking like that in this town he'd probably get beat up! But I guess somehow it works for him; cause Molly said he's like totally dreamy if you get my meaning. Anyway, I almost went with her once to check him, to check the place out. But the whole thing sort of freaked me out. I backed out at the last minute. I never got a second chance to go with her. Cause soon after she just never showed up for work anymore. That was a few weeks ago. She was like me, not from around here. She probably got fed up with small town living and all the rain, and moved back home, or wherever. She was from somewhere back east, Chicago I think . . . ?"

Ian interrupted, "Say Jennifer, do you know of any good camp grounds or RV parks close by?"

Jennifer suddenly had a very thoughtful expression on her face as she gently tapped her pin against her cheek.

"Of course, there's lots of camping near the beaches . . . Warrenton would be maybe the closest. Then there's Seaside . . . it's not too far. I'd guess around a twenty minute drive from here. Oh, and lots of places across the bridge over at Ilwaco, and around Long Beach, which is really nice! They're probably about the same distance away;

also around a twenty minute drive. Hmm, but real close, near to town here, I don't know of any."

Ian smiled and extended his right hand. Jennifer responded by extending hers – they shook hands cordially.

"Jennifer, my name is Ian McDermott, it's been my pleasure to meet you. I want to thank you for all the information – oh, and good luck with school!"

Jennifer smiled bright, "Nice to meet you Ian. My name is Jennifer Dowling."

Ian smiled brightly as he asked, "Jennifer, do you ever go by Jenny . . . ?"

Jennifer looked at him with a slightly surprised look on her face as she responded to his provocative question. "Yeah, my family and friends call me Jenny – why do you ask . . . ?"

Ian grinned as he replied, "Oh, no reason . . . it's just you remind me a bit of a very nice gal who works for a friend of mine – that and Jenny just seems to fit you."

Jennifer smiled and left to turn-in Ian's order to the kitchen.

Ian's food came just a few minutes later. And it was good – very good! Before leaving, Ian wrapped his saved bacon in a napkin and put it in his coat pocket. He then left a sizeable tip at the table for Jennifer, the aspiring Nurse.

Part II

Heading back to his vehicle, Ian spotted Scout who then started barking happily at the sight of him.

Ian unlocked the door of the Jeep and pet Scout; who had been a very good boy – nothing was chewed on, or disturbed in anyway.

Ian retrieved the napkin wrapped bacon from his pocket and gave it to his very appreciative companion. He then put a leash on Scout and walked him to an abandoned lot just across the street from the restaurant parking lot. Scout did his business, then they returned to the Jeep.

"Okay boy, next order of business . . . keep your eyes peeled for a print shop of some kind."

Ian and Scout drove out of the restaurant parking lot and proceeded up the road to the main street of Astoria.

Ian glanced for a second over at Scout, "There . . . right over there! Scout, do you see it? It's just ahead on the right . . . a *FedEx-Kinko's*. They do good work and fast! I'm gonna have them make up some business cards for us. How does *Ian and Scout's Investigations* sound?"

Scout let out a groan then yawned, "Oh, I suppose you'd prefer *Scout and Ian's*?" Ian chuckled as he shook his head.

Scout, as if he understood every word Ian was saying, wagged his tail and barked three times.

Ian glanced at Scout once again . . . this time as he looked into the bright eyes of his four-legged friend he couldn't help smiling. Trying to put his game face on, Ian took a deep breath and exhaled as he spoke, "All right, seriously Scout – what would sound good?"

After much contemplation, Ian began ascending from the depths of his thought. Then, with a sly grin on his face he exclaimed, "Scout, I've got it! I think we're gonna have to go with – **Ian McDermott, PhD Paranormal Investigations.**"

Other works of heart-stopping fiction from the author:

David A. Reuben

The ***Evilution*** *Series:*

Blood of the Lamb – Book I

Is a thrilling, frightening, compelling fiction that gives you some powerful action, drama, ideas, and goose bumps. In this first installment of Reuben's *The Evilution Series* . . .

Masquerading as the powerful Vatican Bishop, Cardinal David Xzytun, evil has finally incarnated with the intent to control – as puppet master a Caesar for his new Roman Empire. His plans of Armageddon and End of Days is about to unfurl in this suspenseful story.

Standing tenuously on the side of hope amidst the encroaching apocalyptic doom is Dr. Paul Bradfield. A man conflicted between rational science and matters of faith – especially when it comes to the unexplainable, supernatural occurrences and horrifying deaths of several of his closest friends. Only Jennifer Dowling, his true love, and Matt Larsen, his slovenly yet brilliant friend, recognize the unholy phenomenon which has fixated on – or, perhaps has emanated from – Father Joseph David, Dr. Bradfield's dearest friend of all.

More questions and mysterious events will surface as each character steps into the devious plots *Evil* has planted in their midst.

Novels by David A. Reuben are available through:

xlibris.com wolfbanebooks.com

bloodofthelamb-davidreuben.com

(And most online book stores/resources)

Coming Soon!

The ***Evilution*** *Series – Book II:*

Blood of the Lamb – **Rubicon Cross**

-And-

Further bone-chilling novels/stories starring:

Ian McDermott – *Paranormal Investigator*